The Writings of Owen Wister

RED MEN AND WHITE

LIN McLEAN

HANK'S WOMAN

THE VIRGINIAN

MEMBERS OF THE FAMILY

WHEN WEST WAS WEST

LADY BALTIMORE

SAFE IN THE ARMS OF CROESUS

U. S. GRANT AND THE SEVEN AGES
OF WASHINGTON

THE PENTECOST OF CALAMITY AND
THE STRAIGHT DEAL

NEIGHBORS HENCEFORTH

The Writings of Owen Wister

SAFE IN THE ARMS OF
CROESUS

Owen Wister

The Writings of Owen Wister

of The American Academy of Arts and Letters

*Membre Correspondant de la Société
des Gens de Lettres*

Honorary Fellow of the Royal Society of Literature

===

Safe in the Arms of Croesus

PRINTED IN THE UNITED STATES OF AMERICA BY
R. R. DONNELLEY & SONS CO., AT THE LAKESIDE PRESS, CHICAGO

PREFACE—*Our Inveterate Family*

"Perhaps it was right to dissemble your love,
But why did you kick me down stairs?"

is a touching remonstrance, to-day embedded in certain books of quotations, and once declaimed in Act 1, Scene 1, of *The Panel*, a play by my great-great uncle, who wrote some dozen plays.

His sister-in-law, my great-grandmother, wrote amusing dramas at that same time—for example, *The Day After the Wedding*, in which the young bride sings, accompanied on the flute by the bridegroom—

When love attends the wedded pair,
Beneath their feet the flowers increase,
And o'er their pathway rises fair
The sunshine of domestic peace.

BRIDEGROOM. You don't execute that last turn quite as it ought to be.
BRIDE. Well, we'll begin again.
When love attends the wedded pair . . .
BRIDEGROOM. Mind your time.
BRIDE. And o'er their pathway rises fair . . .
BRIDEGROOM. Come, let us try it once more.

BRIDE. When love attends the wedded pair . . .
    You interrupt me by beating time.
    Beneath their feet the flowers
        increase . . .
BRIDEGROOM. You are getting too fast.
BRIDE. (*Throws music down.*) Sing it yourself.

This great-grandmother was, according to the *Encyclopædia Britannica*, the daughter of an eminent musician. Her husband wrote *The Point of Honour,* produced in Dublin 1800, and at Covent Garden 1805, and 1842. It was one among a number of plays by him.

Their son, John, a scholar, edited the *British and Foreign Review,* and wrote books both in German and English.

Their daughter, Adelaide, composed and sang music, was the first to sing *Norma* in London, and in 1867 wrote *A Week in a French Country-house,* republished in 1902, with a preface by Thackeray's daughter, in whose house I stayed in 1870. Adelaide transmitted the family gifts to her daughter, Mrs. Evans Gordon, my loveliest cousin, who passed them on to her daughter, Lady Margaret Stanley, in brilliant measure.

Adelaide's sister, Fanny, wrote poems, dramas, and memoirs. Her *Records of a Girlhood* appeared in 1874 in the *Atlantic Monthly,* when W. D. Howells was the editor. Her writings greatly surpass those of her parents.

Their granddaughter, Sarah, my mother, wrote numerous essays, stories, poems, translations, many of these for the *Atlantic Monthly*, but she seldom signed her name to what she published.

Their great-grandson wrote *The Virginian*.

Their great-great-granddaughter has published a volume entitled *Helen and Other Poems*.

Their sister, Sarah, sketched by Sir Joshua Reynolds, hangs over my fireplace; her portrait by him as *The Tragic Muse* is better known, as are many other pictures of her. Her two brothers, authors of the plays I have referred to, were also often painted. Her life has been written more than once, a brief one recently by André Maurois; and besides the *Encyclopædia Britannica*, many books have something to say about Sarah Siddons, her brothers, John Philip and Charles, her nieces, Fanny and Adelaide Kemble.

It's to be seen, therefore, that since the year 1800, our family has been addicted to scribbling; and had this collection of pieces, which are mainly frisky, come out when John Philip Kemble was writing

"But why did you kick me down stairs?" its title might very likely have been *Sketches and Burlesques*. But fashions change, just as much in titles as in hats; and so the book bears the name of the first piece in it, which was the latest to be written. This one brought the letters fluttering in from the four winds, many pro's and some con's. Good business! It isn't modesty that hinders extracts from them being given here; and I could wish nothing better to my readers than that what I write should entertain them as much as what some of them write entertains me.

Take the second piece, *Philosophy Four,* for instance, first published in 1901. It occasioned a grave discussion in Boston newspapers as to whether Harvard undergraduates were ever guilty of such language as some that I placed in their young lips; it brought an accusation that I was a corrupter of youth; a Hebrew wrote me that he wouldn't be like my Christians for anything. I wrote him that I would not be like his patron saint, Jacob, for anything: the worm may laugh, but sometimes turns. Perhaps the most peerless reaction came six years later. I had delivered before a Harvard audience some views about the decadence of American scholarship; and this impelled the editorial mouthpiece of the Local Divinity to say in its choicest language that such sentiments from the author of *Philosophy Four,* were of an audacity! . . . The mouthpiece shuddered to think of it. But William James wrote one in another strain. He was quite of my way of thinking. He had hailed *Philosophy Four* in a delightful letter, "Is *that* what we look like?" he had exclaimed. William James took neither himself nor Harvard too solemnly.

Two of the pieces, *Mother* (for the permission to include this here I thank the courtesy of Messrs. Dodd, Mead and Co.) and *With the Coin of Her Life*, were hoaxes.

Mother appeared first in 1901, in response to an invitation to twenty-five authors to contribute anonymously stories entitled *A House Party* to a syndicate. If you came in, you gave your word to keep it dark, because a prize of one thousand dollars awaited whatever reader should guess most authors right. I don't remember why this enterprise aroused Mark Twain's disapproval, but it did. He doubted if twenty-five authors had been really invited—his name was announced among the others. He telegraphed me: Did I write any of the stories? How could I tell him without breaking my word? I telegraphed him that I had written them all.

In *Mother*, I amused myself by trying to imitate the style of Frank Stockton—another who had been invited. It threw my old friend Alden, editor of *Harper's Magazine*, off the track, and it deceived my mother equally.

In the style of *With the Coin of Her Life*, as well as in choice of subject, I tried to masquerade as Dr. Weir Mitchell. He had ordered me to execute a yarn upon the theme of thirteen at table. He would write one, others would, and all were to be published by *The Century,* and it was again to be a guessing contest. Only three appeared, I think. I meekly obeyed the great doctor, but I did my best to imitate his way of writing, and I took for my heroine the sort of person who came to him for treatment. I got my ophthalmic "dope" from his friend and mine, Dr. George de Schweinitz. It took everybody in—even the trained nurses in charge of Dr. Mitchell's patients—except his brother-in-law, a shrewd lawyer in New York.

In *The Honeymoonshiners,* a revision of *Watch Your Thirst,* published in 1923, the long family inheritance crops out in a form akin to *The Panel.* Words and music by me, it was the second comic opera that I wrote for the Tavern Club of Boston, which gave them both, in 1916 and 1925, respectively. It held, until its final curtain at 11:15, an audience that likes to be let out by 10:30.

The man who knows his Lucian, or his Meilhac and Halévy and his Offenbach, will recognize the skit at once as of that breed; and I shouldn't wonder if John Philip, author of

"Perhaps it was right to dissemble your love,"

might count it as a chip of the old block. But, were I to essay his part of *Coriolanus* or *Hamlet,* it's quite certain that he would kick me down stairs.

OWEN WISTER.

Long House, Bryn Mawr, 1928.

TABLE OF CONTENTS

	PAGE
SAFE IN THE ARMS OF CROESUS	1
PHILOSOPHY FOUR	37
MOTHER	89
WITH THE COIN OF HER LIFE	128
STANWICK'S BUSINESS	172
THE SIMPLE SPELLING-BEE	202
THE HONEYMOONSHINERS	253

SAFE IN THE ARMS OF CROESUS

SAFE IN THE
ARMS OF CROESUS

THE home voyage promised no dullness. Next my chair on deck was that of André Renaud; and the talk of this lively minded Frenchman would cheer the densest fog. Below in the dining-saloon my companions at table were: a gentle lady with eyes full of the past and an unmarried voice; a handsome brute with an important necktie and teeth of strength; a Harvard boy, graduate of the Law School, home-bound for the bottom rung in a busy office, after a wise holiday with work flung to the winds and Europe in his arms; and the youthful editor of *Cute Cracks*, bald before his time, with a blue vital alertness beaming behind his spectacles.

"And so you have been Seeing America First?"

This was Renaud to me, both tucked in our rugs, and the coast fading behind us.

"Not seeing it at all," I replied. "I've made a point of keeping clear of Americans."

"Of that I was sure. And so you should be able to tell me where it is that wicked Americans go when

1

they die. When good ones die, they go to Paris. A wise Bostonian announced this many years ago."

"So you believe in immortality?"

"Completely. If Paris is your American Paradise, what is your American Hell?"

Well, he was up to something. André Renaud was often up to something. He had come from his French University to teach at mine during the Great War, and between us all we had persuaded him to remain.

He now continued, "I had been not yet six months in your inexpressibly amusing country, when I discovered where it is that the wicked Americans go."

"Out with it," said I.

"No. You shall meditate."

The coast of France was fading, fading; a spring and summer of delight were over; a not quite extinct sense of duty was dragging me back to the Statue of Liberty, whose face is turned away from us. Out of my memories I spoke to André:

"Once in my travels I met rudeness. It was in a train. They were Americans. Nobody I saw anywhere was drunk, except several Americans in Paris. But since travel-agencies have turned the vulgar Briton loose on lake and mountain, the American voice has dropped to the third instead of the second worst noise in Europe."

"I heard no noises," said André, "after one re-
ception at your American Library in the rue de
l'Elysée. To that I was compelled officially to go.
I had to welcome one of your popular novelists.
When I asked what he was writing, he answered,
'I am waking them up.' Was it not characteristic?
Then I went to my mother, who is very old. I hid
myself deep in my *petit pays*. I walked among pop-
pies and vineyards, listening to larks in the sky
and to the bell of our little beautiful ancient church.
And, ah, I met leisure once more!" And he spoke
of certain Greek poets and of Horace's debt to them.
He spoke with that grace which drapes the sym-
metry of the Gallic mind. Beside it, our shoulder-
padded education flaps round us like a marked-
down suit. "But I am certain," he concluded,
"that you have been Seeing America First."

"Won't you explain your paradox?"

"My dear fellow! You have been six months
away from your country. Where is the paradox?
How has mankind ever learned the characteristics
of anything except through comparing it with
something else? How should we have discovered
that night is dark if we had never seen day? If
the dog were the only domestic animal in our households would it strike us that dogs cannot climb
trees? To arrive at that generalization we must
have had an opportunity to observe the cat. Look

here. What did you say to me just now about the American voice?"

"That's hearing America. Even the deaf can't help that."

"You quibble. When the travel posters of your splendid railways (through comparison they show me the strong and weak points of our own)—when the posters urge you in all colors of the rainbow to 'See America First,' what they are really advising is that you shall never see America at all. In selling you tickets to places where you will merely meet your own people and your own customs and standards day after day, they make it virtually impossible for you to appreciate how good or how bad your customs are—and, like all the rest of the world, you have plenty of both."

"You perfectly explain," said I, "the impregnable incompetence of every provincial French bank in cashing a letter of credit."

Renaud laughed. "Yes, we French stick too much at home and are interested only in ourselves. If we do not get over that. . . . Well, your Henry James has called us Chinese. What are you? Come, find an epithet for the occasionally great American people."

"One epithet? There isn't any."

"You will not even try?"

"It can't be done. Nothing comes uppermost."

"Perhaps nothing *stays* uppermost. But if we groped among your present characteristics and then groped about in the dictionary—"

"Where is the word that will fit Manhattan, San Francisco, Kansas, Charles Eliot, Bryan, and all the rest of our miscellaneous jungle? What's the meaning of one hundred per cent American? We coined the phrase to hide the facts."

"You're looking at it too close. Of course you cannot see the wood for the trees. Stand back. View it from Europe—as you have done already in the case of the voices and the quack thinking."

"Quack thinking?"

"Haven't you just virtually said that Americans paste names on the outside of bottles and consider this makes the contents correspond to the label? Go on seeing America first. I observe many flowers and many weeds in your jungle—but I'm ready with my main epithet."

"Is your main epithet a flower or a weed?"

"Subconsciously you know it already—it remains for you to become conscious of it. You have nine days. When you find it you'll find also where it is that wicked Americans go when they die."

"Well, perhaps I will try. Hm. Another Bostonian said about 1860 that America's mission was to vulgarize the world. Hardly flattering. But Emerson said our destiny was to legislate for mankind. Highly flattering. Hm. Of course, Emerson resembled Wordsworth in being at times an inspired prophet and at other times an old ass. Well. Of course the typical American resents everything but flattery.''

''Go on!'' cried André. ''Go on! I think, as the children say in their game, you are getting warm.''

But now the trumpeter sounded his call to dress for dinner. So we got out of our rugs and went to our cabins.

Something had gone on before I reached our table: a misty distress was in the face of the gentle lady (she came from St. Paul); the Editor's eyes were brilliant; an alert and roguish mockery sported in the smile of the Harvard boy; and the important man was saying in a voice like heavy bronze:

''Sure we won the War for 'em. But it appears there is such a thing as being too proud to pay.''

I saw the St. Paul lady clasp her hands under the tablecloth.

''England is paying us quite a lot.'' This was the Editor.

''I know the figures.''

''But do you think Belgium. . . . Doesn't it seem as if we ought? . . . The French surely—'' The poor lady left it there.

''Business is business. Loans are loans,'' asserted the important man and ceased attending to the conversation. I certainly did envy him his teeth.

"Not Uncle Shylock, then?" inquired the Harvard boy.

But the important man was far away. "Not Uncle Shylock," repeated the boy, looking innocently at him. "Just Uncle Sham."

The lady's hands were clasped again. She looked as if she would like to leave the table.

"This your first trip?" asked the important man, coming back, but not waiting to hear. "My home's in Los Angeles. I sailed January 29th. Cunard to Cherbourg. Made no stop in New York. Never was east of Chicago before. There's nothing east of Chicago for us Californians. My company manufactures the greatest nerve food on earth. Here's our new ad."

He dealt leaflets about the table, somewhat as if they were cards. They varied as cards do; some said, "Eat Muscatol and forget the Doctor"; others, "Eat Muscatol and forget the Dentist"; or, "Eat Muscatol and forget Worry"; or "Forget Wakefulness"; or Cold Feet, or Drab Thoughts— there must have been a dozen things which eating Muscatol would make you forget. It was Nature's Nerve Food, the cards said.

"Most interesting," murmured the lady from St. Paul, drawing away from her leaflet as if it were a beetle.

"But forgetting so many things—mightn't it make you absent-minded?" suggested the boy.

"It's a grape product," said the man. "Nature's Nerve Food. I've been pushing it among those folks." And he jerked his large head toward Europe. "Slow. That's what I call the British. If they don't drop their 'We've never done it that way,' they'll drop out. They're dense. Los Angeles has one million one hundred thousand inhabitants to-day. By 1935, we'll hit the two million mark."

"Superb!" exclaimed the boy. "Inspirational. Five thousand two hundred and eighty feet make a mile. Allow five feet per capita as the average length of your population." We watched him pencil a rapid sum. "Well, if you park your population end to end in 1935, they'll make a string of Los Angelians 1,893 miles long. Most of the way to Chicago. Simply inspirational!"

"Will you say that again?" asked Muscatol, attentively. Certain words and topics rang up his attention like a telephone.

The Harvard boy said it again. Muscatol whipped a pencil from where it was hooked in his vest pocket, and made some quick notes on his cuff.

"That's good publicity stuff," he remarked with approval. "Mind if I work it up?"

"Delighted!" said the boy, heartily.

"I sailed on January 29th," continued Muscatol. "Cunard to Cherbourg. Europe must have been alive once. I've seen it all I want—London,

Paris, Rome, their whole show. I've got specifications for a pan-Christian temple for our employees to read, swim, exercise, worship, and lunch in. All denominations. Surface area bigger than St. Peter's. Those cathedrals and Michael Angelos are fair bric-à-brac. We'll buy some and move 'em here, maybe. I guess their Reims cathedral would advertise our products among the high brows—if properly handled. Say, the blue water off our California coast makes their Mediterranean look white. This your first trip? I landed at Cherbourg.''

''My seventh,'' said the boy.

''Well, their hotels are falling over one another putting in bathrooms. We're telling Europe where to get off.''

''Isn't it glorious to lead the world in plumbing!'' exclaimed the boy.

''Oh!'' protested the gentle lady. ''We lead it in kindness and generosity to all in misfortune.''

''And in Art and Letters,'' said the boy.

She looked at him reproachfully.

''And in enterprise,'' said the Editor. ''And energy. And resourcefulness.''

She looked at him gratefully.

''And in charm of manner,'' said the boy, ''and courtesy to all nations.''

''I can't bear to hear you say those things!'' exclaimed the lady.

Muscatol had not been attentive to any of this.

Possibly he was planning how to handle Reims for publicity. But he caught the words "manner" and "courtesy," and spoke abruptly.

"Say. Those Europeans are too polite."

"But," said the boy earnestly, "which is more ethical, to be rude and not to mean it, or polite and not to mean it?"

"Surely we all believe in sincerity!" hurried in the lady, quite needlessly. Muscatol had hung up again.

"Well," smiled the boy, disarmingly, "if it's insincere to say 'pardon,' and touch your hat, and keep your criticisms to yourself instead of yelling them across space, I'll give you all the sincerity— if you'll let me have the agreeableness."

"Give us time," pleaded the lady. "We're so young." And she looked at him with pleading affection.

"Oh!" said he, "don't you think we overplay our youth?"

"This your first trip?" suddenly inquired Muscatol.

"My twelfth," replied the boy immediately.

"Well, come out and shake hands with Los Angeles. See our city grow overnight. We'll help you make up the time Harvard wasted for you. If those colleges back East don't drop their high-brow stuff and teach our boys how to make money, they'll be dead as Europe. It's Europe's jealousy that calls us dollar-chasers. When a European catches sight of an American dollar he develops a speed that puts us among the Also Rans."

Just then André Renaud passed us on his way out. He glanced curiously at Muscatol.

"What does America need most?" I inquired, reminded of the main epithet I was to find.

"Bigger and better publicity," said Muscatol, hitting the cloth with his fist.

"Our compartment sleeping-cars are un-American," said the Harvard boy. "They're too private. Undemocratic."

"Well," said Muscatol, dubiously, "maybe the sixteen-section sleeper is more typically American. Those Europeans build high walls round their places. Shut the public out. Americans like to look at one another's yards. Have a right to."

"Where in Europe can we see our neighbor's Monday wash wave in the wind?" asked the boy. "Once a week I pass the shirts and drawers of fifty Homes of Distinction a contractor has just put up outside our gate. Every neighbor can see through his neighbor's window what they're having for dinner and hear the tunes of their phonograph. Publicity, sir, is the breath of our national soul."

The lady of St. Paul seemed to struggle for

gravity; but Muscatol had already hung up, and wouldn't have understood anyhow.

"What does America need most?" I repeated, to fill the silence.

"Perhaps—perhaps—a little humility?" ventured the lady.

"Perhaps a little discipline?" I offered.

"How to get it?" demanded the Editor.

"Eat Muscatol and get it," said the boy.

"Not get: *forget*," corrected the man. The word had rung his number.

"In God we trust; it also pays to advertise," said the boy.

"You bet it pays!"

"Who, I ask you," and the boy looked at us all, "who cares for scenery? What message have the woods? Will a bald rock tell you what soups you need? When a road-side board informs you that you are in Ophelia, the town that built the first Chinese laundry in Petroleum County, why waste money on school histories?"

"We want no books," said Muscatol. "Literature is what the American people want, and our company is handing it to them right now. One million spent on literature this year. Free educational literature. By 1937 I'll have the American people educated up to eating Muscatol three times a day. This your first trip?"

"My fifteenth," said the boy.

The lady pressed her handkerchief to her eyes.

"Take a card," said Muscatol to the boy, handing him one. "I'm head of our publicity department. My name is Cartwell Ross Cartwell."

"Call me Home Sweet Home," said the boy. "Glad to meet you."

"Please excuse me," said the lady, rising hastily, with strange sounds. And she left us.

Cartwell Ross Cartwell stared after her with surprise; then he lighted a handsome cigar.

"Would you think," he inquired, "that little lady would be seasick on a day like this? Too bad. Nice little lady. Well, Mr. Home, come out and shake hands with Los Angeles." And he and his cigar also departed.

"Kindly brush me off," said the boy to the Editor, and turned his back.

"Well," said the Editor, "I would do it, since it's you. But I see nothing to brush. Perhaps you want me to praise your English clothes."

"They speak for themselves," said the boy. "I thought our friend might have chalked Eat and Forget on me."

"He wants bigger and better publicity," said the Editor.

"But she's a sweet old dear," said the boy, pointing to the lady's empty chair.

"Sentimental, though," said I.

"Typical," said the Editor. "We're the super-sentimentalists of the world. Sentimentalism is the mildew of American intelligence. I'll not live to see the day when we no longer burst into sobs over a child that has shot its grandmother in order to be featured on the front page. But you may," he added to the boy.

"You're an optimist!" said the boy.

"No. Nor a pessimist either. I avoid excess. In that I'm un-American. Bryan, our great apostle of temperance, died from over-eating. It's the most humorous event in American history. I doubt if any nation has ever been more mentally preposterous."

"Do you say that sort of thing in your magazines?" the boy inquired.

"Not on your life."

"What do you give them?"

"Any lie they want to hear, and not a truth that they don't. We've doubled our circulation in two years. Advertisers have to pay us top figures."

"Top figures?" said a voice at our backs.

It was Muscatol, come for a pack of leaflets he had left by his plate.

"What's top figures?" he repeated.

"What I charge for one whole-page insertion."

"What do you charge?"

"Ten thousand dollars."

"Meet me in the smoking room. Maybe I'll talk to you. Where do you put your apex at?"

"Of circulation?"

"Your own. Are you forty?"

"Forty-one."

"You've got fourteen years yet. Apexes vary according to a man's vocational nerve output during the period he is capitalizing his personality. When any man under me touches his apex, out he drops, and a younger man gets the job."

"When will a younger man get yours?" asked the Harvard boy.

"In twenty years. I'm thirty-five. Now an editor's job is advertisements. Up to his apex he is out to increase his advertisements, and his policy is aggressive. After his apex, he is afraid of decreasing his advertisements, and his policy is timid. Time to stop. His personality has been capitalized." And with this, away went Muscatol with his leaflets and his cigar.

"Bet he extends his apex when he gets there," said the boy.

"I don't know why he likes you," said the Editor. "But he does."

"He likes everybody," said the boy. "That's what I hate." And he finished his bottle of Pommard.

When I sat down by André in the smoking room
that night, he said:

"Who is your Roman?"

And then, before I took his meaning, he went on:

"His words I did not catch, but his conquering
voice reached me as I passed your table."

"He does not speak loud," said I.

"He has no need. He possesses the voice of the
conqueror. He comes from your West, is it not so?"

"Los Angeles."

"I could not be precise as to his city or state;
but I begin to observe many like him, all from your
West. There he comes."

Muscatol was taking a snug corner with the Editor, behind a table. They were plainly talking business, and at length plainly struck a bargain. The
Harvard boy was across the room, sipping a lonely
liqueur. Muscatol beckoned him to come over, and
the steward brought them further refreshments, and
continued to do so.

"I do not desire the society of your Roman,"
said André. "I have met several superior to him.
That is more than enough. But I admire the preda-
tory power of his eye, and the massive breadth of
his brow, and his vital hair, and his battering-ram
expression. From head to foot he is able, ruthless,
and sensual—the stuff of the eternal conqueror. See
them listen to him! They bend their heads closer,

because he is telling them an intimate anecdote,
very probably from his recent European experience. Now they grow confidential and impart
anecdotes to him. Your Charles Eliot type is extinct. Don't look disgusted, my friend. The Ro-
mans were rough-necks when they started, and in
a thousand years your American type will have de-
veloped a magnificent civilization. His chief de-
lusion at present is to think that he has invented
short cuts to experience."

"A thousand years!" said I. "You talk as if I
could wait."

"I am not offering consolation; I am reminding
you that Rome was not built in a day. If the Ro-
mans when Athens was at her zenith in the fifth
century before Christ had claimed that they were
civilized, all Greece would have smiled—as Europe
smiles at you to-day—except when your bad manners provoke a less indulgent emotion."

"Don't you think our prosperity provokes some
emotion, too?"

"But of course!"

"Do you think anybody ever loves a creditor?"

"Never! Of course Europe is human. I am
speaking of civilization, of which your masses—and
you are a land of masses, not of Charles Eliots—do
not yet comprehend the A B C. But you will have
your turn as Europe has had hers—and it will be

splendid. It is your bad luck to be living in a time
of transition, which is always restless and ugly."

"What do you call the A B C of civilization?"

"Tolerance. Intellectual and moral tolerance,
and to know the difference between idleness and
leisure. Intolerance and aimless haste have always
marked the savage, as they mark your masses.
Christ was tolerant, and He admired the lilies of
the field 'which toil not, neither do they spin.' Consider carefully the Roman at your table. He illus-
trates the main epithet."

"Pushing?" I hazarded at once. "Superficial?"

But André laughed. "And he will go where all
wicked Americans go. What a jolly time he is having with that charming Harvard student and that
acute Editor! He is taking the whole smoking room
into his vast confidence. All attend to him. Therefore, he is happy. Yes, he will go to—you'll tell me
where, before we land. As for me, I shall go to
bed."

I soon followed his example; and later was dimly
roused by the sound of persons tumbling downstairs
to bed, and singing as they fell.

André proved partly right—Muscatol did do his
bit toward my finding the main epithet—but a
younger and greater than he precipitated the
solution.

Wireless brought the news. All other news was struck dumb. No ear listened but to this, no tongue spoke but of it. Under its spell passengers and crew were magically made one beating heart for a while. The emotion of it lingered among us; we might talk of other things, but throughout the days following we came back to it like the burden of a ballad or a song. Our ship steamed west across a sea over which from the west had passed a boy on wings, unknown, alone, unadvertised, with silent daring, without a boast. Out of the world's noise and murk he had sailed up to where the vikings are, and Hector of the glancing helm, and the swift-footed Achilles— an apparition, he and his airship, swimming into our ken like Lohengrin and his swan. Like a breath from the heights he had come and breathed upon our drugged ideals, and they lived. And an American! And already among the legends! Without a Homer to sustain him there, could he remain? Ten thousand arms would reach out to pull down this quiet star that shone so clear above the glare of our hissing fireworks.

I heard the sonorous voice of the clergyman we had on board, saying that with that boy on the platform he could sell religion to South Dakota.

"Always hit it while it's hot."

This was Muscatol, frowning for some reason.

Wireless brought more news. The nations

were choiring anthems to the young viking of the air.

"Only twenty-five!" said the lady at table; and her lips trembled. "When I think of his mother! . . . It makes the world seem brighter."

"He's not being handled right," said Muscatol. And he shook his head somberly.

"Does seem as if unpractical people had got hold of him," said the Editor. He, too, was glum.

"What would be your idea of right handling?" inquired the Harvard boy.

"If he doesn't watch out," declared Muscatol, "he'll overstay his apex. They're not used to him yet. But they'll get used. They'll start thinking about somebody else—and there goes the biggest publicity value we'll ever see."

"Then here's to his being handled wrong!" exclaimed the boy; and he finished a second bottle of stout. "You'll get none ashore," he explained.

"See here," said Muscatol to him, kindly and with true concern, "you don't want him handled wrong. You don't want to talk that high-brow stuff. It's un-American. Sounds snobbish."

"I hope I'm a snob!"

"Now, boy, you know you don't mean that. You've got a big potential asset. Your personality is crying to be capitalized. Honest. You're of us, only you don't know it. If I had the handling of you—"

"Spare my blushes," laughed the boy, and suddenly fired a random shot. He looked from Muscatol to the Editor and back, paused, and took aim. "I know what's the matter with you two! He turned you down!"

There was a thunder-clap of silence.

"A bull's eye!" I shouted.

The gentle lady did not grasp it.

"They both wirelessed," the boy explained.

Still it failed to get home to her.

"Wirelessed Lindbergh. Tried to harness him to their own carts. Wanted to capitalize his personality."

"Oh," breathed the lady, taking it in at length.

"Bet he didn't spend any cash on answering," added the boy. "I'm afraid somebody is handling him wrong."

It was the Editor who first found his speech again.

"I have to be on my job, don't you see? I'd have met any figures he wanted for five thousand words."

All this while Muscatol had been eyeing the boy with considerable intensity.

"You're a peach!" he now broke out. "Put yourself in my hands, and it wouldn't take me two months—"

"To change the subject," said the boy, "what's this new Women of the West movement?"

Everybody attended.

"The fifty thousand earnest Women of the West.

You've heard about it? The next amendment to the Constitution?''

Nobody had heard.

''Why, they're going to change the name of the Battle of the Brandywine to the Battle of Sarsaparilla.''

''What battle was that?'' inquired Muscatol; so we told him.

Lunch was over, and as we separated the lady said to me:

''I wish to scold you.''

''Yes, ma'am,'' said I meekly.

So we sat down together, and she began, with a sweet smile, quite pink with her effort to be bold.

''I am a woman of the West.''

''Oh, he didn't mean your kind! You mustn't scold him, too.''

''I've no intention of it. My people are from New England. My grandfather—but never mind about me. He's a lovely boy.''

''I like him very much.''

''Who could help it? And yet you feel no responsibility for him.''

''Why, no. Why should I?''

''He is too much in the company of that dreadful man.''

''I haven't noticed that. But how should I stop it?''

"You have a bond with him. Didn't you go to Harvard?"

"Yes, ma'am. Some forty years before he did."

"It's more of a bond than he has with that dreadful man, listening to his polluting stories in the smoking room. An insidious influence."

"Dear lady, he's twenty-five years old!"

"Twenty-five. Just the age of the boy who flew over the ocean and uplifted us all. Do you think that other boy would put up with that advertising monster and his quack food? He's true American."

"Who? The monster?"

"No, no, no, never!"

"But he seems so to me."

"I hate to hear you say that!"

"Dear lady, I thank whatever gods there be that a boy I can claim as my fellow-countryman has made me feel again as I used at times to feel in the Great War, and have not felt since till now. I thank whatever gods there be that an American boy has done this thing in an un-American way."

"How can you call his courage un-American?"

"Have Americans a monopoly on courage? Have you never heard of English courage, or French courage? Courage is everywhere. But this boy took thought about every need, tested every inch and bolt, made ready without haste, set off without noise, arrived as if he had done nothing, stood the strain of mobs and kings and medals without a single break, and has flatly declined to capitalize his publicity, as our friend from Los Angeles puts it. How many like him can you count against our native legion of Muscatols?''

"It's terrible to hear you talk as if you didn't love your country!''

"If I didn't love her what should I care what she did? It's like having your mother make a guy of herself in the street.''

"Well, it's because you're old that you feel this way.''

I just caught myself in time not to say, "You must be sixty yourself,'' and instead I replied:

"The lovely boy you're so concerned about is only twenty-five, and he feels very much as I do.''

And then as she groped, baffled, but not refuted, for some supporting plausibility to go on with, all sorts of memories rose to support me, facts, experiences, weaving a steady pattern through the years.

"Listen, dear lady,'' I said. "If any country has a better heart than ours I've yet to learn its name. A better heart, or a more generous hand, or a higher aim. But if you, and people like you, 'can't bear to hear' a word in criticism, isn't that a sort of complacent paralysis? Do you wish the Muscatols to prevail? It's the chip too often on our shoulder, the manner too often bumptious, the too

constant showing off, the too ready loquacity, the
overflowing bluster—if we were only as sure of ourselves as the English are we'd not mention our
superiority so frequently; we'd take ourselves ever
so much more for granted! Listen. When I was
thirteen I came back from a winter in Rome, and
was standing in Chestnut Hill near my town, watching the sun set across a valley called Whitemarsh.

" 'And has thee seen,' said a Quaker lady beside
me as she pointed to the crimson sky, 'in thy
European travels anything equal to that?'

" 'Have you ever,' I answered, 'stood on the
Pincian Hill and seen the sun set behind the dome
of St. Peter's?'

"In Paris when I was twenty-two, a very rich
American lady gave a ball in her house facing the
Arc de Triomphe. Wishing to break a record, she
planned to illuminate the Arc as a feature for her
party. When they told her that she couldn't use a
public monument for a private purpose she offered
to hire the Arc for the evening.

"You will recall that a private American citizen
undertook to explain to Germany that peace was
better than war.

"You will recall that another private American
citizen organized a peace ship when pretty much
all Europe was fighting for its life, and expected a
dozen armies and several fleets to stop on his

account. 'History is bunk,' he had said; and he was going to 'have the boys out of the trenches by Christmas.'

"You may recall that a group of American females sent word to Europe that if Europe gave up wine and took to water we might forget their war debt. There's Monroe Doctrine for you!

"Do you remember that when the French franc was sinking to nothing and France was wrung with misery a young American lighted his cigarette with a French bank-note? . . . That other young Americans pasted French bank-notes on their valises, like hotel labels? . . . That a young American girl went to a fancy ball in Paris with a costume made of French money?"

I had a dozen other illustrations ready, but these seemed sufficient. They were too much for the poor lady.

"But democracy," she faltered, "surely we must expect—surely we ought to have patience!"

"Did it do much good to be patient about slavery? Do you want our democracy to become a thing which can turn any silk purse into a sow's ear?"

She clapped her hands over her ears. "I'll not hear such things!" she exclaimed, and she hurried away.

Well, thought I, her plea for patience made me impatient. But is impatience always a bad thing?

There's too much excuse-making everywhere. There's a lot of shirking disagreeable facts in the name of optimism or patriotism or something. Just like the days of the old Cunard line, before the White Star competition made them sit up. You'd say to your cabin steward, "You haven't given me a clean towel." And he'd say, "Yes, but we have never lost a passenger." You'd say to your saloon steward, "Take these scrambled eggs away, I've found a cockroach in them." And he'd say, "Yes, but we have never lost a passenger." Why eternally be making excuses that don't excuse? Better to be impatient now and then, and speak out your meaning in hotter terms than you mean it. It's over-statement that puts a truth across. Our good qualities are no answer to our bad manners. It's these that set the pace at home and give offense abroad. I'm sorry, though, that I made her mad. No, I'm not. Say what you think when you know you think it. And she believed that boy's modesty about his ocean flight was typically American! Why, it's not our idealism that's so visible to Europe just now; it's the huge glare of our immodesty.

"By jingo!" I said aloud. "I believe I've got André's main epithet. But where do wicked Americans go when they die?"

For a while I walked the deck, and after this exceedingly dull performance in the name of exercise, during which I passed and repassed the Harvard boy and Muscatol and the Editor playing shuffle-board, I settled in my chair to read a detective story. André's chair was vacant.

In time, I found myself at the two-hundredth page of the detective story, and quite unaware of what had so far happened in the plot. At this point I saw the Harvard boy coming along the deck alone, very slowly, very pensively.

"Look here a minute," I said.

He quickened his walk towards me. What was the matter with him?

"Well, sir?" said he, civil, but still preoccupied. Was he reflecting that his student days were over, his last long holiday at an end?

"Tell me where wicked Americans go when they die," I said.

He broke into a smile, and whatever had been in his face left it.

"How much time am I allowed?" he asked.

"Take time, and a cocktail with me."

"Here's with you, sir."

We met André, and I suggested that he join us.

"A cocktail? Yes, indeed. Ah, that is not the least of America's gifts to humanity!"

Before drinking he lifted his glass to the student.

"May I congratulate you on your high honors at graduation?"

"Why, how do you come to know that?"

"We professors hear things. You were recom-
mended as secretary to the most distinguished member of your Supreme Court at Washington."

"Yes."

"He is a great master of English. He can write
his opinions short, yet leave nothing unsaid."

"My father wished me to get down to work."
The cloud was in his face again. "By the time I'm
thirty-five, I suppose I may be making ten thousand
a year. That's an income you can't see with the
naked eye in these days."

"It's a long ladder," said I. "But one reaches
the top."

"Oh, yes. In some forty years." His eye went
to the door, and he frowned.

Muscatol was standing there and hailed him very
audibly, so that heads turned to see what it was.

"Not just now," he answered, rather curtly;
and Muscatol disappeared.

"When did he start calling you by your first
name?" I asked.

"I didn't invite him to. But he needs no invitations. His salary is one hundred thousand a year."
Suddenly the brightness of his look revived. "I
know where they go!"

"Meaning the wicked Americans?"

"Ah!" exclaimed André. "You have asked his
help. Take care. I allow you only one guess."

"Beg pardon, gentlemen," said the smoking-room steward. "If you wish anything to drink to-morrow please order it to-night on account of the twelve-mile limit. You can pay cash, and it shall be sent to your cabins."

He waited for our reply as I spoke to André.

"How many guesses do you give me for the main epithet?"

"One."

"A bottle of champagne to you if I fail, you to pay if I win?"

"Agreed."

"Another between us on similar terms?" said the boy.

"Young sir, I must land sober!"

"Between three strong men what's two bottles?"

"I agree, I agree."

As we ordered the wine, the trumpet sounded for dressing; and there stood Muscatol again at the door.

The boy nodded to him impatiently and rose.

"We'll do our guessing over the coffee," said I; and we separated.

The lady from St. Paul and I were the first at table, the others came some ten minutes late. She noticed their entrance and said to me:

"And so you're leaving him to his evil angel!"

"The Harvard boy? I'm not his good angel!"

"You might have been. I wish I could be."

When the three had sat down with us, the background of further cocktails was plainly discernible.

"Ten thousand when I'm thirty-five," said the boy to the lady, without preamble, and speaking with great care, as if he feared he might fumble it.

"I told you so," said she to me.

"How wonderful of you!" he said to her. "How did you guess it?"

"Fifty thousand in half the time," asserted Muscatol. "Unless I misjudge you. And I don't misjudge usually. Steward, two bottles of Pommery for the last dinner on board."

"To-morrow night we'll be dining in God's Country," said the boy with deliberate fervor.

Muscatol took him literally, of course.

"You bet we will!"

The lady declined the champagne with a cold firmness that made the Editor stare.

"She knows her mind when she chooses," he whispered to me with a cocktail nudge in my ribs.

"Here's to God's Country!" said Muscatol.

The boy would drink but one glass. "I've an ath-ath-letic contest on to-night," he explained. "In-tell-ectional athletics. Intellectual, I mean. Sorry. I give you one toast. Are your glasses charged?" He lifted his without spilling a drop, and said slowly and steadily: "To the chap who flew over the sea. Don't forget I drank to him!" he added earnestly, almost poignantly to me. "Never forget that." A curious effect of cocktails.

"I'll drink to his grit," said Muscatol. "Not to his brains."

"Let—letting himself be handled wrong?" suggested the boy.

"Sure he is."

"Might have leaped at a bound to the top of the ladder," the boy again suggested.

"Sure. He's a business failure."

"I'll drink to him again," whispered the boy to himself; and then to Muscatol, "Ain't it lucky for Am-America there are so few like him and so many like you!"

"That should get under his hide!" I said jocosely.

"He's got no hide to get under," laughed the Editor, with another confidential nudge against my ribs. "Neither have I." And his blue eyes shone like steel drills behind his spectacles.

"I hate—" began the lady, and stopped. Then she rose and left us.

"Why," said Muscatol in surprise, "it's as smooth as a billiard table."

"Perhaps," said I, "it is not the sea that has made her sick."

The athletic contest followed, in due time. The boy had recovered from his cocktails, and his thoughts and utterances were clean-cut once more. We sat in a soft-padded leather corner, behind our coffee cups, he, André, and I.

"May the youngest begin?" he asked, charmingly. Tipsy or sober, he was irresistible. "It flashed on me like an inspiration. Just as if I were a genius! But let me lead up to it. There's America, I thought. There's George Washington. He always wanted to retire beneath his vine and fig tree. First in war and first in peace, but he only spoke once during the whole Constitutional convention. Do Americans want to retire anywhere? Watch 'em parade. Always parading. Elks, Mystic Shriners; and Muscatol is a parade all by himself, all the time. Do Americans speak only once? Listen to 'em. Do you notice much silence? Then the boosters. Publicity. If you're giving a dinner, put it in the paper. If you're getting hanged, put it in the paper. So I said to myself, What do most Americans love most? Answer, Publicity. Therefore, my guess is: Wicked Americans when they die go to Eternal Privacy. Why, that's a poem!" he cried, and chanted it rhythmically. "Milton might have written it."

"I pay for your bottle," said André. "And I know you will succeed in life."

"Oh, yes, I shall succeed!" And a sudden tragic hardness aged his youthful face.

"Your turn," said André to me.

"Well, it took me some time. I'm not a genius."

"Oh, sir, I didn't mean I was!"

"I know you didn't. But in the end it sort of flashed on me, too. The main epithet for America just now is *immodest*."

"I am not sure that I pay for your bottle."

"Understand, I don't mean indecent. We're a decent people—though our young writers are trying hard to be indecent—but they can't do it gracefully. I mean immodest, self-praising, self-advertising, loud."

"I must pay for your bottle also," said André.

But only we two drank them next day—or rather, drank part of one in the seclusion of André's cabin.

The fog which lay thick over the smooth sea during the last night did not seriously delay our ship, for it had lifted when the sun rose. I dislike seeing sunrises, but the fog-horn had kept me sleepless; and in the dark hours I heard people tumbling downstairs, and singing as they fell. Had they done it every night? I don't know. I went to sleep after sunrise and slept sound and late. The steward made me get up for quarantine, and passports, and packing, and all the rest of it that goes on during those final restless hours of bustle as one steams up toward the operatic skyscrapers.

Only the lady and I were at lunch, and the messages which André sent to the boy to come to his cabin for the champagne brought no boy, and no answer. Whether he was sleeping his night off or not, I now believe he hid himself on purpose. At any rate, after our guessing contest over the coffee, I never had another word with him. One further sight of him I did have.

When we had docked, and the gangway was lowered, and the passengers were moving down its slant from the deck to the wharf, I saw him descending in the company of the Editor and Muscatol. And just then, as I waited among the crowded passengers and the stewards and the hand baggage, a gentle hand was laid upon my arm. It was the lady from St. Paul.

"I am to deliver a message to you. He asked me to tell you that he has decided not to practice law in Boston. He is going into that grape-food company in Los Angeles."

We stood looking at each other.

"Going to capitalize his personality," I said after some silence.

"And you could have stopped it!" she exclaimed. Tears were in her eyes.

"Oh, no. The Roman of the West carries heavier guns than mine."

"Deplorable!" she said.

"He's in great luck," I replied. "He will be handled right."

"I do hate to hear you say those things!"

It was the last thing that she did hear me say. The gangway, the wharf's great shed, the trunks and customs presently separated and absorbed us all, and we scattered on our several ways. I caught the six o'clock train for Philadelphia, daylight saving.

Scarce six months later a brilliant Muscatol literature was blazing in every magazine and every landscape. It held the eye, it caught the brain. Quite obviously the boy was being handled right.

Philosophy 4

A STORY OF HARVARD UNIVERSITY

I

TWO frowning boys sat in their tennis flannels beneath the glare of lamp and gas. Their leather belts were loosened, their soft pink shirts unbuttoned at the collar. They were listening with gloomy voracity to the instruction of a third. They sat at a table bared of its customary sporting ornaments, and from time to time they questioned, sucked their pencils, and scrawled vigorous, laconic notes. Their necks and faces shone with the bloom of out-of-doors. Studious concentration was evidently a painful novelty to their features. Drops of perspiration came one by one from their matted hair, and their hands dampened the paper upon which they wrote. The windows stood open wide to the May darkness, but nothing came in save heat and insects; for spring, being behind time, was making up with a sultry burst at the end, as a delayed train makes the last few miles high above schedule speed. Thus it had been since eight o'clock. Eleven was daintily striking now. Its diminutive sonority might have belonged to some

church-bell far distant across the Cambridge silence;
but it was on a shelf in the room,—a timepiece of
Gallic design, representing Mephistopheles, who ca-
ressed the world in his lap. And as the little strokes
boomed, eight—nine—ten—eleven, the voice of the
instructor steadily continued thus:—

"By starting from the Absolute Intelligence, the
chief cravings of the reason, after unity and spirit-
uality, receive due satisfaction. Something tran-
scending the Objective becomes possible. In the
Cogito the relation of subject and object is implied
as the primary condition of all knowledge. Now,
Plato never—"

"Skip Plato," interrupted one of the boys. "You
gave us his points yesterday."

"Yep," assented the other, rattling through the
back pages of his notes. "Got Plato down cold somewhere—oh, here. He never caught on to the subjective, any more than the other Greek bucks. Go
on to the next chappie."

"If you gentlemen have mastered the—the Grreek
bucks," observed the instructor, with sleek intona-
tion, "we—"

"Yep," said the second tennis boy, running a
rapid judicial eye over his back notes, "you've put
us on to their curves enough. Go on."

The instructor turned a few pages forward in

the thick book of his own neat type-written notes
and then resumed,—

"The self-knowledge of matter in motion."

"Skip it," put in the first tennis boy.

"We went to these lectures ourselves," explained
the second, whirling through another dishevelled
note-book. "Oh, yes. Hobbes and his gang. There is
only one substance, matter, but it doesn't strictly
exist. Bodies exist. We've got Hobbes. Go on."

The instructor went forward a few pages more
in his exhaustive volume. He had attended all the
lectures but three throughout the year, taking them
down in short-hand. Laryngitis had kept him from
those three, to which, however, he had sent a sten-
ographic friend, so that the chain was unbroken.
He now took up the next philosopher on the list; but
his smooth discourse was, after a short while, rudely
shaken. It was the second tennis boy questioning
severely the doctrines imparted.

"So he says color is all your eye, and shape isn't?
and substance isn't?"

"Do you mean he claims," said the first boy,
equally resentful, "that if we were all extinguished
the world would still be here, only there'd be no
difference between blue and pink, for instance?"

"The reason is clear," responded the tutor,
blandly. He adjusted his eye-glasses, placed their

elastic cord behind his ear, and referred to his notes.
"It is human sight that distinguishes between colors.
If human sight be eliminated from the universe,
nothing remains to make the distinction, and consequently there will be none. Thus also is it with
sounds. If the universe contains no ear to hear the
sound, the sound has no existence."

"Why?" said both the tennis boys at once.

The tutor smiled. "Is it not clear," said he,
"that there can be no sound if it is not heard?"

"No," they both returned, "not in the least
clear."

"It's clear enough what he's driving at, of
course," pursued the first boy. "Until the waves of
sound or light or what not hit us through our senses,
our brains don't experience the sensations of sound
or light or what not, and so, of course, we can't
know about them—not until they reach us."

"Precisely," said the tutor. He had a suave and
slightly alien accent.

"Well, just tell me how that proves a thunder-
storm in a desert island makes no noise."

"If a thing is inaudible—" began the tutor.

"That's mere juggling!" vociferated the boy.
"That's merely the same kind of toy-shop brain-
trick you gave us out of Greek philosophy yesterday. They said there was no such thing as motion
because at every instant of time the moving body

had to be somewhere, so how could it get anywhere else? Good Lord! I can make up foolishness like that myself. For instance: A moving body can never stop. Why? Why, because at every instant of time it must be going at a certain rate, so how can it ever get slower? Pooh!" He stopped. He had been gesticulating with one hand, which he now jammed wrathfully into his pocket.

The tutor must have derived great pleasure from his own smile, for he prolonged and deepened and variously modified it, while his shiny little calculating eyes travelled from one to the other of his ruddy scholars. He coughed, consulted his notes, and went through all the paces of superiority. "I can find nothing about a body's being unable to stop," said he, gently. "If logic makes no appeal to you, gentlemen—"

"Oh, bunch!" exclaimed the second tennis boy, in the slang of his period, which was the early eighties. "Look here. Color has no existence outside of our brain—that's the idea?"

The tutor bowed.

"And sound hasn't? and smell hasn't? and taste hasn't?"

The tutor had repeated his little bow after each.

"And that's because they depend on our senses? Very well. But he claims solidity and shape and distance do exist independently of us. If we all died,

they'd be here just the same, though the others
wouldn't. A flower would go on growing, but it
would stop smelling. Very well. Now you tell me
how we ascertain solidity. By the touch, don't we?
Then, if there was nobody to touch an object, what
then? Seems to me touch is just as much of a sense
as your nose is.'' (He meant no personality, but the
first boy choked a giggle as the speaker hotly followed up his thought.) ''Seems to me by his rea-
soning that in a desert island there'd be nothing at
all—smells or shapes—not even an island. Seems
to me that's what you call logic.''

The tutor directed his smile at the open window.
''Berkeley—'' said he.

''By Jove!'' said the other boy, not heeding him,
''and here's another point: If color is entirely in
my brain, why don't that ink-bottle and this shirt
look alike to me? They ought to. And why don't a
Martini cocktail and a cup of coffee taste the same
to my tongue?''

''Berkeley,'' attempted the tutor, ''demon-
strates—''

''Do you mean to say,'' the boy rushed on, ''that
there is no eternal quality in all these things which
when it meets my perceptions compels me to see
differences?''

The tutor surveyed his notes. ''I can discover no
such suggestions here as you are pleased to make,''

said he. "But your orriginal rresearches," he continued most obsequiously, "recall our next subject,
—Berkeley and the Idealists." And he smoothed
out his notes.

"Let's see," said the second boy, pondering; "I
went to two or three lectures about that time.
Berkeley—Berkeley. Didn't he—oh, yes! he did.
He went the whole hog. Nothing's anywhere except
in your ideas. You think the table's there, but it
isn't. There isn't any table."

The first boy slapped his leg and lighted a cigarette. "I remember," said he. "Amounts to this:
If I were to stop thinking about you, you'd evaporate."

"Which is balls," observed the second boy, judi-
cially, again in the slang of his period, "and can be
proved so. For you're not always thinking about
me, and I've never evaporated once."

The first boy, after a slight wink at the second,
addressed the tutor. "Supposing you were to happen to forget yourself," said he to that sleek gentleman, "would you evaporate?"

The tutor turned his little eyes doubtfully upon
the tennis boys, but answered, reciting the language of his notes: "The idealistic theory does not
apply to the thinking ego, but to the world of exter-
nal phenomena. The world exists in our conception
of it."

"Then," said the second boy, "when a thing is inconceivable?"

"It has no existence," replied the tutor, complacently.

"But a billion dollars is inconceivable," retorted the boy. "No mind can take in a sum of that size; but it exists."

"Put that down! put that down!" shrieked the other boy. "You've struck something. If we get Berkeley on the paper, I'll run that in." He wrote rapidly, and then took a turn around the room, frowning as he walked. "The actuality of a thing," said he, summing his clever thoughts up, "is not disproved by its being inconceivable. Ideas alone depend upon thought for their existence. There! Anybody can get off stuff like that by the yard." He picked up a cork, and a foot-rule, tossed the cork, and sent it flying out of the window with the foot-rule.

"Skip Berkeley," said the other boy. "How much more is there?"

"Necessary and accidental truths," answered the tutor, reading the subjects from his notes. "Hume and the causal law. The duality, or multiplicity, of the ego."

"The hard-boiled ego," commented the boy with the ruler; and he batted a swooping June-bug into space.

"Sit down, idiot," said his sprightly mate.

Conversation ceased. Instruction went forward. Their pencils worked. The causal law, etc., went into their condensed notes like Liebig's extract of beef, and drops of perspiration continued to trickle from their matted hair.

II

Bertie and Billy were sophomores. They had been alive for twenty years, and were young. Their tutor was also a sophomore. He, too, had been alive for twenty years, but never yet had become young. Bertie and Billy had colonial names (Rogers, I think, and Schuyler), but the tutor's name was Oscar Maironi, and he was charging his pupils five dollars an hour each for his instruction. Do not think this excessive. Oscar could have tutored a whole class of irresponsibles, and by that arrangement have earned probably more; but Bertie and Billy had preëmpted him on account of his fame for high standing and accuracy, and they could well afford it. All three sophomores alike had happened to choose Philosophy 4 as one of their elective courses, and all alike were now face to face with the Day of Judgment. The final examinations had begun. Oscar could lay his hand upon his studious heart and await the Day of Judgment like—I had nearly said a Christian! His notes were full: Three hundred pages about Zeno and Parmenides and the

rest, almost every word as it had come from the professor's lips. And his memory was full, too, flowing like a player's lines. With the right cue he
could recite instantly: "An important application
of this principle, with obvious reference to Heracleitos, occurs in Aristotle, who says—" He could
do this with the notes anywhere. I am sure you
appreciate Oscar and his great power of acquiring
facts. So he was ready, like the wise virgins of
parable. Bertie and Billy did not put one in mind
of virgins: although they had burned considerable
midnight oil, it had not been to throw light upon
Philosophy 4. In them the mere word Heracleitos
had raised a chill no later than yesterday,—the chill
of the unknown. They had not attended the lectures of the "Greek bucks." Indeed, profiting by
their privilege of voluntary recitations, they had
dropped in but seldom on Philosophy 4. These
blithe grasshoppers had danced and sung away the
precious storing season, and now that the bleak
hour of examinations was upon them, their waked-up
hearts had felt aghast at the sudden vision of
their ignorance. It was on a Monday noon that this
feeling came fully upon them, as they read over the
names of the philosophers. Thursday was the day
of the examination. "Who's Anaxagoras?" Billy
had inquired of Bertie. "I'll tell you," said Bertie,
"if you'll tell me who Epicharmos of Kos was."

And upon this they embraced with helpless laughter. Then they reckoned up the hours left for them to learn Epicharmos of Kos in,—between Monday noon and Thursday morning at nine,—and their quailing chill increased. A tutor must be called in at once. So the grasshoppers, having money, sought out and quickly purchased the ant.

Closeted with Oscar and his notes, they had, as Bertie put it, salted down the early Greek bucks by seven on Monday evening. By the same midnight they had, as Billy expressed it, called the turn on Plato. Tuesday was a second day of concentrated swallowing. Oscar had taken them through the thought of many centuries. There had been intermissions for lunch and dinner only; and the weather was exceedingly hot. The pale-skinned Oscar stood this strain better than the unaccustomed Bertie and Billy. Their jovial eyes had grown hollow to-night, although their minds were going gallantly, as you have probably noticed. Their criticisms, slangy and abrupt, struck the scholastic Oscar as flippancies which he must indulge, since the pay was handsome. That these idlers should jump in with doubts and questions not contained in his sacred notes raised in him feelings betrayed just once in that remark about "orriginal rresearch."

"Nine—ten—eleven—twelve," went the little timepiece; and Oscar rose.

"Gentlemen," he said, closing the sacred notes, "we have finished the causal law."

"That's the whole business except the ego racket, isn't it?" said Billy.

"The duality, or multiplicity, of the ego remains," Oscar replied.

"Oh, I know its name. It ought to be a soft snap after what we've had."

"Unless it's full of dates and names you've got to know," said Bertie.

"Don't believe it is," Billy answered. "I heard him at it once." (This meant that Billy had gone to a lecture lately.) "It's all about Who am I? and How do I do it?" Billy added.

"Hm!" said Bertie. "Hm! Subjective and objective again, I suppose, only applied to oneself. You see, that table is objective. I can stand off and judge it. It's outside of me; has nothing to do with me. That's easy. But my opinion of—well, my—well, anything in my nature—"

"Anger when it's time to get up," suggested Billy.

"An excellent illustration," said Bertie. "That is subjective in me. Similar to your dislike of water as a beverage. That is subjective in you. But here comes the twist. I can think of my own anger and judge it, just as if it were an outside thing, like a table. I can compare it with itself on different mornings or with other people's anger. And I trust that you can do the same with your thirst."

"Yes," said Billy; "I recognize that it is greater at times and less at others."

"Very well. There you are. Duality of the ego."

"Subject and object," said Billy. "Perfectly true, and very queer when you try to think of it. Wonder how far it goes? Of course, one can explain the body's being an object to the brain inside it. That's mind and matter over again. But when my own mind and thought can become objects to themselves—I wonder how far that does go?" he broke off musingly. "What useless stuff!" he ended.

"Gentlemen," said Oscar, who had been listening to them with patient, Oriental diversion, "I—"

"Oh," said Bertie, remembering him. "Look here. We mustn't keep you up. We're awfully obliged for the way you are putting us on to this. You're saving our lives. Ten to-morrow for a grand review of the whole course."

"And the multiplicity of the ego?" inquired Oscar.

"Oh, I forgot. Well, it's too late to-night. Is it much? Are there many dates and names and things?"

"It is more of a general inquiry and analysis," replied Oscar. "But it is forty pages of my notes." And he smiled.

"Well, look here. It would be nice to have to-morrow clear for review. We're not tired. You leave us your notes and go to bed."

Oscar's hand almost moved to cover and hold his precious property, for this instinct was the deepest in him. But it did not so move, because his intelligence controlled his instinct nearly, though not quite, always. His shiny little eyes, however, became furtive and antagonistic—something the boys did not at first make out.

Oscar gave himself a moment of silence. "I could not brreak my rule," said he then. "I do not ever leave my notes with anybody. Mr. Woodridge asked for my History 3 notes, and Mr. Bailey wanted my notes for Fine Arts 1, and I could not let them have them. If Mr. Woodridge was to hear—"

"But what in the dickens are you afraid of?"

"Well, gentlemen, I would rather not. You would take good care, I know, but there are sometimes things which happen that we cannot help. One time a fire—"

At this racial suggestion both boys made the room joyous with mirth. Oscar stood uneasily contemplating them. He would never be able to understand them, not as long as he lived, nor they him. When their mirth was over he did somewhat better, but it was tardy. You see, he was not a specimen of the first rank, or he would have said at once what he said now: "I wish to study my notes a little myself, gentlemen."

"Go along, Oscar, with your inflammable notes, go along!" said Bertie, in supreme good-humor. "And we'll meet to-morrow at ten—if there hasn't been a fire. Better keep your notes in the bath, Oscar."

In as much haste as could be made with a good appearance, Oscar buckled his volume in its leather cover, gathered his hat and pencil, and, bidding his pupils a very good night, sped smoothly out of the room.

III

Oscar Maironi was very poor. His thin gray suit in summer resembled his thick gray suit in winter. It does not seem that he had more than two; but he had a black coat and waistcoat, and a narrow-brimmed, shiny hat to go with these, and one pair of patent-leather shoes that laced, and whose long soles curved upward at the toe like the rockers of a summer-hotel chair. These holiday garments served him in all seasons; and when you saw him dressed in them, and seated in a car bound for Park Square, you knew he was going into Boston, where he would read manuscript essays on Botticelli or Pico della Mirandola, or manuscript translations of Armenian folk-songs; read these to ecstatic, dim-eyed ladies

in Newbury Street, who would pour him cups of
tea when it was over, and speak of his earnestness
after he was gone. It did not do the ladies any harm;
but I am not sure that it was the best thing for
Oscar. It helped him feel every day, as he stepped
along to recitations with his elbow clamping his
books against his ribs and his heavy black curls
bulging down from his gray slouch hat to his collar,
how meritorious he was compared with Bertie and
Billy—with all Berties and Billies. He may have
been. Who shall say? But I will say at once that
chewing the cud of one's own virtue gives a sour
stomach.

Bertie's and Billy's parents owned town and
country houses in New York. The parents of Oscar
had come over in the steerage. Money filled the
pockets of Bertie and Billy; therefore were their
heads empty of money and full of less cramping
thoughts. Oscar had fallen upon the reverse of this
fate. Calculation was his second nature. He had
given his education to himself; he had for its
sake, toiled, traded, outwitted, and saved. He had
sent himself to college, where most of the hours not
given to education and more education, went to toiling and more toiling, that he might pay his meagre
way through the college world. He had a cheaper
room and ate cheaper meals than was necessary.
He tutored, and he wrote college specials for several

newspapers. His chief relaxation was the praise
of the ladies in Newbury Street. These told him of
the future which awaited him, and when they gazed
upon his features were put in mind of the dying
Keats. Not that Oscar was going to die in the least.
Life burned strong in him. There were sly times
when he took what he had saved by his cheap meals
and room and went to Boston with it, and for a few
hours thoroughly ceased being ascetic. Yet Oscar
felt meritorious when he considered Bertie and
Billy; for, like the socialists, merit with him meant
not being able to live as well as your neighbor.
You will think that I have given to Oscar what is
familiarly termed a black eye. But I was once inclined to applaud his struggle for knowledge, until
I studied him close and perceived that his love was
not for the education he was getting. Bertie and
Billy loved play for play's own sake, and in play
forgot themselves, like the wholesome young crea-
tures that they were. Oscar had one love only:
through all his days whatever he might forget, he
would remember himself; through all his days he
would make knowledge show that self off. Thank
heaven, all the poor students in Harvard College
were not Oscars! I loved some of them as much as I
loved Bertie and Billy. So there is no black eye
about it. Pity Oscar, if you like; but don't be so
mushy as to admire him as he stepped along in the

night, holding his notes, full of his knowledge, thinking of Bertie and Billy, conscious of virtue, and
smiling his smile.

They were not conscious of any virtue, were Bertie and Billy, nor were they smiling. They were
solemnly eating up together a box of handsome
strawberries and sucking the juice from their red-
dened thumbs.

"Rather mean not to make him wait and have
some of these after his hard work on us," said Bertie. "I'd forgotten about them."

"He ran out before you could remember, anyway," said Billy.

"Wasn't he absurd about his old notes?" Bertie
went on, a new strawberry in his mouth. "We don't
need them, though. With to-morrow we'll get this
course down cold."

"Yes, to-morrow," sighed Billy. "It's awful to
think of another day of this kind."

"Horrible," assented Bertie.

"He knows a lot. He's extraordinary," said
Billy.

"Yes, he is. He can talk the actual words of the
notes. Probably he could teach the course himself.
I don't suppose he buys any strawberries, even
when they get ripe and cheap here. What's the matter with you?"

Billy had broken suddenly into merriment. "I
don't believe Oscar owns a bath," he explained.

"By Jove! so his notes will burn in spite of everything!" And both of the tennis boys shrieked foolishly.

Then Billy began taking his clothes off, strewing them in the window-seat, or anywhere that they happened to drop; and Bertie, after hitting another cork or two out of the window with the tennis racket, departed to his own room on another floor and left Billy to immediate and deep slumber. This was broken for a few moments when Billy's room-mate returned happy from an excursion which had begun in the morning.

The room-mate sat on Billy's feet until that gentleman showed consciousness.

"I've done it," said the room-mate, then.

"The hell you have!"

"You couldn't do it."

"The hell I couldn't!"

"Great dinner."

"The hell it was!"

"Soft-shell crabs, broiled live lobster, salmon, grass-plover, dough-birds, rum omelette. Bet you five dollars you can't find it."

"Take you. Go to bed." And Billy fell again into deep, immediate slumber.

The room-mate went out into the sitting room, and noting the signs there of the hard work which had gone on during his absence, was glad that he did not take Philosophy 4. He was soon asleep also.

IV

Billy got up early. As he plunged into his cold
bath he envied his room-mate, who could remain at
rest indefinitely, while his own hard lot was hurry-
ing him to prayers and breakfast and Oscar's in-
exorable notes. He sighed once more as he looked
at the beauty of the new morning and felt its air
upon his cheeks. He and Bertie belonged to the same
club-table, and they met there mournfully over the
oatmeal. This very hour to-morrow would see them
eating their last before the examination in Philosophy 4. And nothing pleasant was going to happen
between,—nothing that they could dwell upon with
the slightest satisfaction. Nor had their sleep entirely refreshed them. Their eyes were not quite
right, and their hair, though it was brushed, showed
fatigue of the nerves in a certain inclination to
limpness and disorder.

> "Epicharmos of Kos
> Was covered with moss,"

remarked Billy.

> "Thales and Zeno
> Were duffers at keno,"

added Bertie.

In the hours of trial they would often express
their education thus.

"Philosophers I have met," murmured Billy, with scorn. And they ate silently for some time.

"There's one thing that's valuable," said Bertie next. "When they spring those tricks on you about the flying arrow not moving, and all the rest, and prove it all right by logic, you learn what pure logic amounts to when it cuts loose from common sense. And Oscar thinks it's immense. We shocked him."

"He's found the Bird-in-Hand!" cried Billy, quite suddenly.

"Oscar?" said Bertie, with an equal shout.

"No, John. John has. Came home last night and waked me up and told me."

"Good for John," remarked Bertie pensively.

Now, to the undergraduate mind of that day the Bird-in-Hand tavern was what the golden fleece used to be to the Greeks,—a sort of shining, remote, miraculous thing, difficult though not impossible to find, for which expeditions were fitted out. It was reported to be somewhere in the direction of Quincy, and in one respect it resembled a ghost: you never saw a man who had seen it himself; it was always his cousin, or his elder brother in '79. But for the successful explorer a dinner and wines were waiting at the Bird-in-Hand more delicious than anything outside of Paradise. You will realize, therefore, what a thing it was to have a room-mate who had attained. If Billy had not been so dog-tired last night, he would have sat up and made John tell him everything from beginning to end.

"Soft-shell crabs, broiled live lobster, salmon, grass-plover, dough-birds, and rum omelette," he was now reciting to Bertie.

"They say the rum there is old Jamaica brought in slave-ships," said Bertie, reverently.

"I've heard he has white port of 1820," said Billy; "and claret and champagne."

Bertie looked out of the window. "This is the finest day there's been," said he. Then he looked at his watch. It was twenty-five minutes before Oscar. Then he looked Billy hard in the eye. "Have you any sand?" he inquired.

It was a challenge to Billy's manhood. "Sand!" he yelled, sitting up.

Both of them in an instant had left the table and bounded out of the house.

"I'll meet you at Pike's," said Billy to Bertie. "Make him give us the black gelding."

"Might as well bring our notes along," Bertie called after his rushing friend; "and get John to tell you the road."

To see their haste, as the two fled in opposite directions upon their errands, you would have supposed them under some crying call of obligation, or else to be escaping from justice.

Twenty minutes later they were seated behind the black gelding and bound on their journey in search of the Bird-in-Hand. Their notes in Philosophy 4 were stowed under the buggy-seat.

"Did Oscar see you?" Bertie inquired.

"Not he," cried Billy, joyously.

"Oscar will wonder," said Bertie; and he gave the black gelding a triumphant touch with the whip.

You see, it was Oscar that had made them run so; or, rather, it was Duty and Fate walking in Oscar's displeasing likeness. Nothing easier, nothing more reasonable, than to see the tutor and tell him they should not need him to-day. But that would have spoiled everything. They did not know it, but deep in their childlike hearts was a delicious sense that in thus unaccountably disappearing they had won a great game, had got away ahead of Duty and Fate. After all, it did bear some resemblance to an escape from justice.

Could he have known this, Oscar would have felt more superior than ever. Punctually at the hour agreed, ten o'clock, he rapped at Billy's door and stood waiting, his leather wallet of notes nipped safe between elbow and ribs. Then he knocked again. Then he tried the door, and as it was open, he walked deferentially into the sitting room. Sonorous snores came from one of the bedrooms. Oscar peered in and saw John; but he saw no Billy in the other bed.

Then, always deferential, he sat down in the sitting room and watched a couple of prettily striped coats hanging in a half-open closet.

At that moment the black gelding was flirtatiously crossing the drawbridge over the Charles on the Allston Road. The gelding knew the clank of those suspending chains and the slight unsteadiness of the meeting halves of the bridge as well as it knew oats. But it could not enjoy its own entirely premeditated surprise quite so much as Bertie and Billy were enjoying their entirely unpremeditated flight from Oscar. The wind rippled on the water; down at the boat-house Smith was helping some one embark in a single scull; they saw the green meadows toward Brighton; their foreheads felt cool and unvexed, and each new minute had the savor of fresh forbidden fruit.

"How do we go?" said Bertie.

"I forgot I had a bet with John until I had waked him," said Billy. "He bet me five last night I couldn't find it, and I took him. Of course, after that I had no right to ask him anything, and he thought I was funny. He said I couldn't find out if the landlady's hair was her own. I went him another five on that."

"How do you say we ought to go?" said Bertie, presently.

"Quincy, I'm sure."

They were now crossing the Albany tracks at Allston. "We're going to get there," said Bertie; and
he turned the black gelding toward Brookline and
Jamaica Plain.

The enchanting day surrounded them. The suburban houses, even the suburban street-cars, seemed
part of one great universal plan of enjoyment.
Pleasantness so radiated from the boys' faces and
from their general appearance of clean white flannel
trousers and soft clean shirts of pink and blue that
a driver on a passing car leaned to look after them
with a smile and a butcher hailed them with loud
brotherhood from his cart. They turned a corner,
and from a long way off came the sight of the tower
of Memorial Hall. Plain above all intervening tene-
ments and foliage it rose. Over there beneath its
shadow were examinations and Oscar. It caught
Billy's roving eye, and he nudged Bertie, pointing
silently to it. "Ha, ha!" sang Bertie. And beneath
his light whip the gelding sprang forward into its
stride.

The clocks of Massachusetts struck eleven. Oscar
rose doubtfully from his chair in Billy's study.
Again he looked into Billy's bedroom and at the
empty bed. Then he went for a moment and watched
the still forcibly sleeping John. He turned his eyes
this way and that, and after standing for a while

moved quietly back to his chair and sat down with
the leather wallet of notes on his lap, his knees together, and his unblacked shoes touching. In due
time the clocks of Massachusetts struck noon.

In a meadow where a brown amber stream ran,
lay Bertie and Billy on the grass. Their summer
coats were off, their belts loosened. They watched
with eyes half closed the long water-weeds moving
gently as the current waved and twined them. The
black gelding, brought along a farm road and
through a gate, waited at its ease in the field beside
a stone wall. Now and then it stretched and cropped
a young leaf from a vine that grew over the wall,
and now and then the warm wind brought down
the fruit blossoms all over the meadow. They fell
from the tree where Bertie and Billy lay, and the
boys brushed them from their faces. Not very far
away was Blue Hill, softly shining; and crows high
up in the air came from it occasionally across here.

By one o'clock a change had come in Billy's
room. Oscar during that hour had opened his satchel
of philosophy upon his lap and read his notes attentively. Being almost word perfect in many parts of
them, he now spent his unexpected leisure in acquiring accurately the language of still further
paragraphs. "The sharp line of demarcation which

Descartes drew between consciousness and the material world," whispered Oscar with satisfaction, and knew that if Descartes were on the examination paper he could start with this and go on for nearly twenty lines before he would have to use any words of his own. As he memorized, the chambermaid, who had come to do the bedrooms three times already and had gone away again, now returned and no longer restrained her indignation. "Get up, Mr. Blake!" she vociferated to the sleeping John; "you ought to be ashamed!" And she shook the bedstead. Thus John had come to rise and discover Oscar. The patient tutor explained himself as John listened in his pyjamas.

"Why, I'm sorry," said he, "but I don't believe they'll get back very soon."

"They have gone away?" asked Oscar, sharply.

"Ah—yes," returned the reticent John. "An unexpected matter of importance."

"But, my dear sir, those gentlemen know nothing! Philosophy 4 is to-morrow, and they know nothing."

"They'll have to stand it, then," said John, with a grin.

"And my time. I am waiting here. I am engaged to teach them. I have been waiting here since ten. They engaged me all day and this evening."

"I don't believe there's the slightest use in your

waiting now, you know. They'll probably let you know when they come back."

"Probably! But they have engaged my time. The girl knows I was here ready at ten. I call you to witness that you found me waiting, ready at any time."

John in his pyjamas stared at Oscar. "Why, of course they'll pay you the whole thing," said he, coldly; "stay here if you prefer." And he went into the bathroom and closed the door.

The tutor stood awhile, holding his notes and turning his little eyes this way and that. His young days had been dedicated to getting the better of his neighbor, because otherwise his neighbor would get the better of him. Oscar had never suspected the existence of boys like John and Bertie and Billy. He stood holding his notes, and then, buckling them up once more, he left the room with evidently reluctant steps. It was at this time that the clocks struck one.

In their field among the soft new grass sat Bertie and Billy some ten yards apart, each with his back against an apple tree. Each had his notes and took his turn at questioning the other. Thus the names of the Greek philosophers with their dates and doctrines were shouted gayly in the meadow. The foreheads of the boys were damp to-day, as they had been last night, and their shirts were opened to the

air; but it was the sun that made them hot now, and
no lamp or gas; and already they looked twice as
alive as they had looked at breakfast. There they
sat, while their memories gripped the summarized
list of facts essential, facts to be known accurately;
the simple, solid, raw facts, which, should they happen to come on the examination paper, no skill could
evade nor any imagination supply. But this study
was no longer dry and dreadful to them: they
turned it to a sporting event. "What about Heracleitos?" Billy as catechist would put at Bertie.
"Eternal flux," Bertie would correctly snap back at
Billy. Or, if he got it mixed up, and replied, "Everything is water," which was the doctrine of another Greek, then Billy would credit himself with
twenty-five cents on a piece of paper. Each ran a
memorandum of this kind; and you can readily see
how spirited a character metaphysics would assume
under such conditions.

"I'm going in," said Bertie, suddenly, as Billy
was crediting himself with a fifty-cent gain.
"What's your score?"

"Two seventy-five, counting your break on Parmenides. It'll be cold."

"No, it won't. Well, I'm only a quarter behind
you." And Bertie pulled off his shoes. Soon he
splashed into the stream where the bend made a hole
of some depth.

"Cold?" inquired Billy on the bank.

Bertie closed his eyes dreamily. "Delicious," said he, and sank luxuriously beneath the surface with slow strokes.

Billy had his clothes off in a moment, and, taking the plunge, screamed loudly. "You liar!" he yelled, as he came up. And he made for Bertie.

Delight rendered Bertie weak and helpless; he was caught and ducked; and after some vigorous wrestling both came out of the icy water.

"Now we've got no towels, you fool," said Billy.

"Use your notes," said Bertie, and he rolled in the grass. Then they chased each other round the apple trees, and the black gelding watched them by the wall, its ears well forward.

While they were dressing they discovered it was half-past one, and became instantly famished. "We should have brought lunch along," they told each other. But they forgot that no such thing as lunch could have induced them to delay their escape from Cambridge for a moment this morning. "What do you suppose Oscar is doing now?" Billy inquired of Bertie, as they led the black gelding back to the road; and Bertie laughed like an infant. "Gentlemen," said he, in Oscar's manner, "we now approach the multiplicity of the ego." The black gelding must have thought it had humorists to deal with this day.

Oscar, as a matter of fact, was eating his cheap

lunch away over in Cambridge. There was cold mut-
ton, and boiled potatoes with hard brown spots in
them, and large pickled cucumbers; and the salt was
damp and would not shake out through the holes
in the top of the bottle. But Oscar ate two helps of
everything with a good appetite, and between
whiles looked at his notes, which lay open beside
him on the table. At the stroke of two, he was again
knocking at his pupils' door. But no answer came.
John had gone away somewhere for indefinite hours
and the door was locked. So Oscar wrote: "Called,
two P.M.," on a scrap of envelope, signed his name
and put it through the letter-slit. It crossed his
mind to hunt other pupils for his vacant time,
but he decided against this at once, and returned to
his own room. Three o'clock found him back at the
door, knocking scrupulously. The idea of perform-
ing his side of the contract, of tendering his goods
and standing ready at all times to deliver them,
was in his commercially mature mind. This time he
had brought a neat piece of paper with him, and
wrote upon it, "Called, three P.M.," and signed it
as before, and departed to his room with a sense of
fulfilled obligations.

Bertie and Billy had lunched at Mattapan quite
happily on cold ham, cold pie, and doughnuts. Mattapan, not being accustomed to such lilies of the

field, stared at their clothes and general glory, but observed that they could eat the native bill-of-fare as well as anybody. They found some good, cool beer, moreover, and spoke to several people of the Bird-in-Hand, and got several answers: for instance, that the Bird-in-Hand was at Hingham; that it was at Nantasket; that they had better inquire for it at South Braintree; that they had passed it a mile back; and that there was no such place. If you would gauge the intelligence of our population, inquire your way in a rural neighborhood. With these directions they took up their journey after an hour and a half,—a halt made chiefly for the benefit of the black gelding, whom they looked after as much as they did themselves. For a while they discussed club matters seriously, as both of them were officers of certain organizations, chosen so on account of their recognized executive gifts. These questions settled, they resumed the lighter theme of philosophy, and made it (as Billy observed) a near thing for the Causal law. But as they drove along, their minds left this topic on the abrupt discovery that the sun was getting down out of the sky, and they asked each other where they were and what they should do. They pulled up at some cross-roads and debated this with growing uneasiness. Behind them lay the way to Cambridge,—not very clear, to be sure; but you could always go where you had come

from, Billy seemed to think. He asked, "How
about Cambridge and a little Oscar to finish off
with?" Bertie frowned. This would be failure.
Was Billy willing to go back and face John the
successful?

"It would only cost me five dollars," said Billy.

"Ten," Bertie corrected. He recalled to Billy the
matter about the landlady's hair.

"By Jove, that's so!" cried Billy, brightening.
It seemed conclusive. But he grew cloudy again the
next moment. He was of opinion that one could go
too far in a thing.

"Where's your sand?" said Bertie.

Billy made an unseemly rejoinder, but even in
the making was visited by inspiration. He saw the
whole thing as it really was. "By Jove!" said he,
"we couldn't get back in time for dinner."

"There's my bonny boy!" said Bertie, with pride;
and he touched up the black gelding. Uneasiness
had left both of them. Cambridge was manifestly
impossible; an error in judgment; food compelled
them to seek the Bird-in-Hand. "We'll try Quincy,
anyhow," Bertie said. Billy suggested that they
inquire of people on the road. This provided a new
sporting event: they could bet upon the answers.
Now, the roads, not populous at noon, had grown
solitary in the sweetness of the long twilight. Voices
of birds there were; and little, black, quick brooks,

full to the margin grass, shot under the roadway through low bridges. Through the web of young foliage the sky shone saffron, and frogs piped in the meadow swamps. No cart or carriage appeared, however, and the bets languished. Bertie, driving with one hand, was buttoning his coat with the other, when the black gelding leaped from the middle of the road to the turf and took to backing. The buggy reeled; but the driver was skilful, and fifteen seconds of whip and presence of mind brought it out smoothly. Then the cause of all this spoke to them from a gate.

"Come as near spillin' as you boys wanted, I guess," remarked the cause.

They looked, and saw him in huge white shirtsleeves, shaking with joviality. "If you kep' at it long enough, you might a-most learn to drive a horse," he continued, eying Bertie. This came as near direct praise as the true son of our soil—Northern or Southern—often thinks well of. Bertie was pleased, but made a modest observation, and "Are we near the tavern?" he asked. "Bird-in-Hand!" the son of the soil echoed; and he contemplated them from his gate. "That's me," he stated with complacence. "Bill Diggs of the Bird-in-Hand has been me since April, '65." His massy hair had been yellow, his broad body must have weighed two hundred and fifty pounds, his wide face was canny,

red, and somewhat clerical, resembling Henry Ward
Beecher's.

"Trout," he said, pointing to a basket by the gate.
"For your dinner." Then he climbed heavily but
skilfully down and picked up the basket and a rod.
"Folks round here say," said he, "that there ain't
no more trout up them meadows. They've been
a-sayin' that since '74; and I've been a-sayin' it
myself, when judicious." Here he shook slightly
and opened the basket. "Twelve," he said. "Six-
teen yesterday. Now you go along and turn in the
first right-hand turn, and I'll be up with you soon.
Maybe you might make room for the trout." Room
for him as well, they assured him; they were in luck
to find him, they explained. "Well, I guess I'll trust
my neck with you," he said to Bertie, the skilful
driver; " 'tain't five minutes' risk." The buggy
leaned, and its springs bent as he climbed in, wedg-
ing his mature bulk between their slim shapes. The
gelding looked round the shaft at them. "Pro-
testin', are you?" he said to it. "These light-weight
stoodents spile you!" So the gelding went on, expressing, however, by every line of its body, a sense
of outraged justice. The boys related their difficult
search, and learned that any mention of the name
Diggs would have brought them straight. "Bill
Diggs of the Bird-in-Hand was my father, and my
grandf'ther, and his father; and has been me sence

I come back from the war and took the business in
'65. I'm not commonly to be met out this late.
About fifteen minutes earlier is my time for gettin'
back, unless I'm plannin' for a jamboree. But to-
night I got to settin' and watchin' that sunset, and
listenin' to a darned red-winged black-bird, and I
guess Mrs. Diggs has decided to expect me some-
wheres about noon to-morrow or Friday. Say, did
Johnnie send you?" When he found that John had
in a measure been responsible for their journey, he
filled with gayety. "Oh, Johnnie's a bird!" said he.
"He's that demure on first appearance. Walked in
last evening and wanted dinner. Did he tell you
what he ate? Guess he left out what he drank.
Yes, he's demure."

You might suppose that upon their landlord's
safe and sober return fifteen minutes late, instead
of on the expected noon of Thursday or Friday,
their landlady would show signs of pleasure; but
Mrs. Diggs from the porch threw an uncordial eye
at the three arriving in the buggy. Here were two
more like Johnnie of last night. She knew them by
the clothes they wore and by the confidential tones
of her husband's voice as he chatted to them. He had
been old enough to know better for twenty years.
But for twenty years he had taken the same extreme
joy in the company of Johnnies, and they were bad
for his health. Her final proof that they belonged

to this hated breed was when Mr. Diggs thumped
the trout down on the porch, and after briefly remarking, "Half of 'em boiled, and half broiled
with bacon," himself led away the gelding to the
stable instead of intrusting it to his man Silas.

"You may set in the parlor," said Mrs. Diggs,
and departed stiffly with the basket of trout.

"It's false," said Billy, at once.

Bertie did not grasp his thought.

"Her hair," said Billy. And certainly it was an
unusual-looking arrangement.

Presently, as they sat near a parlor organ in the
presence of earnest family portraits, Bertie made a
new poem for Billy,—

> "Said Aristotle unto Plato,
>   'Have another sweet potato?'"

And Billy responded,—

> "Said Plato unto Aristotle,
>   'Thank you, I prefer the bottle.'"

"In here, are you?" said their beaming host at
the door. "Now, I think you'd find my department
of the premises cosier, so to speak." He nudged
Bertie. "Do you boys guess it's too early in the
season for a silver-fizz?"

We must not wholly forget Oscar in Cambridge.
During the afternoon he had not failed in his

punctuality; two more neat witnesses of this lay on
the door-mat beneath the letter-slit of Billy's room.
And at the appointed hour after dinner a third
joined them, making five. John found these cards
when he came home to go to bed, and picked them
up and stuck them ornamentally in Billy's looking-
glass, as a greeting when Billy should return. The
eight o'clock visit was the last that Oscar paid to
the locked door. He remained through the evening
in his own room, studious, contented, unventilated,
indulging in his thick notes, and also in the thought
of Billy's and Bertie's eleventh-hour scholarship.
"Even with another day," he told himself, "those
young men could not have got fifty per cent." In
those times this was the passing mark. To-day I
believe you get an A, or a B, or some other letter
denoting your rank. In due time Oscar turned out
his gas and got into his bed; and the clocks of Massachusetts struck midnight.

Mrs. Diggs of the Bird-in-Hand had retired at
eleven, furious with rage, but firm in dignity in
spite of a sudden misadventure. Her hair, being the
subject of a sporting event, had remained steadily
fixed in Billy's mind,—steadily fixed throughout
an entertainment which began at an early hour to
assume the features of a celebration. One silver-fizz
before dinner is nothing; but dinner did not come

at once, and the boys were thirsty. The hair of Mrs.
Diggs had caught Billy's eye again immediately
upon her entrance to inform them that the meal
was ready; and whenever she re-entered with a new
course from the kitchen, Billy's eye wandered back
to it, although Mr. Diggs had become full of anecdotes about the Civil War. It was partly Grecian:
a knot stood out behind to a considerable distance.
But this was not the whole plan. From front to
back ran a parting, clear and severe, and curls fell
from this to the temples in a manner called, I believe
by the enlightened, *à l'Anne d'Autriche*. The color
was gray, to be sure; but this propriety did not save
the structure from Billy's increasing observation.
As bottles came to stand on the table in greater
numbers, the closer and the more solemnly did Billy
continue to follow the movements of Mrs. Diggs.
They would without doubt have noticed him and his
foreboding gravity but for Mr. Diggs's experiences
in the Civil War.

The repast was finished—so far as eating went.
Mrs. Diggs with changeless dudgeon was removing
and washing the dishes. At the revelers' elbows
stood the 1820 port in its fine, fat, old, dingy bottle,
going pretty fast. Mr. Diggs was nearing the end
of Antietam. "That morning of the 18th, while
McClellan was holdin' us squattin' and cussin'," he
was saying to Bertie, when some sort of shuffling

sound in the corner caught their attention. We can never know how it happened. Billy ought to know, but does not, and Mrs. Diggs allowed no subsequent reference to the casualty. But there she stood with her entire hair at right angles. The Grecian knot extended above her left ear, and her nose stuck through one set of *Anne d'Autriche.* Beside her Billy stood, solemn as a stone, yet with a sort of relief glazed upon his face.

Mr. Diggs sat straight up at the vision of his spouse. "Flouncing Florence!" was his exclamation. "Geewhittaker, Mary, if you ain't the most unmitigated sight!" And wind then left him.

Mary's reply arrived in tones like a hornet stinging slowly and often. "Mr. Diggs, I have put up with many things, and am expecting to put up with many more. But you'd behave better if you consorted with gentlemen."

The door slammed and she was gone. Not a word to either of the boys, not even any notice of them. It was thorough, and silence consequently held them for a moment.

"He didn't mean anything," said Bertie, growing partially responsible.

"Didn't mean anything," repeated Billy, like a lesson.

"I'll take him and he'll apologize," Bertie pursued, walking over to Billy.

"He'll apologize," went Billy, like a cheerful piece of mechanism. Responsibility was still quite distant from him.

Mr. Diggs got his wind back. "Better not," he advised in something near a whisper. "Better not go after her. Her father was a fightin' preacher, and she's—well, begosh! she's a chip of the old pulpit." And he rolled his eye towards the door. Another door slammed somewhere above, and they gazed at each other, did Bertie and Mr. Diggs. Then Mr. Diggs, still gazing at Bertie, beckoned to him with a speaking eye and a crooked finger; and as he beckoned, Bertie approached like a conspirator and sat down close to him. "Begosh!" whispered Mr. Diggs. "Unmitigated." And at this he and Bertie laid their heads down on the table and rolled about in spasms.

Billy from his corner seemed to become aware of them. With his eye fixed upon them like a statue, he came across the room, and, sitting down near them with formal politeness, observed, "Was you ever to the battle of Antietam?" This sent them beyond the limit; and they rocked their heads on the table and wept as if they would expire.

Thus the three remained, during what space of time is not known: the two upon the table, convalescent with relapses, and Billy like a seated idol, unrelaxed at his vigil. The party was seen through the windows by Silas, coming from the stable to inquire if the gelding should not be harnessed. Silas leaned his face to the pane, and envy spoke plainly in it. "O my! O my!" he mentioned aloud to himself. So we have the whole household: Mrs. Diggs reposing scornfully in an upper chamber; all parts of the tavern darkened, save the one lighted room; the three inside that among their bottles, with the one outside looking covetously in at them; and the gelding stamping in the stable.

But Silas, since he could not share, was presently of opinion that this was enough for one sitting, and he tramped heavily upon the porch. This brought Bertie back to the world of reality, and word was given to fetch the gelding. The host was in no mood to part with them, and spoke of comfortable beds and breakfast as early as they liked; but Bertie had become entirely responsible. Billy was helped in, Silas was liberally thanked, and they drove away beneath the stars, leaving behind them golden opinions, and a host who decided not to disturb his helpmate by retiring to rest in their conjugal bed.

Bertie had forgotten, but the playful gelding had not. When they came abreast of that gate where Diggs of the Bird-in-Hand had met them at sunset, Bertie was only aware that a number of things had happened at once, and that he had stopped the horse after about twenty yards of battle. Pride filled him,

but emptied away in the same instant, for a voice
on the road behind him spoke inquiringly through
the darkness.

"Did anyone fall out?" said the voice. "Who
fell out?"

"Billy!" shrieked Bertie, cold all over. "Billy,
are you hurt?"

"Did Billy fall out?" said the voice, with plaintive cadence. "Poor Billy!"

"He can't be," muttered Bertie. "Are you?" he
loudly repeated.

There was no answer; but steps came along the
road as Bertie checked and pacified the gelding.
Then Billy appeared by the wheel. "Poor Billy fell
out," he said mildly. He held something up, which
Bertie took. It had been Billy's straw hat, now a
brimless fabric of ruin. Except for smirches and
one inexpressible rent which dawn revealed to
Bertie a little later, there were no further injuries,
and Billy got in and took his seat quite competently.

Bertie drove the gelding with a firm hand after
this. They passed through the cool of the unseen
meadow swamps, and heard the sound of the hollow
bridges as they crossed them, and now and then
the gulp of some pouring brook. They went by the
few lights of Mattapan, seeing from some points
on their way the beacons of the harbor, and again
the curving line of lamps that drew the outline of

some village built upon a hill. Dawn showed them
Jamaica Pond, smooth and breezeless, and encir-
cled with green skeins of foliage, delicate and new.
Here multitudinous birds were chirping their tiny,
overwhelming chorus. When at length, across the
flat suburban spaces, they again sighted Memorial
tower, small in the distance, the sun was lighting it.

Confronted by this, thoughts of hitherto ban-
ished care, and of the morrow that was now to-day,
and of Philosophy 4 coming in a very few hours,
might naturally have arisen and darkened the end
of their pleasant excursion. Not so, however. Memorial tower suggested another line of argument.
It was Billy who spoke, as his eyes first rested upon
that eminent pinnacle of Academe.

"Well, John owes me five dollars."

"Ten, you mean."

"Ten? How?"

"Why, her hair. And it was easily worth
twenty."

Billy turned his head and looked suspiciously at
Bertie. "What did I do?" he asked.

"Do! Don't you know?"

Billy in all truth did not.

"Phew!" went Bertie. "Well, I don't, either.
Didn't see it. Saw the consequences, though. Don't
you remember being ready to apologize? What do
you remember, anyhow?"

Billy consulted his recollections with care: they
seemed to break off at the champagne. That was
early. Bertie was astonished. Did not Billy remember singing "Brace up and dress the Coun-
tess," and "A noble lord the Earl of Leicester"?
He had sung them quite in his usual manner, con-
versing freely between whiles. In fact, to see and
hear him, no one would have suspected— "It must
have been that extra silver-fizz you took before
dinner," said Bertie. "Yes," said Billy; "that's
what it must have been." Bertie supplied the gap
in his memory,—a matter of several hours, it
seemed. During most of this time Billy had met
the demands of each moment quite like his usual
agreeable self—a sleep-walking state. It was only
when the hair incident was reached that his conduct
had noticeably crossed the line. He listened to all
this with interest intense.

"John does owe me ten, I think," said he.

"I say so," declared Bertie. "When do you
begin to remember again?"

"After I got in again at the gate. Why did I
get out?"

"You fell out, man."

Billy was incredulous.

"You did. You tore your clothes wide open."

Billy, looking at his trousers, did not see it.

"Rise, and I'll show you," said Bertie.

"Goodness gracious!" said Billy.

Thus discoursing, they reached Harvard Square. Not your Harvard Square, gentle reader, that place populous with careless youths and careful maidens and reticent persons with books, but one of sleeping windows and clear, cool air and few sounds; a Harvard Square of emptiness and conspicuous sparrows and milk wagons and early street-car conductors in long coats going to their breakfast; and over all this the sweetness of the arching elms.

As the gelding turned down toward Pike's, the thin old church clock struck. "Always sounds," said Billy, "like cambric tea."

"Cambridge tea," said Bertie.

"Walk close behind me," said Billy, as they came away from the livery stable. "Then they won't see the hole."

Bertie did so; but the hole was seen by the street-car conductors and the milk men, and these sympathetic hearts smiled at the sight of the marching boys, and loved them without knowing any more of them than this. They reached their building and separated.

V

One hour later they met. Shaving and a cold bath and summer flannels, not only clean but beautiful, invested them with the radiant innocence of

flowers. It was still too early for their regular
breakfast, and they sat down to eggs and coffee at
the Holly Tree.

"I waked John up," said Billy. "He is satisfied."

"Let's have another order," said Bertie. "These
eggs are delicious." Each of them accordingly ate
four eggs and drank two cups of coffee.

"Oscar called five times," said Billy; and he
threw down those cards which Oscar had so neatly
written.

"There's multiplicity of the ego for you!" said
Bertie.

Now, inspiration is a strange thing, and less obe-
dient even than love to the will of man. It will decline to come when you prepare for it with the
loftiest intentions, and, lo! at an accidental word
it will suddenly fill you, as at this moment it filled
Billy.

"By gum!" said he, laying his fork down. "Multiplicity of the ego. Look here. I fall out of a
buggy and ask—"

"By gum!" said Bertie, now also visited by
inspiration.

"Don't you see?" said Billy.

"I see a whole lot more," said Bertie, with excitement. "I had to tell you about your singing."
And the two burst into a flare of talk.

To hear such words as cognition, attention, re-
tention, entity, and identity, freely mingled with
such other words as silver-fizz and false hair,
brought John, the egg-and-coffee man, as near surprise as his impregnable nature permitted. Thus
they finished their large breakfast, and hastened
to their notes for a last good bout at memorizing
Epicharmos of Kos and his various brethren. The
appointed hour found them crossing the college
yard toward a door inside which Philosophy 4
awaited them: three hours of written examination!
But they looked more roseate and healthy than most
of the anxious band whose steps were converging
to that same gate of judgment. Oscar, meeting
them on the way, gave them his deferential "Good
morning," and trusted that the gentlemen felt
easy. Quite so, they told him, and bade him feel
easy about his pay, for which they were, of course,
responsible. Oscar wished them good luck and
watched them go to their desks with his little eyes,
smiling in his particular manner. Then he dismissed
them from his mind, and sat with a faint remnant
of his smile, fluently writing his perfectly accurate
answer to the first question upon the examination
paper.

Here is that paper. You will not be able to answer all the questions, probably, but you may be
glad to know what such things are like.

PHILOSOPHY 4

1. Thales, Zeno, Parmenides, Heracleitos, Anaxagoras. State briefly the doctrine of each.

2. Phenomenon, noumenon. Discuss these terms. Name their modern descendants.

3. Thought=Being. Assuming this, state the difference, if any, between (1) memory and anticipation; (2) sleep and waking.

4. Democritus, Pythagoras, Bacon. State the relation between them. In what terms must the objective world ultimately be stated? Why?

5. Experience is the result of time and space being included in the nature of mind. Discuss this.

6. Nihil est in intellectu quod non prius fuerit in sensibus. Whose doctrine? Discuss it.

7. What is the inherent limitation in all ancient philosophy? Who first removed it?

8. Mind is expressed through what? Matter through what? Is speech the result or the cause of thought?

9. Discuss the nature of the ego.

10. According to Plato, Locke, Berkeley, where would the sweetness of a honeycomb reside? Where would its shape? its weight? Where do you think these properties reside?

Ten questions, and no Epicharmos of Kos. But no examination paper asks everything, and this one did ask a good deal. Bertie and Billy wrote the full time allotted, and found that they could have filled an hour more without coming to the end of their thoughts. Comparing notes at lunch, their information was discovered to have been lacking here and there. Nevertheless, it was no failure; their inner convictions were sure of fifty per cent at least, and this was all they asked of the gods. "I was ripping about the ego," said Bertie. "I was rather splendid myself," said Billy, "when I got going. And I gave him a huge steer about memory." After lunch both retired to their beds and fell into sweet oblivion until seven o'clock, when they rose and dined, and after playing a little poker went to bed again pretty early.

Some six mornings later, when the Professor returned their papers to them, their minds were washed almost as clear of Plato and Thales as were their bodies of yesterday's dust. The dates and doctrines, hastily memorized to rattle off upon the great occasion, lay only upon the surface of their minds, and after use they quickly evaporated. To their pleasure and most genuine astonishment, the Professor paid them high compliments. Bertie's discussion of the double personality had been the most intelligent which had come in from any of the class. The illustration of the intoxicated hack-driver who had fallen from his hack and inquired who it was that had fallen, and then had pitied himself, was, said the Professor, as original and perfect an illustration of our subjective-objectivity as he had met with in all his researches. And Billy's suggestions concerning the inherency of time and space in the mind the Professor had also found very striking and independent, particularly his reason-

ing based upon the well-known distortions of time
and space which hashish and other drugs produce
in us. This was the sort of thing which the Professor had wanted from his students: free comment
and discussions, the *spirit* of the course, rather than
any strict adherence to the letter. He had constructed his questions to elicit as much individual
discussion as possible and had been somewhat disappointed in his hopes.

Yes, Bertie and Billy were astonished. But their
astonishment did not equal that of Oscar, who had
answered many of the questions in the Professor's
own language. Oscar received seventy-five per cent
for this achievement—a good mark. But Billy's
mark was eighty-six and Bertie's ninety. "There
is some mistake," said Oscar to them when they
told him; and he hastened to the Professor with
his tale. "There is no mistake," said the Professor.
Oscar smiled with increased deference. "But," he
urged, "I assure you, sir, those young men knew
absolutely nothing. I was their tutor, and they
knew nothing at all. I taught them all their information myself." "In that case," replied the
Professor, not pleased with Oscar's tale-bearing,
"you must have given them more than you could
spare. Good morning."

Oscar never understood. But he graduated con-
siderably higher than Bertie and Billy, who were

not able to discover many other courses so favorable to "orriginal rresearch" as was Philosophy 4. That is twenty years ago. To-day Bertie is treasurer of the New Amsterdam Trust Company, in Wall Street; Billy is superintendent of passenger traffic of the New York and Chicago Air Line. Oscar is successful too. He has acquired a lot of information. His smile is unchanged. He has published a careful work entitled "The Minor Poets of Cinquecento," and he writes book reviews for the *Evening Post*.

Mother

WHEN handsome young Richard Field—he was very handsome and very young—announced to our assembled company that if his turn should really come to tell us a story, the story should be no invention of his fancy, but a page of truth, in which himself was the hero and a lovely, innocent girl was the heroine, his wife at once looked extremely uncomfortable. She changed the reclining position in which she had been leaning back in her chair, and she sat erect, with a hand closed upon each arm of the chair.

"Richard," she said, "do you think that it is right of you to tell any one, even friends, anything that you have never yet confessed to me?"

"Ethel," replied Richard, "although I cannot promise that you will be entirely proud of my conduct when you have heard this episode of my past, I do say that there is nothing in it to hurt the trust you have placed in me since I have been your husband. Only," he added, "I hope that I shall not have to tell any story at all."

"Oh, yes, you will!" we all exclaimed together; and the men looked eager while the women sighed.

The rest of us were much older than Richard,

we were middle-aged, in fact; and human nature is so constructed, that when it is at the age when making love keeps it busy, it does not care so much to listen to tales of others' love-making; but the more it recedes from that period of exuberance, and ceases to have love adventures of its own, the greater become its hunger and thirst to hear about this delicious business which it can no longer personally practise with the fluency of yore. It was for this reason that we all yearned in our middle-aged way for the tale of love which we expected from young Richard. He, on his part, repeated the hope that by the time his turn to tell a story was reached we should be tired of stories and prefer to spend the evening at the card tables or in the music room.

We were a house party, no brief "week-end" affair, but a gathering whose period for most of the guests covered a generous and leisurely ten days, with enough departures and arrivals to give that variety which is necessary among even the most entertaining and agreeable people. Our skilful hostess had assembled us in the country, beneath a roof of New York luxury, a luxury which has come in these later days to be so much more than princely. By day, the grounds afforded us both golf and tennis, the stables provided motor cars and horses to ride or drive over admirable roads, through beautiful scenery that was embellished by a magnificent autumn season. At nightfall, the great house itself received us in the arms of supreme comfort, fed us sumptuously, and after dinner ministered to our middle-aged bodies with chairs and sofas of the highest development.

The plan devised by our hostess, Mrs. Davenport, that a story should be told by one of us each evening, had met with courtesy, but not with immediate enthusiasm. But Mrs. Davenport had chosen her guests with her usual wisdom, and after the first experiment, story telling proved so successful that none of us would have readily abandoned it. When the time had come for Richard Field to entertain the company with the promised tale from his life experience, his hope of escaping the ordeal had altogether vanished.

Mrs. Field, it had been noticed as early as breakfast time, was inclined to be nervous on her husband's account. Five years of married life had not cured her of this amiable symptom, and she made but a light meal. He, on the other hand, ate heartily and without signs of disturbance. Apparently he was not even conscious of the glances that his wife so frequently stole at him.

"Do at least have some omelet, my dear," whispered Mrs. Davenport urgently. "It's quite light."

But Mrs. Field could summon no appetite.

"I see you are anxious about him," Mrs.

Davenport continued after breakfast. "You are surely not afraid his story will fail to interest us?"

"No, it is not that."

"It can't be that he has given up the one he expected to tell us and can think of no other?"

"Oh, no; he is going to tell that one."

"And you don't like his choice?"

"He won't tell me what it is!"

Mrs. Davenport put down her embroidery. "Then, Ethel," she said with severity, "the fault is yours. When I had been five years married, Mr. Davenport confided everything to me."

"So does Richard. Except when I particularly ask him."

"There it is, Ethel. You let him see that you want to know."

"But I do want to know. Richard has had such interesting experiences, so many of them. And I do so want him to tell a thoroughly nice one. There's the one when he saved a man from drowning just below our house, the second summer, and the man turned out to be a burglar and broke into the pantry that very night, and Richard caught him in the dark with just as much courage as he had caught him in the water, and with just as few clothes, only it was so different. Richard makes it quite thrilling. And I mentioned another to him. But he just went on shaving. And now he has gone out walking, and I believe it's going to be something I would rather not hear. But I mean to hear it.''

At lunch Mrs. Field made a better meal, although it was clear to Mrs. Davenport that Richard on returning from his walk had still kept his intentions from Ethel.

''She does not manage him in the least,'' Mrs. Davenport declared to the other ladies, as Ethel and Richard started for an afternoon drive together. ''She will not know anything more when she brings him back.''

But in this Mrs. Davenport did wrong to Ethel's resources. The young wife did know something more when she brought her husband back from their drive through the pleasant country. They returned looking like an engaged couple, rather than parents whose nursery was already a song of three little voices.

''He has told her,'' thought Mrs. Davenport at the first sight of them, as they entered the drawing-room for afternoon tea. ''She does understand some things.''

And when after dinner the ladies had withdrawn to the library, and waited for the men to finish their cigars, Mrs. Davenport spoke to Ethel. ''My dear, I congratulate you. I saw it at once.''

''But he hasn't. Richard hasn't told me anything.''

"Ethel! Then what is the matter?"

"I told him something. I told him that if it was going to be any story about—about something I shouldn't like, I should simply follow it with a story about him that he wouldn't like."

"Ethel! You darling!"

"Oh, yes, and I said I was sure you would all listen, even though I was not an author myself. And I have it ready, you know, and it's awfully like Richard, only a different side of him from the burglar one."

"But my dear, what did he do when you—"

This inquiry was, however, cut short by the entrance of the men. And from the glance that came from Richard's eyes as they immediately sought out his wife, Mrs. Davenport knew that he could not have done anything very severe to Ethel when she made that threat to him during their drive.

Richard at once made his way to the easy-chair arranged each night in a good position for the narrator of the evening, and baptised "The Singstool" by Mr. Graves. Mr. Graves was an ardent Wagnerian, and especially devoted to The Mastersingers of Nüremberg.

"Shall we have," he whispered to Mr. Hillard, "a Beckmesser fiasco to-night, or will it be a Walter success?"

But Mr. Hillard, besides being an author and critic, cared little for the too literary cleverness of Mr. Graves. He therefore heavily crushed that gentleman's allusion to Wagner's opera. "I remember," he said, "the singing contest between Beckmesser and Walter, and I doubt if we are to be afflicted with anything so dull in this house."

Richard had settled himself in the easy-chair, and was looking thoughtfully at various objects in the room, while the small-talk was subsiding around him.

"Why, Mr. Field," said Mrs. Davenport, "you look as if you could find nothing to suggest your story to you."

"On the contrary," said Richard, "it is the number of things that suggest it. This newspaper here, that has arrived since I was last in the room, has a column which reminds me very forcibly of the experience that I have selected to tell you. But I think the most appropriate of all is that picture." He pointed to the largest picture on the wall. "'Breaking Home Ties' is the title, I remember very well. It is a replica of the original that drew such crowds in the Art Building at the World's Fair."

While Richard was saying this, his wife had possessed herself of the newspaper, and he now observed how eagerly she was scanning its pages. "It is the financial column, Ethel, that recalls my story."

Ethel, after a hopeless glance at this, resumed her seat near the sofa by Mrs. Davenport.

"There were many paintings," continued Richard, "in that Art Building, of merit incomparably greater than 'Breaking Home Ties'; and yet the crowd never looked at those, because it did not understand them. But at any hour of the day, if you happened to pass this picture, it took you some time to do so. You could pass any of John Sargent's pictures, for instance, at a speed limited only by your own powers of running; but you could never run past 'Breaking Home Ties.' You had to work your way through the crowd in front of that just as you have to do at a fire, or a news office during a football game. The American people could never get enough of that mother kissing her boy good-bye, while the wagon waits at the open door to take him away from her upon his first journey into the world. The idea held a daily pathos for them. Many had themselves been through such leave takings; and no word so stirs the general heart as the word 'mother.' Song writers know this; and the artist knew it when he decided to paint 'Breaking Home Ties.' And 'Mother' is the title of my story to-night."

" 'Mother!' " This was Ethel's bewildered echo. "Whose Mother?" she softly murmured to herself.

Richard continued. "It concerns the circumstances under which I became engaged to my wife.''

There was a movement from Ethel as she sat by the sofa.

''Not all the circumstances, of course,'' the narrator continued, with a guarded candour in his tone. ''There are certain circumstances which naturally attend every engagement between happy and—and devoted—young people, that they keep to themselves quite carefully, in spite of the fact that any one who has been through the experience of being engaged two or three times—''

There was another movement from Ethel by the sofa.

''—or even only once, as is my case,'' the narrator went on, ''anybody, I say, who has been through the experience of being engaged only once, can form a very correct idea of the circumstances that attend the happy engagements of all young people. I imagine they prevail in all countries, just as the feeling about 'mother' prevails. Yes, 'Mother' is the right title for my story, as you shall see. Is it not strange that if you add 'in-law' to the word 'mother,' how immediately the sentiment of the term is altered?—as strongly indeed as when you prefix the word 'step' to it. But it is with neither of these composite forms of mother that my story deals.

"Ethel has always maintained that if I had really understood her, it never would have happened. She says—"

"Richard, I—"

"My dear, you shall tell your story afterwards, and I promise to listen without a word until you are finished. Mrs. Field says that if I had understood her nature as a man ought to understand the girl he has been thinking about for several years, I should have known she cared nothing about my income."

"I didn't care! I'd have"—but Mrs. Field checked her outburst.

"She was going to say," said Mr. Field, "that had I asked her to marry me when I became sure that I wished to marry her, she would have been willing to leave New York and go to the waste land in Michigan that was her inheritance from a grand-father, and there build a cabin and live in it with me; and that while I shot prairie chickens for dinner she would have milked the cow, which some member of the family would have been willing to give us as a wedding present instead of a statue of the Winged Victory, or silver spoons and forks, had we so desired."

Richard made a pause here, and looked at his wife as if he expected her to correct him. But Ethel was plainly satisfied with his statement, and he therefore continued.

"I think it is ideal when a girl is ready to do so much as that for a man. But I should not think it ideal in a man to allow the girl he loved to do it for him. Nor did I then know anything about the lands in Michigan—though this would have made no difference. Ethel had been accustomed to a house several stories high, with hot and cold water in most of them, and somebody to answer the door-bell."

"The door-bell!" exclaimed Ethel. "I could have gone without hearing that."

"Yes, Ethel, only to hear the welkin ring would have been enough for you. I know that you are sincere in thinking so. And the ringing welkin is all we should have heard in Michigan. But the more truly a man loves a girl, the less can he bear taking her from an easy to a hard life. I am sure that all the men here agree with me."

There was a murmur and a nod from the men, and also from Mrs. Davenport. But the other ladies gave no sign of assenting to Richard's proposition.

"In those days," said he, "I was what in the curt parlance of the street is termed a six-hundred-dollar clerk. And though my ears had grown accustomed to this appellation, I never came to feel that it completely described me. In passing Tiffany's window twice each day (for my habit was to walk to and from Nassau Street) I remember that seeing a thousand-dollar clock exposed for sale caused me annoyance. Of course my salary as a clerk brought me into unfavorable comparison with the clock; and I doubt if I could make you understand my sometimes feeling when I passed Tiffany's window that I should like to smash the clock.

"I met Ethel frequently in society, dancing with her, and sitting next her at dinners. And by the time I had dined at her own house, and walked several afternoons with her, my lot as a six-hundred-dollar clerk began to seem very sad to me. I wrote verses about it, and about other subjects also. From an evening passed with Ethel, I would go next morning to the office and look at the other clerks. One of them was fifty-five, and he still received six hundred dollars—his wages for the last thirty years. I was then twenty-one; and though I never despaired to the extent of believing that years would fail to increase my value to the firm by a single cent, still, for what could I hope? If my salary were there and then to be doubled, what kind of support was twelve hundred dollars to offer Ethel, with her dresses, and her dinners, and her father's carriage? For two years I was wretchedly unhappy beneath the many hours of gaiety that came to me, as to every young man."

"Those two years we could have been in Michigan," said Ethel, "had you understood."

"I know. But understanding, I believe that I should do the same again. At the office when not busy, I wrote more poetry, and began also to write prose, which I found at the outset less easy. When my first writings were accepted (they were four sets of verses upon the Summer Resort) I felt that I could soon address Ethel; for I had made ten dollars outside my salary. Had she not been in Europe that July, I believe that I should have spoken to her at once. But I sent her the paper; and I have the letter that she wrote in reply."

"I—" began Ethel. But she stopped.

"Yes, I know now that you kept the verses," said Richard. "My next manuscript, however, was rejected. Indeed, I went on offering my literary productions nearly every week until the following January before a second acceptance came. It was twenty-five dollars this time, and almost made me feel again that I could handsomely support Ethel. But not quite. After the first charming elation at earning money with my pen, those weeks of refusal had caused me to think more soberly. And though I was now bent upon becoming an author and leaving Nassau Street, I burned no bridges behind me, but merely filled my spare hours with writing and with showing it to Ethel.

"It was now that the second great perturbation of my life came to me. I say the second, because the first had been the recent dawning belief that Ethel thought about me when I was not there to remind her of myself. This idea had stirred—but you will understand. And now, what was my proper, my honorable course? It was a positive relief that at this crisis she went to Florida. I could think more quietly. My writing had come to be quite often accepted, sometimes even solicited. Should I speak to her, and ask her to wait until I could put a decent roof over her head, or should I keep away from her until I could offer such a roof? Her father, I supposed, could do something for us. But I was not willing to be a pensioner. His business—were he generous—would be to provide cake and butter; but the bread was to be mine—and bread was still a long way off, according to New York standards. These things I thought over while she was in Florida; yet when once I should find myself with her again, I began to fear that I could not hold myself from—but these are circumstances which universal knowledge renders it needless to mention, and I will pass to the second perturbation.

"A sum of money was suddenly left me. Then for the first time I understood why I had during my boyhood been so periodically sent to see a cross old brother of my mother's, who lived near Cold Spring on the Hudson, and whom we called Uncle Snaggletooth when no one could hear us. Uncle

Godfrey (for I have called him by his right name ever since) died and left me what in those old days, six years ago, was still a large amount. To-day we understand what true riches mean. But in those bygone times, six years ago, a million dollars was a sum considerable enough to be still seen, as it were, with the naked eye. That was my bequest from Uncle Godfrey, and I felt myself to be the possessor of a fortune.''

At this point in Richard's narrative, a sigh escaped from Ethel.

"I know," he immediately said, "that money is always welcome. But it is certainly some consolation to reflect how slight a loss a million dollars is counted to-day in New York. And I did not lose all of it.

"I met Ethel at the train on her return from Florida, and crossed with her on the ferry from Jersey City to Desbrosses Street. There I was obliged to see her drive away in the carriage with her father.''

"Mr. Field," said Mrs. Davenport, "what hour did that train arrive at Jersey City?''

Richard looked surprised. "Why, seven-fifteen P.M.," he replied. "The tenth of March.''

"Dark!" Mrs. Davenport exclaimed. "Mr. Field, you and Ethel were engaged before the ferry boat landed at Desbrosses Street.''

Richard and Ethel both sat straight up, but remained speechless.

"Pardon my interruption," said Mrs. Davenport, smiling. "I didn't want to miss a single point in this story—do go on!"

Richard was obliged to burst out laughing, in which Ethel, after a moment, followed him, though perhaps less heartily. And as he continued, his blush subsided.

"With my Uncle Godfrey's legacy I was no longer dependent upon my salary, or my pen, or my father's purse; and I decided that with the money properly invested, I could maintain a modest establishment of my own. Ethel agreed with me entirely; and, after a little, we disclosed our plans to our families, and they met with approval. This was in April, and we thought of October or November for the wedding. It seemed long to wait; but it came near being so much longer, that I grow chilly now to think of it.

"Of course, I went steadily on with my work at the office in Nassau Street, nor did I neglect my writing entirely. My attention, however, was now turned to the question of investing my fortune. Just round the corner from our office was the firm of Blake and Beverly, Stocks and Bonds. Thither my steps began frequently to turn. Mr. Beverly had business which brought him every week to the room of our president; and so having a sort of acquaintance with him, I felt it easier to consult him than to seek any other among the brokers, to which class I was a well-nigh total stranger. He very kindly consented to be my adviser. I was well pleased to find how much I had underrated the interest-bearing capacity of my windfall. 'Four per cent!' he cried, when I told him this was the extent of my expectations. 'Why, you're talking like a trustee.' And then seeing that his meaning was beyond me, he explained in his bluff, humorous manner: 'All a trustee cares for, you know, is his reputation for safety. It's not his own income he's nursing, and so he doesn't care how small he makes it, provided only that his investments would be always called safe. Now there are ways of being safe without spending any trouble or time upon it; and those are the ways a trustee will take. For example,' and here he arose, and unhooking a file of current quotations from the wall, placed it in my lap as I sat beside him. 'Now here are Government three's selling at 108⅜. They are as safe as the United States; and if I advised you to buy them, it would cost me no thought, and my character for safety would run no risk of a blemish. That is the sort of bond that a trustee recommends. But see what income it gives you. Roughly speaking, about twenty-eight thousand dollars.'

" 'That would not do at all,' said I, thinking of Ethel and October.

" 'Certainly not for you,' returned Mr. Beverly, gaily. 'If you were a timorous old maid, now, who would really like all her money in her stocking in gold pieces, only she's ashamed to say so! But a young fellow like you with no responsibility, no wife, and no butcher's bill—it's quite another thing!'

" 'Quite,' said I, 'oh, quite!' "

"Richard," interrupted Ethel, "do you have to make yourself out so simple?"

"My dear, you forget that I said I should invent nothing, but should keep myself to actual experiences. The part of my story that is coming now is one where I should be very glad to draw upon my imagination.

"Mr. Beverly now ran his finger up and down various columns. 'Here again,' said he, 'is a typical trustee bond, and nets you a few thousand dollars more at present prices. New York Central and Hudson River 3½'s. Or here are West Shore 4's at 113⅝. But you see it scales down to pretty much the same thing. The sort of bond that a trustee will call safe does not bring the owner more than about three and one-half per cent.'

" 'Why, there are some six per cent bonds!' I said; and I pointed them out to him.

" 'Selling at 137⅞, you see,' said Mr. Beverly.
'Deducting the tax, there you are scaled down
again.' He pencilled some swift calculations.
'There,' said he. And I nearly understood them.
'Now I'm not here to stop your buying that sort
of petticoat and canary-bird wafer,' continued Mr.
Beverly. 'It's the regular trustee move, and nobody
could criticise you if you made it. It's what I call
thoughtless safety, and it brings you about 3½
per cent, as I have already shown you. Anybody
can do it.'

"These words of Mr. Beverly made me feel that
I did not want to do what anybody could do. 'There
is another kind of safety which I call thoughtful
safety,' said he. 'Thoughtful, because it requires
you to investigate properties and their earnings,
and generally to use your independent judgment
after a good deal of work. And all this a trustee
greatly dislikes. It rewards you with five and even
six per cent, but that is no stimulus to a trustee.'

"Something in me had leaped when Mr. Beverly
mentioned six per cent. Again I thought of Ethel
and October, and what a difference it would be to
begin our modest housekeeping on sixty instead of
forty thousand dollars a year, outside of what I was
earning.

"Mr. Beverly now rang a bell. 'You happen to
have come,' said he, 'on a morning when I can really

do something for you out of the common. Bring me (it was a clerk he addressed) one of those Petunia circulars. Now here you can see at a glance for yourself.' He began reading the prospectus rapidly aloud to me while I followed its paragraphs with my own eye. His strong, well-polished thumb-nail ran heavily but speedily down the columns of figures and such words as gross receipts, increase of population, sinking fund, redeemable at 105 after 1920, churned vigorously and meaninglessly through my brain. But I was not going to let him know that to understand the circular I should have to take it away quietly to my desk in Nassau Street, and spend an hour with it alone.

" 'What is your opinion of Petunia Water sixes?' he inquired.

" 'They are a lead-pipe cinch,' I immediately answered; and he slapped me on the knee.

" 'That's what I think!' he cried. 'Anyhow, I have taken 20,000 for mother. Do what you like.'

" 'Oh, well,' said I, delighted at this confidence, 'I think I can afford to risk what you are willing to risk for your mother, Mrs. Beverly. Where is Petunia, did you say?'

"He pulled down a roller map on the wall as you draw down a window-blind, and again I listened to statements that churned in my brain. Petunia was a new resort on the sea-coast of New Hampshire.

One railway system did already connect it with
both Portsmouth and Portland, but it was not a
very direct connection at present. Yet in spite of
this, the population had increased 23 and seven-
tenths per cent in five years, and now an electric
railway was in construction that would double the
population in the next five years. This was less
than what had happened to other neighboring re-
sorts under identical conditions; yet with things
as they now were, the company was earning two
per cent on its stock, which was being put into im-
provements. The stock was selling at 30, and if a
dividend was paid next year, it would go to par.
But Mr. Beverly did not counsel buying the stock.
'I did not let mother have any,' he said, 'though I
took some myself. But the bonds are different.
You're getting the last that will be sold at par. In
three days they will be placed before the public at
102½ and interest.'

"I was well pleased when I left Mr. Beverly's
office. In a few days I was still more pleased to
learn that I could sell my Petunia sixes for 104
if I so wished. But I did not wish it, and Mr. Beverly told me that he should not sell his mother's
unless they went to 110. 'In that case,' said he, 'it
might be worth while to capitalize her premium.'

"I liked the idea of capitalizing one's premium.
If you had fifty bonds that cost you par, and sold

them at 110, you would then buy at par fifty-five
bonds of some other rising kind, and go on doing
this until—I named no limit for this process; but
my delighted mind saw visions of eighty and a hundred thousand a year—comfort at least, if not afflu-
ence in New York—and I explained to Ethel what
the phrase capitalizing one's premium meant. I
showed her the Petunias, too, and we read what it
said on the coupons aloud together. Ethel was at
first not quite satisfied with the arrangement of the
coupons. 'Thirty dollars on January first, and
thirty on July first,' she said. 'That seems a long
while to wait for those payments, Richard. And
there are only two in every year, though you pay
them a thousand dollars all at once. It does not
seem very prompt on their part.' I told her that
this was the rule. 'But,' she urged, 'don't you
think that a man like Mr. Beverly might be able
to get them to make an exception if he explained
the circumstances? Other people may be satisfied
with waiting for little crumbs in this way, but why
should we?' I soon made her understand how it
was, however, and I explained many other facts
about investments and the stock market to her, as I
learned them. It was a great pleasure to do this.
We came to talk about finance even more than we
talked of my writings, for during that spring I invested a good deal more rapidly than I wrote. The

Petunias had taken only one-twentieth of my million dollars; and though Mr. Beverly warned me to rush hastily into nothing, and pointed out the good sense of distributing my eggs in a number of baskets, still we both agreed that the sooner all my money was bringing me five or six per cent, the better.

"I have come to think that it might be well were women taught the elements of investing as they are now taught French and Music. I would not have the French and Music dropped, but I would add the other. It might be more of a protection to women than being able to read a French novel, and perhaps some day we shall have it so. But of course it had been left totally out of Ethel's education; and at first she merely received my instruction and took my opinions. It was not long, however, before she began to entertain some of her own, obliging me not infrequently to reason with her. I very well remember the first occasion that this happened.

"We had been as usual talking about Stocks, as we walked on the Riverside Drive on a Sunday afternoon in May. Ethel had been for some moments silent. 'Richard,' she finally began, 'if I had had the naming of these things, I should never have called them securities. Insecurities comes a great deal nearer what they are. What right has a thing that says on its face it is worth a thousand dollars

to go bobbing up and down in the way most of them
do ? I think that securities is almost sarcastic. And
have you noticed the price of those Petunias ? '

"I had, of course, noticed it; but I had not
mentioned it to Ethel. 'I read the papers now,' she
explained, 'morning and evening. Of course the
market is off a little on account of the bank statement. But that is not enough to account for the
Petunias.'

" 'Ethel, you are nervous,' I said. 'And it is
the papers which make you so. The Petunias are a
first lien on the whole property, of which the as-
sessed valuation—'

" 'What is the good,' she interrupted, 'of a first
lien on something which depends on politics for its
existence, if the politicians change their minds ?
Did you not see that bill they're thinking of passing ? '

"I was startled by what Ethel told me, for the
article in the paper had escaped my notice. But
Mr. Beverly explained it to me in a couple of
minutes. 'Ha !' he jovially exclaimed, on my enter-
ing his office on Monday morning; 'you want to
know about Petunias. They opened at 85 I see.'
He then ran the tape from the ticker through his
clean strong hands. 'Here they are again. Five
thousand sold at 83. Now, if they go to 70, I'll very
likely take ten thousand more for mother. It's all

Frank Smith's bluff, you know. He wants a jag of
the water-works stock, more than they say they
agreed he should have. So he's shaking this bill
over them, which would allow the city to build its
own water-plant, and of course run the present company out of business. Not a thing in it! All bluff.
He'll get the stock, I suppose. What's that?' he
broke off to a clerk who came with a message.
'Wants 500 preferred does he? Buyer 30? Very
well, he can't have it. Say so from me. Now,' he
resumed to me, 'take a cigar by the way. And don't
buy any more Petunias until I tell you the right
moment. Do you see where your Amalgamated
Electric has gone to?'

"I had seen this. It had scored a 20-point rise
since my purchase of it; and I felt very sorry that
I had not taken Mr. Beverly's advice and bought
a thousand shares. It had been on a day when I felt
unaccountably cautious, and I had taken only two
hundred and fifty shares of Amalgamated Electric.
There are days when one is cautious and days when
one is venturesome; and they seem to have nothing
to do with results.

" 'They're going to increase the dividend,' said
Mr. Beverly, as I smoked his excellent cigar. 'It's
good for twenty points higher by the end of the
week. I have just got mother a few more shares.'

"I left Mr. Beverly's office the possessor of two

thousand shares of Amalgamated Electric, and also
entirely reassured about my Petunias. He always
made me feel happy. His keen laughing brown eyes,
and crisp well-brushed hair, and big somewhat
English way of chaffing (he had gone to Oxford,
where he had rowed on a winning crew) carried
a sense of buoyant prosperity that went with his
wiry figure and good smart London clothes. His
face was almost as tawny as an Indian's with the
outdoor life that he took care to lead. I was always
flattered when he could spare any time to slap me
on the shoulder and crack a joke.

"Amalgamated Electric had risen five more
points before the board closed that afternoon. This
was the first news that I told Ethel.

"'Richard,' said she, 'I wish you would sell
that stock to-morrow.'

"But this I saw no reason for; and on Tuesday
it had gained seven points further. Ethel still more
strongly urged me to sell it. I must freely admit
that." And the narrator paused reflectively.

"Thank you, Richard," said Ethel from the sofa.
"And I admit that I could give you no reason for
my request, except that it all seemed so sudden.
And—yes—there was one other thing. But that
was even more silly."

"I believe I know what you mean," replied Richard, "and I shall come to it presently. If any one
was silly, it was not you.

"I did not sell Amalgamated Electric on Wednesday, and on Thursday a doubt about the increased dividend began to be circulated. The stock, nevertheless, after a forenoon of weakness, rallied. Moreover, a check for my first dividend came from the Pollyopolis Heat, Light, Power, Paving, Pressing, and Packing Company.

" 'What a number of things it does!' exclaimed Ethel, when I showed her the company's check.

" 'Yes,' I replied, and quoted Browning to her: "Twenty-nine distinct damnations. One sure if the other fails." 'Beverly's mother has a lot of it.'

"But Ethel did not smile. 'Richard,' she said, 'I do wish you had more investments with ordinary simple names, like New York Central, or Chicago and Northwestern.' And when I told her that I thought this was really unreasonable, she was firm. 'Yes,' she replied, 'I don't like the names—not most of them, at least. Dutchess and Columbia Traction sounds pretty well; and besides that, of course one knows how successful these electric railways are. But take the Standard Egg Trust, and the Patent Pasteurized Infant Rubber Feeder Company.'

" 'Why, Ethel!' I exclaimed, 'those are both based upon great inventions, Mr. Beverly—'

"But she interrupted me earnestly. 'I know about these inventions, Richard, for I have procured the prospectuses. And I wish that I could

have told you my own feeling about them before
you bought any of the stock.'

" 'I do not think you can fully have taken it in,
Ethel.'

" 'I trust that it may not have fully taken you
in,' she replied. 'Have you noticed what those
stocks are selling for at present?'

"Of course I had noticed this. I had paid 63 for
Standard Egg, and it was now 48, while 11 was the
price of Patent Pasteurized Feeder, for which I
had paid 20. But this, Mr. Beverly assured me,
was a normal and even healthy course for a new
stock. 'Had they gone up too soon and too high,'
he explained, 'I should have suspected some crooked
manipulation and advised selling at once. But this
indicates a healthy absorption preliminary to a
natural rise. I should not dream of letting mother
part with hers.'

"The basis of Standard Egg was not only a
monopoly of all the hens in the United States, but
a machine called a Separator, for telling the age
and state of an egg by means of immersion in water.
Perfectly good eggs sank fast and passed out
through one distributor; fairly nice eggs did not
reach the bottom, and were drawn off through another sluice, and so on. This saved the wages of the
egg twirlers, whose method of candling eggs, as it
was called, was far less rapid than the Separator.

And when I learned that one house in St. Louis alone twirled 50,000 eggs in a day, the possible profits of the Egg Trust became clear to me. But they were not so clear to Ethel. She said that you could not monopolize hens. That they would always be laying eggs and putting it in the power of competitors to hatch them by incubators. Nor did she have confidence in the Pasteurized Feeder. 'Even if you get the parents to adopt it,' she said, 'you cannot get the children. If they do not like the taste of the milk as it comes out of the bottle through the Feeder, they will simply not take it.'

" 'Well,' I answered, 'old Mrs. Beverly is holding to hers.'

"When I said this, Ethel sat with her mouth tight. Then she opened it and said: 'I hate that woman.'

" 'Hate her? Why you have never so much as laid eyes on her.'

" 'That is not at all necessary. I consider it indecent for a gray-haired woman with grandchildren to be speculating in the stock market every week like a regular bull or bear.'

"Every point in this outburst of Ethel's seemed to me so unwarrantable that I was quite dazed. I sat looking at her, and her eyes filled with tears. 'Oh, Richard!' she exclaimed, 'she will ruin you, and I hate her!'

" 'My dear Ethel,' I replied, 'she will not. And only see how you are making it all up out of your head. You have never seen her, but you speak of her as a gray-haired grandmother.'

" 'She must be, Richard. You have told me that Mr. Beverly is a married man and about forty-five. No doubt he has older sisters and brothers. But if he has not, his mother can hardly be less than sixty-five, and he has probably been married for several years. He might easily have a daughter coming out, next winter, and a son at Harvard or Yale; and if their grandmother's hair is not gray, that is quite as unnatural as her speculating in monopolized eggs in this way at her age. She must be a very unladylike person.'

"Ethel, I saw, was excited. Therefore I made no more point of theories concerning the appearance and family circle of old Mrs. Beverly. But in justice to myself I felt obliged to remind her, first, that I was investing, not speculating, and second, that it was Mr. Beverly's advice I was following, and not that of his mother. 'Had he not spoken of her,' I said, 'I should have remained unaware of her existence.'

" 'She is at the bottom of it all the same,' said Ethel. 'Everything you have bought has been because she bought it.'

" 'That is not quite the right way to put it,' I

replied. 'I was willing to buy these securities because Mr. Beverly thought so highly of them that
he felt justified in—'

" 'There is no use,' interrupted Ethel, 'in our
going round this circle as if we were a pair of squir-
rels. I do not ask you to hate that woman for my
sake, but I cannot change my own feeling. Do you
remember, Richard, about the City of Philippi
Sewer Bonds? You did not want to buy them at
first. You told me yourself that you thought new
towns in Texas were apt to buzz suddenly and then
die because all the people hurried away to some
newer town and left the houses and stores standing
empty. But Mr. Beverly's mother got some, and
all your hesitation fled. And now I see that the
Gulf, Galveston, and Little Rock is going to build
a branch that may make Philippi a perfectly evaporated town. If you sold these bonds to-day, how
much would you lose?'

"I did not enjoy telling Ethel how much, but I
had to. 'Only fifteen thousand dollars,' I said.

" 'Only!' Ethel said. 'Well, I hope his mother
will lose a great deal more than that.'

"It is seldom that Ethel taps her foot, but she
had begun to tap it now; and this inclined me to
avoid any attempt at a soothing reply, in the hope
that silence might prove still more soothing, and
that thus we might get away from old Mrs. Beverly.

" 'She cannot possibly be less than sixty-five, Ethel presently announced. 'And she is far more likely to be seventy.'

"I thought it best to agree to any age that Ethel chose to give the old lady.

" 'Do you suppose,' Ethel continued, 'that she does it by telephone?'

" 'My dearest,' I responded, 'he must do it all for her, of course, you know.'

" 'I doubt that very much, Richard. And she strikes me as being the sort of character for whom a mere telephone would not be enough excitement. The nerves of those people require more and more stimulants to give them any sensation at all. I believe that she sits in his private office and watches the ticker.'

" 'Why not give her a ticker in her bedroom while you are about it, Ethel?' I suggested.

"But Ethel could not smile. 'I think that is perfectly probable,' she answered. And then, 'Oh, Richard, isn't it mean!' At this I took her hand, and she—but again I abstain from dwelling upon those circumstances of the engaged which are familiar to you all.

"The change of May into June, and the change of June into July, did not mellow Ethel's bitter feelings. I remember the day after Petunias defaulted on their interest, that she exclaimed, 'I hope

I shall never meet her!' We always called Mr. Beverly's mother 'she' now. 'For if I were to meet her,' continued Ethel, 'I feel I should say something that I should regret. Oh, Richard, I suppose we shall have to give up that house on Park Avenue!'

"I put a cheerful and even jocular face on the matter, for I could not bear to see Ethel so depressed. But it was hard work for me. Some few of my investments were evidently good; but it always seemed as if it was into these that I had happened to put not much money, while the bulk of my fortune was entangled in the others. Besides the usual Midsummer faintness that overtakes the stock market, my own specialties were a good deal more than faint. On the 20th of August I took the afternoon train to spend my two weeks' holiday at Lenox; and during much of the journey I gazed at the Wall Street edition of the afternoon paper that I had purchased as I came through the Grand Central Station. Ethel and I read it in the evening.

"'I wonder what she's buying now?' said Ethel, vindictively.

"'Well, I can't help feeling sorry for her,' I answered, with as much of a smile as I could produce.

"'That is so unnecessary, Richard! She can easily afford to gratify her gambling instinct.'

" 'There you go, Ethel, inventing millions for her just as you invented grandchildren.'

" 'Not at all. Unless she constantly had money lying idle, she could not take these continual plunges. She is an old woman with few expenses, and she lives well within her income. You would hear of her entertaining if it was otherwise. So instead of conservatively investing her surplus, she makes ducks and drakes of it in her son's office. Is he at Hyde Park now?' Hyde Park was where the old Beverly country seat had always been.

" 'No,' I answered. 'He went to Europe early last month.'

" 'Very likely he took her with him. She is probably at Monte Carlo.'

" 'Scarcely in August, I fancy. And I'll tell you what, Ethel. I have been counting it up. She has lost twenty-four thousand dollars in Standard Egg alone. It takes a good deal of surplus to stand that.'

" 'Serve her right,' said Ethel. 'And I would say so to her face.'

"September brought freshness to the stock market but not to me. Mr. Beverly, like the well-to-do man that he was, remained away in Europe until October should require his presence as a guiding hand in the office. Thus was I left without his buoyant consolation in the face of my investments.

"Petunias were being adjusted on a four per

cent basis; Dutchess and Columbia Traction was
holding its own; I could not complain of Amalgamated Electric, though it was now lower than when
I had bought it, while had I sold it on that Wednesday in May when Ethel begged me, before the increased dividend turned out a mistake, I should
have made money. But Philippi Sewers were
threatened; Pasteurized Feeders had been numb
since June; Pollyopolis Heat, Light, Power, Paving, Pressing, and Packing was going to pass its
quarterly dividend; and Standard Egg had gone
down from 63 to $7\frac{1}{8}$. My million dollars on paper
now was worth in reality less than a quarter of
that sum, and although we could still make both
ends meet fairly well in some place where you
wouldn't want to live, like Philadelphia, in New
York we should drop into a pinched and dwarfed
obscurity.

"I must say now, and I shall never forget, that
Ethel during these gloomy weeks behaved much
better than I did. The grayer the outlook became,
the more words of hope and sense she seemed to
find. She reminded me that, after all, my Uncle
Godfrey's legacy had been a thing unlooked for,
something out of my scheme of life; that I had my
youth, my salary, and my writing; and that she
would wait till she was as old as Mr. Beverly's
mother.

"It was the thought of that lady which brought from Ethel the only note of complaint she uttered in my presence during that whole dreary month.

"We were spending Sunday with a house party at Hyde Park; and driving to church, we passed an avenue gate with a lodge. 'Rockhurst, sir,' said the coachman. 'Whose place?' I inquired. 'The old Beverly place, sir.' Ethel heard him tell me this; and as we went on, we saw a carriage and pair coming down the avenue toward the gate with that look which horses always seem to have when they are taking the family to church on Sunday morning.

"'If I see her,' said Ethel to me as we entered the door, 'I shall be unable to say my prayers.'

"But only young people came into the Beverly pew, and Ethel said her prayers and also sang the hymns and chants very sweetly.

"After the service, we strolled together in the old and lovely graveyard before starting homeward. We had told them that we should prefer to walk back. The day was beautiful, and one could see a little blue piece of the river, sparkling.

"'Here is where they are all buried,' said Ethel, and we paused before brown old headstones with Beverly upon them. 'Died 1750; died 1767,' continued Ethel, reading the names and inscriptions. 'I think one doesn't mind the idea of lying in such a place as this.'

"Some of the young people in the pew now came along the path. 'The grandchildren,' said Ethel. 'She is probably too old to come to church. Or she is in Europe.'

"The young people had brought a basket with flowers from their place, and now laid them over several of the grassy mounds. 'Give me some of yours,' said one to the other, presently; 'I've not enough for grandmother's.'

"Ethel took me rather sharply by the arm. 'Did you hear that?' she asked.

" 'It can't be she, you know,' said I. 'He would have come back from Europe.'

"But we found it out at lunch. It was she, and she had been dead for fifteen years.

"Ethel and I talked it over in the train going up to town on Monday morning. We had by that time grown calmer. 'If it is not false pretences,' said she, 'and you cannot sue him for damages, and if it is not stealing or something, and you cannot put him in prison, what are you going to do to him, Richard?'

"As this was a question which I had frequently asked myself during the night, having found no satisfactory answer to it, I said: 'What would you do in my place, Ethel?' But Ethel knew.

" 'I should find out when he sails, and meet his steamer with a cowhide.'

" 'Then he would sue me for damages.'

" 'That would be nothing, if you got a few good cuts in on him.'

" 'Ethel,' I said, 'please follow me carefully. I should like dearly to cowhide him, and for the sake of argument we will consider it done. Then comes the lawsuit. Then I get up and say that I beat him because he made me buy Standard Egg at 63 by telling me that his mother had some, when really the old lady had been dead for fifteen years. When I think of it in this way, I do not feel—'

" 'I know,' interrupted Ethel, 'you are afraid of ridicule. All men are.'

"Had Ethel insisted, I believe that I should have cowhided Mr. Beverly for her sake. But before his return our destinies were brightened. Copper had been found near Ethel's waste lands in Michigan, and the family business man was able to sell the property for seven hundred thousand dollars. He did this so promptly that I ventured to ask him if delay might not have brought a greater price. 'Well,' he said, 'I don't know. You must seize these things. Blake and Beverly might have got tired waiting.'

" 'Blake and Beverly!' I exclaimed. 'So they made the purchase. Is Mr. Beverly back?'

" 'Just back. To tell the truth I don't believe they're finding so much copper as they hoped.'

"This turned out to be true. And I am not sure

that the business man had not known it all the while.
'We looked over the property pretty thoroughly
at the time of the Tamarack excitement,' he said.
And in a few days more, in fact, it was generally
known that this land had returned to its old state
of not quite paying the taxes.

"Then I paid my visit to Mr. Beverly, but with
no cowhide. 'Mr. Beverly,' said I, 'I want to an-
nounce to you my engagement to Miss Ethel Lan-
sing, whose Michigan copper land you have lately
acquired. I hope that you bought some for your
mother.'

"Those," concluded Mr. Richard Field, "are the
circumstances attending my engagement which I
felt might interest you. And now, Ethel, tell your
story, if they'll listen."

"Richard," said Ethel, "that is the story I was
going to tell."

With the Coin of Her Life

A STORY OF THIRTEEN AT TABLE

IT must be that I am growing old; tell-tale memory reveals this every day. Why else, for instance, should I forget where I dined last Tuesday, yet remember as vividly as if it were yesterday the buzzing of a fly at the window upon that morning I was forty, while I sat reading Cornelia Dean's note? Birthday tokens from "grateful patients" were on my table, but I looked at the note. Short it was and spoke not of birthdays; it asked one single question,—might Cornelia see me before I began my official day?—yet the handwriting clearly betrayed agitation. I gave orders that as soon as Miss Dean came she should be admitted to my office through the "door of privilege." Outside "the door of practice" some patients were already waiting; I had caught a glimpse of them when my secretary had passed through to the front office at half-past nine with my dictated mail. The busy clicks of the typewriter now reached me clearly. Half-read beside my portfolio lay a scientific review in which Playfair, over in London, before the British Medical Association, praised my recent book; and the proofs of my more recent article upon certain phases of neuras-

128

thenia awaited revision. Yet, after setting my table
in order and dipping a pen in ink, my eyes would
still wander to Cornelia's note, and presently, two
or three minutes before ten, the door of privilege
opened for her.

She looked at the clock. "Don't mind that," I
said. "They all can wait."

"Yes, they must," she murmured. "And you
must help me." She sat down heavily, like one at
the end of all resource.

I was concerned by the change in my friend's
usually cheerful, apple-fresh countenance, and I
asked her gravely, "What's the matter?"

"It's my niece."

Cornelia had several nieces, some grown up and
married, yet I guessed instantly that she meant a
niece of whom she never spoke, a young girl
from the interior of the State, upon whom family
silence and a ban had fallen: she had gone upon
the stage. Even Cornelia, advanced though she was
for her generation and ready to jest about her prej-
udices, remained old-fashioned enough to forbid
her house to many a Parisian novel, also, for example, declining to countenance the play of "Camille."
"With the unspeakable morals of the French," she
once said, "it seems extraordinary that their verb
aimer should be regular." Cornelia was good company.

"It's my niece," she repeated, "it's my poor Nancy," her baffled mind halting at the consciousness of all there was in it. "I have induced her to come to you at last. She's in there now." Cornelia threw a glance at the door of practice. "She doesn't know I'm here."

Still I looked at her gravely; she made me feel grave. "Does she need me as a doctor or as a friend?"

"Let it be both. She's quite likely to tell you she never was better in her life. The point is," Cornelia declared, "she doesn't want to be cured."

"You don't mean that she is tired of life?"

"No. It's different from that. It's different from anything." Again Cornelia's mind seemed to halt. "But, at any rate, I've got her here, and you're going to make it all right, aren't you, my friend? There was something about her letters—something she didn't mean to put there—which frightened me, so I just took the train for Buffalo. She was boarding in the most horrible place—the sort of place where the kitchen smell clings to the very roof and the window-panes; gas on the staircase all day. She refuses to go to her mother's—do you wonder?—or to any of them, or to any of us, except me. She has come to her Aunt Cornelia. By that I am repaid for the way the rest of the family have taken my writing to her regularly all through the two years."

"But why does the child need me?"

"A sound person doesn't believe that they're—haunted. She tells me she has begun to see it."

"What has she begun to see?"

"It, the thing, whatever it is, just off to one side of where she's looking. To the right side—almost round the corner. She doesn't mind it, you understand. That is what has seemed to me so—" Cornelia did not finish, but fixed her troubled eyes on mine. "I believe that she has been trying to see it, you know, for some time. It's what I seem to have felt in her letters, though it never came in definitely. Anyhow, she sees it now. She calls it her triumph."

I said lightly: "Well, these images are not uncommon. You might suppose, to read the medical books, that every next man and woman had them. Sometimes we nerve specialists cure them, sometimes we send the patient to the oculist. And sometimes, of course, no one is able to cure them. Does your niece happen to complain of headaches?"

Cornelia shook her head. "She complains of nothing. But, then, she wouldn't speak of it if she had them."

I thought she would, or that such headaches as I meant would make themselves known, and I had hoped to hear of headaches. Without them, "the image" took on a significance more sinister. This

there was no reason to tell Cornelia to-day, and I continued: "We meet every sort of image, you know. Some patients see chairs, tables; there was a mother who saw her six children in a row, just to the right. It was so real that sometimes she put out her hand, expecting to touch them. I had an army officer who always saw a razor-back hog. He was gradually set straight by rest, good food, and but little else. What does your niece see?"

"What she sees," said Cornelia, "I am to know, she promises, on the day when she has made the thing come straight in front of her." For a moment the grotesque side of this touched Cornelia's wholesome Middle-States humor. "To be bringing up a ghost," she smiled, "seems more like what they might do in Boston."

I laughed myself, but it was chiefly for Cornelia's sake; her news of her niece was indeed not good. I thought it over, and hesitated. "I wonder if there's something you're not telling me," I ventured at last.

Her eyes dropped. "No; I do not think that she— I couldn't believe—I am certain there has been nothing of that sort. Although there is a young man—but I don't believe he's the thing she sees," she added quickly, as if to herself.

"You mustn't leave me groping, Cornelia," I remonstrated. "It's hard enough already."

"It is not easy for me," my friend pursued, and I perceived that her emotion was not growing less.

"You have become very fond of your niece," I said gently.

"Ah, I love her!" Cornelia rose precipitately; the effort to check her tears was successful; she walked to the window and stood looking out for a moment upon my garden. "He may be the cause of it," she resumed. "I hadn't thought of that. He cannot care for her, you know, or he would have been to see her. He knows where she is, because she has written him. He's very handsome. About thirty, I should fancy."

"Then you've seen him."

"Indeed, I have not. She has his photograph, with his name signed across it in a thick, fulsome handwriting. An actor, English by birth, she says."

"Oh, she talks about him?"

"Yes; that is why I'm not clear as to the nature of her feeling. What she says is, that he will be the making of her."

"Has he said that?"

"I don't know what he may have boasted. It seems she has acted in plays where he was the hero. What a set of brutes we have all been to abandon her!"

"Not all of you."

"All, all," Cornelia vehemently insisted. "For

my letters should have been kinder. If she had ever
felt she had a home with me, no matter what, she
might have come to me long ago. But her running
off the minute she was twenty-one was so dreadful!
I couldn't feel kind at first. It was the others be-
having like such stones that made me write, not
any sympathy with what she had done. One of *us*
—to exhibit herself upon the public stage! And
how can she have any talent? Though not even if she
had genius— But she's not famous. She admits this
to herself. Only, she says she knows now that she's
going to be.''

"Knows now?"

"Yes; she has become sure of it lately. But
oughtn't she to have made a name for herself after
two whole years of drudgery? That is what I wish
to make her feel—that she has no talent. Don't you
sometimes hypnotize—"

"Cornelia!" I cried, laughing. "I have seen
some rather appalling results come of hypnotism,
but nothing quite so awful as what you lightly suggest. The destruction of a talent! I should de-
serve a thunderbolt. But let us be serious—and
avoid hypnotism as much as we can; I trust it less
and less—however, never mind my medical opinions
just now. This young man—you have told me all
you know? When did he come into it?"

"The summer engagement, the stock company in

Buffalo. He was the leading young man. She's had four months of him, if you count the month since they closed. June 5 till October 3," Cornelia finished. This fond aunt had her niece's dates at her finger-ends!

"Then she has had him," I smiled, "much longer than needful to disturb the heart."

"But if it's not the heart?"

"Ah, wait till I've seen her. Perhaps she'll tell me all the things you've skipped."

"I've skipped nothing."

"We haven't even mentioned appetite, digestion, sleep, exercise, habits of life when she was acting, and all the rest of the prosy physical details."

Cornelia looked puzzled while I closely questioned her upon matters less romantic than the young man. She could tell me only a part of what I needed to know; she had not been observing those things. "I supposed it was a mental or nervous disorder," she explained, "requiring—well, not pills, but the character-dosing you give."

"There are no miracles in my medicine-chest, Cornelia—or in any one's. But you give me a bad account of your niece's body, and I hope it may be good news. Mental disorder is often secondary, following organic disturbances, and departs of itself, once we have set the body in order, without any form of influence exerted through the mind of the patient.

And remember, Cornelia, science does not record one single instance of organic disease cured by such means. We'll hope she won't even need pills.''

After Cornelia had gone I sat thinking over what she told me. Might the histrionic temperament give us some special form of disease, subspecies, so to speak, of ailments already classified in the books? Actors are a strange people, unexpectedly emotional, unexpectedly callous, their minds illumined, yet with great blind spots between, and in their fiber delicacy and coarseness stirred together to a blend. They are self-centered in a particular manner, compelled to think continually of their bodies, their voices, their faces, their total selves, in fact, as an instrument upon which they play like a violin to move and hold a mass of spectators. A mind, a will, an attention perpetually strained to such an unnatural attitude, might well in the end produce abnormalities. A special form of palsy affects the hands of writers and telegraph operators; why to the brain that is always watching its possessor should there not come—I paused here and brought my thoughts back from the great dim space that looms beyond the frontiers of knowledge, push them however far we may. No professional temptation besets the modern doctor more dangerous than to treat his patient as an object for study instead of as a brother to heal. It is because I never, even in my

most ardent hours of speculation, forgot that my
duty was to my patient first and to science next,
that I have been in some measure successful. If
Cornelia was right about the headaches, then I had a
disease to deal with, threatening and mysterious in
all instances, but additionally clouded in this case
by something wholly novel. There were physical
causes both plentiful and plain for any amount of
nervous disorder and exhaustion—a life of bad food
and bad air in perpetual trains, theaters, and hotels,
with irregular hours, to which doubtless overwork
and mental strain had been added.

It was not until I had seen six or seven patients
that the young girl's turn arrived. Will you understand my recognizing her at once in spite of her
being altogether different from what I had expected? I did do so, though she was short, fair and
vivacious. It was not by her clothes, which were
quiet and good, or by her hair, which was lovely and
simple in arrangement, or by any one thing in itself; and this is, I take it, what we mean by having
"personality." She had this beyond question—
whatever it be—and whatever else requisite to her
calling she did not have. I had looked for pale
cheeks; I did not immediately detect that her rosy
color came not from serene health, but from its very
opposite.

With her gray eyes fixed upon me she stood a

moment at the door, and then stepping forward she broke into an enchanting smile. "I am going to tell you my real name, after all. I had made up my mind to say I was Miss Evelyn Shenstone, which is my stage name. I'm Nancy, you know."

I laughed rather helplessly, but with excellent result, for she exclaimed: "Why, you're not going to be like the others! You knew who I was, too!" she added almost instantly, with another quick, full look into my eyes. Her voice also went home with a certain force.

Again I laughed helplessly; one had to. "Well, Miss Shenstone—"

"Nancy! Nancy! That's not a bit nice in you."

"Well, Miss Nancy (perhaps I'll be able to drop the 'Miss' presently), who are the others, and why am I not going to be like them?"

"Because you aren't as dull as ditch-water and dead as a door nail. Even Aunt Cornelia, who's a darling—has she been here? Of course she has."

I do not see to-day, any better than I did then, how one was to cope with such a patient, so sweet was she, so engaging, so surprising. I told myself, however, that presently my tact would dominate her, and thereafter I should soon be winding her round my little finger. Meanwhile I nodded to signify that her Aunt Cornelia had paid me a visit.

The girl's eyes sparkled. "She loves me, she

wants me to be happy, but it has all got to be in her way. I can't make her see—oh, anything! Because it makes her happy to do her own marketing, and just now to get awfully delicious things for me (as if I cared what I eat! She was lamenting this morning it was too early for ducks), and because it is her rule to decant her own Madeira and to call only on people who live in certain streets (and not on all of those even, and some of the other streets are much wider and cleaner, better, anyhow) and to light the furnace on the first of November, no matter what the thermometer says, and never till then— why, what do you suppose she said this morning at breakfast, reading the paper? 'Not a respectable death to-day!' And so she put the paper down. That's Aunt Cornelia, and she wants me to be happy like that. But you'll not tell me what she tells me. You"—the girl's voice here sank low, yet gained in volume, and her little body might have been tall, so much presence did it give forth—"you know, you understand it, for in your own way you have it yourself—the consecration—the ideal. I knew you had before I came, and now I see you have."

The searching, melodious cadence of her final words left me silent.

"There is Scripture for it," she said.

"I suppose there is Scripture for almost everything," I replied.

"Ah, don't talk like that! That's not yourself. You can't even imitate an old fogy well. It's about the man who buried his talent in a napkin instead of using it and making it bear increase. He was punished for it, you remember, in the New Testament. And so should I be if I did what Aunt Cornelia wishes. Why, you, with your discoveries in a new field, and your duty never to drop it, but to go on, on,—why, you'd pay for it with the coin of your life. It's the only coin that ever buys the star."

She took my breath away, and still I merely looked at her, waiting for some appropriate thing to say to this creature. I might have said—some doctors would have said: "Tut! tut! my dear; sit down and show me your tongue!" but this or anything like it, would, I knew, have ended there and then any chance of helping her. Her confidence must be won, or Cornelia would have called vainly upon me.

"I am not an artist yet," Nancy now said, "but I am going to be one."

"So you shall," I exclaimed. "So you shall, if the talent is there!"

"Then you do belong to us!" she cried. "I knew it."

"I think I belong to your Aunt Cornelia," I said, smiling; "and I should tell her that talent—the real thing—is forever justified of itself. That

doesn't mean, you know, that I have passed upon
yours.''

"No, no. Come and see me in something,—there'll
be something by the New Year,—that's all I ask
of you.''

"Come and see you?" I replied. If this were to
abet her and array myself against Cornelia, I could
enter into no such pact. I had to turn it over
quickly; she was watching me with all her eyes, and I
had learned that those eyes could see other things besides images. "Come and see you—yes; if meanwhile you'll come and see me a little.''

She moved swiftly up to me and took both my
hands. "I'll come and see you now," she laughed.
"I knew you belonged to us.''

We sat down then. Hitherto we had conducted
the interview standing, I, where I had risen from
my chair upon her entrance, behind my broad study-
table, with its roses and tokens and strewn papers,
she at some little distance away, with the door of
practice as a mahogany background. Thus had the
first part of our scene taken place (she had only
moved a step or two forward) until the final impulse which brought her close to the table. If it
were a battle, I had certainly won the first position: she had not come into that room prepared to
run up and shake hands with me. Well, I must keep
it, my first position, must follow it up, and secure

a second, if possible, while she was here this morning; she must promise me to await my professional permission before she took a new engagement.

"I wish you would tell me," I began, "all about it."

"About what?" She was instantly on the verge of suspicion.

"How you get into it,—your profession, I mean, —what the process, the mystery, is. When a man wants to become a doctor, he enters a medical school, and all that. I know how one becomes a lawyer, a clergyman, a merchant; but what you people do, I don't at all know."

She liked my calling her "you people"; this her extraordinary eyes showed to me even as I spoke the words: I was not treating her like a stage-struck miss, but as of "the profession."

"We do a hundred sorts of things. What I did was to go to the office of a manager, exactly as a cook goes to an intelligence-office. Only I had no references. I made a very bad supe at first. It was great luck to get any job at all, with the throng of applicants he had. My eyes and hair were a value, of course,—he could see that at a glance,—and he happened to need a small woman for a very small part. So I got it, and the South liked me. The South has liked me from the first. It is my voice. Then— well, then one thing led to another; they were all little, little things. Sometimes it was awful. The men sometimes—I traveled with a musical show twice—but why go into all that? It is past, and my future is very close now.'' For a flashing instant her facè, over this assertion, nay, proclamation of her coming fame, gleamed like resolute steel—steel ground and polished to an edge by hard stones of drudgery.

"You see, I am very strong, nothing tires me; it's nothing to me if I sleep or not, and I am a quick study. In Buffalo I could take a new part in the morning and go on in the evening. Then my Celtic temperament is worth any looks I haven't got, always given my eyes and hair. I suit the classic or romantic. I don't do in comedy; I wish I did.'' She had now got herself going,—I did not have to push her, she ran along without end—the life, the plays, the parts, the notices—she always had good notices now, in Boston, Toledo, Richmond, Atlanta; and Chicago last May had given her the best she had ever received. She named the standard parts she should like to play (Camille was one of them, and I wondered if Cornelia knew it), she graduated the cities according to the warmth of their audiences, she played for me, in short, a multitudinous set of variations upon the perpetual theme of self. This was the wonder of it, how, without being in one way in the least vain, nay, evidently quite humble in some ways,—her every thought, her every throb, was merely a circumference that whirled around her as its center.

In her thus pouring it out, this jumble of fact, opinion, and ambition, she incidentally gave me plentiful ground for astonishment that she should still retain any digestion at all. One single meal a day, and coffee instead of the other two, had been with her so common an occurrence that she fairly stared at me when I interrupted her to make sure I had rightly understood her to say that such a diet had been frequent. "Oh, for economy!" she explained in answer to my question, and she hurried on to something of more interest to her.

But the unknown "thing" remained unknown. She avoided it with an art which concealed art; I should never have dreamed that, for all her talk, I was listening to a person afflicted probably with focal brain disease, who was fostering a hemiopic hallucination. If she were not going to speak of "the image," then it was for me also to be silent about it, at least upon this first day; I might lose all I had gained of her confidence; wherefore, when at length the copious flow of biography ceased, I was ready with a suggestion which I hoped might cause her mind to open and admit me as medical adviser. I threw off some opinions about coffee, adding that I had been obliged to give it up except

in the morning, and intimated the likelihood that
most of what she had taken had not been real coffee
at all; this was the only way in which I could account for her not being a bed-ridden wreck. Did
she ever have "sick-headaches"? I asked casually,
and I know that she spoke the truth when she replied
that she did not. Feeling my way according to the
measure of her attention which I hoped I was winning, I talked about good food, regular hours, and
the number of business men who broke down because
they neglected both. I informed her that her profession probably bore on the nerves more acutely
than any other save the stock gambler's, and that a
great actor, like a great engine, would stop unless
the boiler was full of steam. "Do you remember
Matthew Arnold's remark," I continued—"that
genius is largely a question of energy?"

The expression in her eyes changed. "Did he say
that?" And encouraged by this sign that she was
coming into closer touch with me, I pursued my
talk. But I was misled by her eyes. I then began to
perceive what later I completely learned, that she
could fix on you a gaze of absorbed attention, and
yet not be open to a word you uttered. I bade her
reflect how much more likely to please her acting
would be if she were in robust health; I gave it as my
guess that she was far from well at the present moment, in spite of her opinion to the contrary, and

that I could make her much fitter for work by January if she would be guided by me and obey me.

"Whatever your Aunt Cornelia thinks about the stage for you," I concluded, "it's never anything but your welfare that she wishes. And just now she desires to be sure you are strong. I have promised her to do what I can for you."

The girl, though all the while I had been talking she had never taken her eyes from my face, now seemed in some way to waken and look at me with a new scrutiny—a look of smiling friendliness and ease, yet one in which I read my defeat.

"If I were not myself," she said, "I should like to be the sort of person you are and do the sort of thing that you do. It must be glorious"—her gaze and voice expanded upon the words—"to touch the sick and heal them! To talk with a maimed human creature, and learn through subtle art his needs, and make him whole! You deal with the mystery of pain. But I could not give up . . . give up. . . ." She touched her breast above the heart, and slowly shook her head. Spontaneous or studied, the pantomime spoke her thought to perfection.

She had finished in a sort of reverie, with her voice dropped to a very low register. There was in it a thrill which gave me a sudden and strange uneasiness; but this passed with the thought, Why deliver a commonplace so elaborately? Most of us

would say the same: we may very well envy our
neighbor his lot, but we would not take the lot if
the neighbor had to go with it. Moreover, her performance struck me as a trifle overdone to be sincere; and if it was applause she was watching my
eyes for, she saw none there. I was moved to tell her
that if she had come merely to try her art on me,
she had better go.

But although brutality is at times my final resource with patients, it is never my first: it is after
I have spent weeks in plumbing their perversions
that I employ it in certain cases. To-day I had become sure of but one fact—that I had a nature to
deal with that was far less open than it wished to
seem. She had set up her histrionic gift as a screen
between us, had treated me to a little scene on the
trite subject of one's identity being too precious to
part with; that no career, however enviable, would
be worth exchanging for it. Well, play-acting was
hardly needed to persuade me of that! I now suspected one fact more—that any exercise of her art,
even so slight as this one had been, was at present
dangerous for her. A flush of brilliance, new and
sudden, mounted in her face, and I caught in her
eyes the same strange thing which had thrilled in
her voice. She stopped observing me, she was seeing—whatever had just arrived. With a disturbance, cold and unaccountable in me as a physician,

I observed her looking steadily out into my garden. I involuntarily followed her gaze, and, childish as this must seem, with apprehension; and the fact that of course I saw nothing through the window where she was so extraordinarily staring, made the whole moment we were living in seem like a vibrant intake of breath. In my fifteen years of experience I had seen three patients afflicted with the malady from which she obviously suffered—yet they had not frightened me. She began to smile as she closely watched her visitant, and suddenly she gave an exclamation of delight and clasped her hands. That this had escaped her was instantly evident by the attempt she made to cover it up, or, rather, to account to me for it. "Why, you've got Dante there!"

A death-mask of this poet hung, it is true, between my office's two back windows that looked on the garden, and she was now contemplating it with animation. She did not wish to give me time, either, to speak; she quoted quickly:

"Nel mezzo del cammin di nostra vita
Mi ritrovai per una selva oscura."

She repeated the lines well, and with an accent remarkably good when you remember that she came from the central regions of our State.

"Do you know the whole thing?" I inquired.

She chose not to take note of the irony I could

not help putting into my question. "I love it! I
love it! If somebody would only turn Francesca
into a play for me!"

"It has been done several times," I said coldly.
"Stripped of Dante's verse and setting, it falls in-
evitably to a somewhat stale intrigue. Miss Nancy,
—well, Nancy, if you permit it,—you make it un-
commonly hard for a poor doctor. What shall I
report to your Aunt Cornelia?"

"Can't you tell her that I kept my promise, and
that I'm glad I did, and that I'll come to see you
again, if you'll let me?"

"I cannot tell her that last part for this reason:
you are not well enough to be out of her house.
You should be in bed at this moment, with a trained
nurse to care for you. And it is I who should be
coming to see you. You are deeply fatigued, much
overwrought, and if you are not willing to be advised by me, I cannot answer for the consequences.
Do what I wish,—it is merely to rest and exist regularly for a while,—and it may avert a grave illness.
Don't you love your aunt enough for that?"

She looked from me to Dante, from Dante to me,
she gave a glance—one stolen look of comprehension
—at whatever was looking in at us, and then turned
upon me a face of bright bewilderment. "I would
do anything for Aunt Cornelia, in reason; but what
does she want? Look at me! Send me to bed? Why,

I'm a horse and an ox for strength!'' She turned
on a little more bewilderment into her expression
as she continued to smile upon me with parted, incredulous lips.

I decided to let her have it straight—not alone
what I knew, but also a professional guess I had
made during the last few seconds. ''You understand me perfectly. If you will press your eye, it
will remain single. If it were really in the garden,
it would become double. And—it will never come
straight in front of you, although you thought just
now that it had taken a step in that direction.''

I expected to surprise a sign from her, but I had
reckoned without allowing for the frightful adroit-
ness of minds partially unhinged, as I made sure
that hers must be. I could not detect a tremor or
a blink of comprehension; the smile, the parted lips,
the eyes, merely grew to a brighter friendliness.
''That's too much medical language for me all at
once. Now, I'm not going to promise anything to-
day except that I will really take care of myself.
If you will not let me come back, then I know you'll
come to Aunt Cornelia's.''

She gave me her hand, which must have been
freezing cold to its deepest fiber; even after she
had gone I seemed to feel the lingering ice of its
touch.

I assume that I attended properly to the rest of

my patients that day, both those who came to consult, and those whom I drove out to visit after office hours, but of this I can recall nothing. The one thing I remember is that I sent to Cornelia's house to ascertain if the young girl were there, and received a message that she had returned in safety. To such a pitch had my anxiety risen that I was prepared to learn she had fled from our hampering solicitude. No sign seemed worse to me than the uncanny skill by which she had baffled my attempts to come to a frank understanding with her, and all the signs were bad. Her relation to "the image," wherein a progress had taken place under my very eyes—this foretold evil rapidly advancing. That my guess had been right was almost certain, and herein lay my single item of success: I had been able so to frame my remarks that her very ignoring them was proof she understood them. She understood them in sooth only too well, otherwise she would have inquired what I meant; but even her enfevered cleverness had not been able at a stroke to devise an escape from revealing this to me. Now, henceforth, she knew that I knew the fact of "the image" and its shift of position was something shared between us two, whether or not she decided this should draw us together or push us apart.

I took the skeins and shreds I had gathered of this case, and from them made out a partial pattern:

she had a fixed idea; its precise nature I could
not trace until I had discovered what she saw.
Herein it was that her case presented to me something wholly new. Was eclipse to be her heritage—
partial eclipse of sight and perhaps total eclipse of
mind? Was hers a case of visual hallucination in
that portion of a field over which darkness would at
some future moment sweep at a stroke? Such fate
would come from a lesion in one of the occipital
lobes of the brain. (Let me apologize for such technical words; no others seem available.)

What did she see, and why did she wish "it" to
be in front of her? I found myself repelling the
absurd idea that it was in truth any phantom from
the spirit world; but here again let me confess something that seems utterly childish : more than once I
looked uncomfortably through my garden window
while I sat in the gathering dusk.

In the letter which I sent Cornelia that evening
I made a clean breast of my discomfiture. I confessed that after certain remarks of mine had seemed
to have a happy effect, and to bring Nancy and myself into a relation of downright comradeship, my
clumsiness (so I must suppose it) had spoilt all.
Something too like a lecture, too paternal, in the tone
that, through my anxiety, I had finally taken, had
driven her off again into the deep recesses of her
secret. I had not given up; it would not do for either

of us to give up. "Make her go to bed and rest, if you can," I concluded. "I cannot urge this too strongly. Her state baffles me, and I am altogether alarmed about it. Get her to bed. I don't wonder that your heart goes out to her, but I should humbly counsel you not to be too parental."

In the matter of getting Nancy to bed, Mother Nature stepped in to our assistance. The next day I was called to see her by a note from Cornelia; her niece had not been able to get up that morning. It was in a state of collapse that I found the young girl. The flush her cheeks had worn yesterday was deeper, her eyes searched me more brightly than ever; the appearance of energy was lasting after energy itself had disappeared. It was like a conflagration, where the house has fallen in, but the flames still leap toward the sky. Ambition was burning that fragile body up, nerve after nerve, or would, if it were not stopped. Youth was on her side against the consuming element of her fixed idea. It had to be drugs this first day, much as I disliked such resource, but sleep or torpor was immediately essential, and these the drugs duly gave us. It is curious that with all the little things I remember connected with this time, what I forget is, how long it lasted. I suppose this must be because I came every day, and the days were much alike. Trained nurses and diet are not interesting in a story, and I shall

pass them over, together with as much of the medical treatment as can be omitted, without harm to the
story. I followed a course which I find more and
more safe to adopt in nervous maladies partly aris-
ing from fatigue: I began with the body, and
watched to see if a return to its normal state would
not be followed by a corresponding improvement in
the mind. I abstained wholly from anything in the
nature of what has come to be loosely and injuriously
termed "suggestion." That is, I abstained at first.
From one common precaution I was saved: there was
no need to discourage all talk of symptoms between
my patient and her masseuse and nurse; Nancy could
hardly be brought to speak of symptoms even to me,
and about the arch-symptom of all, "the image," I
never succeeded in extracting a word from her. If
she saw it, and there's no doubt she must at times
have seen it, she had profited with swift subtlety by
that one slip when she revealed to me in my study
that she was looking at it; she knew now how to
watch it surreptitiously. Isolation I decided at once
would be of no help, might be actually injurious,
and here I think still to-day that I made no mistake,
and that such happy progress toward cure as I did
achieve resulted as much from the good, wholesome
society of her Aunt Cornelia as it did from the milk
and massage and all the rest of the treatment which
I ordered and from time to time modified.

Stay, I have forgotten one thing. On that first visit to her room I noticed at once the photograph of the handsome actor. From his crimson velvet frame and above his flamboyant signature he seemed to gaze at me as if he could tell me "something to my advantage," as the phrase goes when queer people advertise queer things in the papers. It was not a bad face, yet as I looked at the opulent eyes (I find no other word for them), I wondered what it was that he had done—if he had done anything— to Nancy.

"Take it out," I told Cornelia, when we were alone in the sitting-room. "I want to keep from her sight any objects which might hold her obsession before her mind. You can set up her young star in his velvet frame in here."

"That I decline to do," said Cornelia. "He shall go into a drawer in the dark."

Several days passed before Cornelia had any news to give me of this. From the effect of the drugs Nancy sank away fast from the flush of cheek and brightness of eye, and lay pale enough and passive enough for a long while. "She hasn't noticed it yet," Cornelia told me on a number of successive afternoons as soon as I arrived; after that, it dropped out of both our minds until about a week, perhaps more, was gone, when Cornelia met me on the stairs with, "She has spoken to the nurse."

"Just now?" I asked.

"No. This morning when they opened the shutters."

"Then she spoke as soon as she noticed," I suggested.

"That seems likely," said Cornelia. "But there has not been a syllable to me about it."

We went to Nancy's room together, and no syllable about it was dropped then either, so that on the following afternoon, with Nancy lying among her pillows, I introduced the subject myself. As if with no special aim, I rose from my chair by the bedside and walked about the room, stopping before a picture here, and picking up a book there, talking the while of a dance to which some of my young people had been the night before, and of which I deplored the prematurely grown-up character. "Boys and girls," I said, "begin to play at society a deal too early for their good—Didn't you have a photograph on this table? I don't see it."

I had addressed Cornelia, but it was Nancy who from her pillows replied at once. "Yes; Mr. Richard Bellegarde, the actor. Aunt Cornelia has removed him as being hurtful to my morals." She spoke with the quietest self-possession and sweetness.

Cornelia Dean stared at me, opened her mouth, and shut it. To help her out, I exclaimed: "Oh, morals be hanged till we have got her on her feet again! Let her have it back."

Nancy was shaking her head and smiling. "You mustn't interfere with Aunt Cornelia's plans for my welfare."

Still to assist Cornelia, for whom her niece was proving a good deal too much, I said to Nancy, "Your Mr. Bellegarde seems a handsome fellow, whether he is a good actor or not."

"Only one in the country is better," said Nancy. "Give me your hand, Auntie darling." Cornelia, reduced to obedience, did so, and the young girl began to stroke it as she talked. "New York found him out last week, and now the world is his. I am in love with his art, Auntie, but not in the least with him. And he shall soon be in love with mine, though not in the least—"

Suddenly my study and the garden window came into my mind, and I discerned the reason; for an instant her eyes with strange, intimate intensity, had become fixed upon a corner of the room. It was for an instant only, that this gaze and the pause between her words lasted—"not in the least in love with me," she finished imperturbably. "I can do without the photograph, Doctor." She followed the words with a gentle laugh.

"Come away," I said to Cornelia. "She mustn't talk any more to-day."

"But isn't it good," exclaimed Cornelia, when we had reached her sitting-room, "isn't it good to hear her laugh again!"

It was not good. I had caught her once more with "the image" so to speak; but that laugh of hers boded worse than "the image," although I did not tell Cornelia this. I heard something in it that escaped an untrained hearing—the cunning of a sick mind all alert to foil us. In her words, too, I heard the huddled, dodging mockery of a spirit playing hide-and-go-seek with us, its well-wishers; she could "do without the photograph." I think that this was a "false lead," as they say, I believe, on the stage; I think she meant me to suppose from it that as she had the young man's image present with her in another way, she did not need his picture. At any rate, from that day, I fully agreed with Cornelia that she saw not the actor but something else. Of course I questioned the nurse as to what Nancy had said to her, and she to Nancy, when the shutters were opened and the photograph discovered to be gone. The one remark, "Why they've taken my photograph away!" had been all. With her rapid formidable cleverness the girl had made the whole thing out for herself. I cautioned the nurse not to encourage or permit her patient to talk "theater"; in this case talking "theater" amounted to the same thing as talking "symptoms." I don't wish to exaggerate the difficulties of my problem, because I failed to solve it until it was too late; I must in all humility record merely my mistakes: one, undoubt-

edly, was to remove that photograph. Yet even after
this, Nancy's trust was almost restored. It was only
one part of her nature that was in rebellion against
us, the rest—all that was wholesome and sweet and
affectionate—was with us, and on that I counted, to
that I directed my treatment, and as time went on
it responded. Order came back to her bodily forces,
sleep, appetite, and strength followed, and the new
color of her cheeks, the new light in her eyes, deceived me into thinking we had won her.

One sunny December morning, I advised her to go
for a short drive. That afternoon when I saw her,
I knew we had slipped back. Utterly puzzled, I
asked Cornelia to send for her coachman. The man
could tell me nothing, evidently concealed nothing
and I asked him through what streets he had driven.
With this hopeless clue I then took the same drive.
It was just when the futility of my proceeding had
decided me to desist that I saw upon a high hoard-
ing, which screened some excavations where a hotel
was going up, a huge theatrical poster in three
colors. From this the opulent eyes of Richard Bellegarde stared full at me, always as if they knew
"something to my advantage." He was blazoned in
company with a well-known actress, whose face also
stared out of the bill, and the pair were announced
as presently to visit us with a brilliant repertory.
Here was the key to Nancy's change, but neither

Cornelia nor I could be sure what it unlocked; would she, we asked each other, have been disturbed by the poster if Bellegarde's face had appeared upon it in solitary glory?

"She'd have missed the photograph sooner, if it was that," Cornelia declared.

"How do you know she didn't miss it at once?" I demanded.

"Perhaps she only found herself out when she saw the other woman," suggested Cornelia.

We made no advance along these lines, but I discovered in two or three days that Nancy was advancing somewhere by herself. Inspired by that sad, expert mistrust which is forced upon all nerve specialists by the fathomless and versatile cunning of our patients, I arrived at an unexpected evening hour, when Nancy was at dinner downstairs with Cornelia. Breakfast and lunch were still carried up to her room. There I hastily ascended. I lifted the rug and found beneath it the newspaper whose presence, somewhere accessible to her in secret, I had divined. Not a servant in the house admitted any knowledge of this newspaper—but I pass over the domestic convulsion which thereupon rent poor Cornelia's household; all of us have had cooks and waitresses leave us. The forbidden sheet—I had positively prohibited any journals containing theatrical news— was full of the triumphs of Bellegarde's company;

it was easy to suspect this to be only one of several instances when the injurious element had been introduced into Nancy's room, even as poison is conveyed to a prisoner.

"If your sleep is going to fail you now," I said to my patient one or two days later, "you'll never be able to return to work in January," and as I then saw coming into her eyes the look which I had learned to translate as defiance, I hastened to add, "Not that we'll try to stop you. I'll allow no such thing as that. I simply mean there will not be enough of you to stand the racket."

Well, she turned this over; evidently by the next afternoon the force of it, not as relating to her getting well for her doctor's sake, or her aunt's, or her own, but for the sake of her profession, had been recognized. She opened her gray eyes upon me. "What am I to do, please?"

The little talk we had upon this passed off with a smoothness quite unexpected; what I wanted her to do was to allow herself to go to sleep without the use of drugs, and as I was now concealing from her a part of my intention, I feared her keen penetration would see through my plans. I do not think that she had a suspicion of what I had in mind. I had at length decided (with Cornelia's full knowledge and consent, of course) to exert some mental influence upon my patient. The state of her body left little

now to desire, but her mind, if it had begun to re-
cover, had received a set-back from the poster, as I
have already said, and needed direct-healing. Therefore I induced a light hypnosis, and to my patient
while in this state I gave a peremptory order of
oblivion: she was to forget the poster, the actor,
and "the image." It was thus that I sought to
destroy the fixed idea. I told Cornelia that perhaps
one such experiment would suffice, and that perhaps any number might fail of effect, but that I
could imagine no harm coming from the trial. "In
your niece," I said, "the spirit is again setting fire
to its house. We had the house pretty much rebuilt,
and now we must keep the spirit in order, if we
can."

We cannot tell what else of evil might have happened had I not taken this step, but what did
happen was assuredly its direct and amazing consequence.

My visit had been made soon after twelve. I
lunched at home, and drove out again upon my
rounds. When I re-entered my study at about half
past five, Cornelia Dean was waiting for me. "She
is gone," she said; and to my bewildered question,
she answered merely, "gone. Gone away; from my
house, from the town." She put into my hand a
note which Nancy had left for her.

"My darling Aunt: Don't stop loving me. Everything is all right, and will be more all right. But I could not stay with you and be robbed. The doctor will understand me. Give him all sorts of messages of thanks and affection; tell him that I know how well he meant. He'll soon see how mistaken he was. Your Nancy always and always.''

We sat for a while in silence over this startling message, exchanging with our eyes the defeat and the foreboding that so filled us with pain. Then Cornelia told me the little else she knew, giving all blame to herself. She had allowed Nancy to go out for a drive with the nurse. At a drug shop the young girl had wanted some cologne, and the nurse went in to get it. On her return to the coupé, she found it empty. The coachman was as thunderstruck as herself. The girl must have stepped out on the street side, and got instantly into a car. The man seemed to remember that one had stopped opposite the carriage.

We were still searching for her when a telegram from New York told us of her safe arrival at a friend's, and next morning another followed to say she had found an engagement and should be in our town playing a small part within ten days, when she would come to see us. It was now poor Cornelia (she decided that no sort of attempt to restrain her niece should be made) who fell ill. By the time I had her somewhat mended, the company had been

playing a week in town. I had written Nancy that
she must not see her aunt just yet, and Nancy had
written that she would come to see me as soon as she
was less busy with rehearsals. I did not acquaint
Cornelia with the fact that Nancy's company was
Bellegarde's company. It appeared that Miss Evelyn Shenstone played, among other parts, the nurse
or maid, or whatever she is, in "Camille," which
they gave on Monday, Wednesday, and Saturday
nights. Two papers had given her one line of favorable comment, and ten or twenty lines of publicity,
in obedience to their code that no matter what cruel
pain such things inflict upon unoffending, helpless
private people, the public "has a right" to know
all about it. Nor did they stop with revealing her
true name, and the respectable disapproval felt by
her family at her choice of calling; they hinted at
further matters of interest. Mr. Richard Bellegarde believed in a great future for Miss Shenstone,
while the lady star of his company was rumored to
entertain a different opinion.

I leaned my head in my hand after finishing these
nauseating paragraphs, and reflected that with their
daily injection of vice, violence and sophistication
into American homes, these newspapers are on the
whole America's worst enemy. It seemed my duty to
come in with some support and countenance for
Nancy. Accordingly I did two things: I took a box

for the Saturday night's performance of "Camille,"
to which I invited a number of friends of Cornelia
and her family, and I arranged a supper after the
performance at my own house. To this were bidden,
besides my box party, Nancy, Bellegarde, and the
star actress, with a few other friends to make up an
assemblage large enough to seem marked and formal. All my guests accepted, save Cornelia.

At the play a surprise awaited us. The manager
in a speech before the curtain craved our indul-
gence; the star had been suddenly incapacitated, her
part would be taken by Miss Shenstone. The excitement of mingled curiosity and anxiety into which
the news threw me was soon supplanted by interest
and a dawning conviction that Nancy had a right
to be an actress. She bore, she even profited by, the
sudden strain of this demand. After the first ten
minutes she began to play with an exaltation which
by the end of the act captured the house, and drove
from my mind all thought of Bellegarde, in whom
I naturally felt a peculiar, if not a hostile, interest.
His real eyes were precisely like the poster and the
photograph; beyond these, and his black hair, I recall noticing nothing at the theater. My guests
thought that he played very well. That scene between the heroine and the father of Armand called
forth much enthusiasm from every one except myself; I had begun to be frightened by the appear-

ance of Nancy and the marvelous manner of her acting, though doubtless I should never have been so but for my previous knowledge of her. She was called before the curtain several times after this act.

"How beautiful she looks!" exclaimed my neighbor.

"She looks frightfully ill," I said.

"But she ought to in this part," my neighbor reminded me.

This I had not thought of; I hoped the appearance would prove merely the result of art; I hoped that her eyes, as they so strangely gazed upon the audience, beheld nothing less corporeal. My mind now suddenly illumined, gave, so to speak, a start; into it a thought had leaped, seemingly from outside. Of course this unexpected flash was (to use a chemical simile) produced merely by the uniting of separate trains of thought which must have been for some time approaching each other. Nancy's acting depended on "the image," or she thought it did. It stood for her, whatever it was, as some guide or source. It must then be—what? On the threshold of certainty my mind halted, but its new preoccupation lost me the final act, which I stared at without in the least seeing.

Richard Bellegarde did not wait for Nancy, for whom I sent my carriage back to the theater. In this he showed tact, if not good feeling. He arrived before several of the others, full of enthusiasm for Nancy's performance. If he had other thoughts about her, he concealed them well. It was with real or excellently feigned freedom that he spoke of the young girl while my supper party was assembling and removing its wraps, and he had the good taste to make no reference whatever to the newspapers. Of himself, he was, of course, a little more full than he was of Nancy. "She says she owes everything to me, and I'll not deny that she does owe a lot. She hadn't an idea of pantomime till I took hold of her. You see, over in England I studied under the Bancrofts, and they—he especially—well, if you couldn't suit him in your pantomime, you couldn't stay. D' ye know, some of your comic actors here are better than the others? But I used to say to Nancy when we were rehearsing in Buffalo, 'My dear little girl, don't do it that way! If you could only see yourself as others see you, you'd do it all right in no time.' "

Another flash in my mind followed these words, but my arriving guests broke, for the moment, this colloquy. "It" was herself she saw!—But in what presentment? Bellegarde also was disappointed in being interrupted; with a civility good but perhaps a little too lustrously august, he bowed to the various friends I brought up to him, but hovered aloof, handsome and rapt, beside my fireplace. Nancy, of course, was surrounded, which gave me no chance to watch her, even after we sat down to table; there, though sitting at my right, she was still beflowered with compliments and questions. Bellegarde I changed, placing him at my left, in order to continue our talk at the first possible moment. So sunk was I in what he had revealed to me that I forgot to order removed the empty chair intended for the actress star. From her I had found a note, excusing herself a trifle abruptly, on the score of "indisposition." I had made no reference to her absence, and I hoped that no one else would do so.

"Odd little lady," Bellegarde, on his first chance, resumed to me. "As I was saying, she got all that pantomime from me, though she didn't get it in a hurry, I can tell you! She continued awfully bad, and I said to her every day, 'Don't do it that way! If you could only be in two places at once—on the stage, and in front watching your own mistakes!' She knows she owes it all to me."

"Has she told you so?" I inquired, observing him attentively.

"Dear me, yes! Queer little lady!"

"Miss Shenstone is a great friend of mine," I remarked.

He took the hint, but excused himself. "And of mine. You mustn't mind us stage folk and our ways

with each other. It makes for familiarity. No offense is meant.''

On this point Nancy now certainly bore him out.
Across me she lifted her glass to him. ''Here's how,
Jack!'' Then she added : ''You don't yet know all.''

Thus I learned that Mr. Richard Bellegarde, who
now pledged Nancy in a bumper of champagne and
with a glance that set me wretchedly wondering
about them once more, had been baptized John, and
that his true name was Bagstock.

''But,'' he continued, ''I succeeded with her—put
her on the right track. She told me she was going
to see herself, watch herself from in front. That
would show her better than talking where she fell
short. Imagination, what!''

The empty chair now struck my attention for
the first time, and I directed it should be removed.
But even as the man placed his hand upon it, a low
exclamation came from Nancy. She was looking apparently at him, and my heart sank.

''Whom was it intended for?'' asked one of my
guests.

''Why,'' exclaimed another, ''you were going to
ask—''

''She couldn't come,'' I said hastily.

My guest met it with equal haste.   ''Oh! of
course!'' she murmured.

The silence it brought on us was a mere moment;

talk waked up briskly again with the happy inspiration of some one down the table. "Well, it's lucky we haven't another, for then we should be thirteen!"

Nancy leaned once more across me. "We are thirteen, Jack. . . . Do you understand?" They did not hear her, nor see her next action. They were all gay again; only their host, myself, sat cold, as he saw his guest of honor lift her glass, and where the empty chair had been, pledge across the table her conjured visitant, "the image," now at last evidently in front of her. Then suddenly, still holding her glass, she rose, the triumph on her face obliterated by staring horror; there came from her a wild, long, piercing shriek, and as the glass fell shivering among the silver and flowers, her hands began to make a blind groping. I started to support her swaying body, but Bellegarde, as if in answer to that groping gesture, had already rushed behind me, and caught her in his arms. The eclipse had come! Darkness had covered one half of her sight, engulfing "the image" in its descent.

We carried her to Cornelia's house—Cornelia had not been well enough to accept my invitation—and under her aunt's roof, not at once, but before spring, Nancy died. It was a merciful aberration that possessed her mind during those last weeks; she remembered nothing of her art or her ambition, and her affectionate nature shed a sort of happiness upon herself, even if it could not upon us who watched her.

Even to this day I ask myself what was the true cause of that appalling cry which Nancy gave. I cannot feel sure; I shall never feel sure. That for a triumphant moment she saw "the image" full in front of her (as she had always been determined she should see it) I have no doubt whatever; the direction of her gaze was unmistakable. Was it swept to the center of the field by the rush of oncoming blindness? Perhaps so. But why that awful shriek? Did she see the looming night close in? Or—had she at last come face to face with the image of her true self, that hidden, ultimate self, which none of us has seen or guessed in mortal life, and had its glory or its terror proved more than her fragile strength could bear? These are odd thoughts for a scientific man; they shall be the last of my confessions.

It is all long ago. Cornelia is dead now, leaving in our town a great blank for me, and one less of the few with whom I am at happy ease. You may wonder about Bellegarde; I have often wondered.

Stanwick's Business

I HAD, that hot afternoon, after all the prelimi-
naries of ticket and baggage were serenely accomplished, a luxurious little margin of minutes
before my train's departure to the New Jersey coast;
so that amid the press and gasp of obviously des-
perate travelers in front of me at the Bureau of Information (where I merely wanted the new summer
time-table) I stood reflecting how great among our
lesser blessings it is to have enough time at a railway station—especially when the whole world, apparently, is (as I saw it put in a newspaper head-
line) "Rushing to Neptune's arms." I was making
this comfortable reflection when Stanwick came up
behind me and, in his inveterate way, apprised me
of his imminence by giving me a slap on the back
at which even the bystanders turned round. I never
knew him to fail in this demonstration. Of course,
I turned round myself; and my greeting to him
was, I cannot choose but suspect, moderate. I've
nothing against Stanwick; his good humor is sleepless, he is always eager to back his opinion with a
bet, or to beat you at golf, tennis, billiards and

172

dominoes, or to swallow more food or drink than
you can; his railroad stories command a thrilled and
enormous public, and there is an egregious go to
them—as there is to him. For he walks with an
egregious go, and he sits down with an egregious
go, and there's an egregious go about his shirt linen;
and when I see him coming—though I've absolutely
nothing against Stanwick—I am apt to speed from
his approach. I hoped we weren't taking the same
train this afternoon. But, as it immediately turned
out, we were.

"Going to the shore?" his large voice inquired,
and told me, without waiting, that Salamis Grove
was his point. "Best place in Jersey!" he declared
heartily. "Best surf, best hotels, best sport. I've
tried all the others—Charlemagne Beach, Amalfi
Park, Sneak-box River, Squankawan, Shakespeare-
by-the-Sea—the whole bunch of 'em, and give me
Salamis. Where have you been lately?" he now
asked, and again saved me the effort of answering
by informing me that he had been to Scranton.
"Yes. Been to Scranton. Getting material for big
railroad wreck story—hot stuff! Are you going to
the shore? Salamis Park in my opinion—"; but
you need not hear Stanwick's further opinion of
this spot. Indeed, I did not hear it myself. Stanwick (as you will doubtless have noticed) has the
jovial monologue habit. Every fifty or sixty words

he drops you a question, and goes immediately on
with the monologue. Thus is created for him the
illusion that he is hearing all your news, while at
the same time he is spared the wear and tear of listening to you. But the jovial monologue habit
spares you, also; I didn't learn Stanwick's opinions any more than he learned my destination; I
merely said "Ah-ha" and "Um-um" at him now
and then, and thought of something else. He would
soon ask me if I had read his new story, and I would
say yes, because he would never stop long enough
to find out the truth.

Still, my previous serenity was growing troubled.
We were approaching the window of the Information Bureau at the usual speed of three inches a
minute. A piebald cluster of us pressed forward
together. Most of us carried chattels, and all of us
glared with mournful, unanimous eyes at the young
man in the information window. A white lady with
a basket of plums was asking him the best way to go
to Skaneateles; a black clergyman from time to time
very sadly inquired if the Tuskegee Convention
special car started from this station; behind him
a stumpy woman with emigrant hair poked a scrawl
of paper up at everybody in general, and hoarsely
ejaculated the word "Smork"; two Italians with
restless feet paid no heed to my freshly polished, de-
fenseless shoes; while a stolid agriculturist pressed a

live rooster against my heart. There were more of us; but now my body from neck to heels was latticed with trickling streams of sweat, and my endurance gave forth a sigh. I said: "All I want is a time-table to Shakespeare-by-the-Sea."

The young man in the window lifted his eye from the volume whence he was gradually extracting the route to Skaneateles. "Then you want Long Branch Division," he remarked, and he reached me the time-table.

Stanwick broke his monologue. "Long Branch? That's my train. Going pretty soon, isn't it?"

I told him, in nine minutes.

The young man lifted his eye again and spoke in the cold voice of supremacy. "Four o'clock just gone. Next train 5:58 to-morrow morning."

"The dickens!" Stanwick cried out.

"It's nothing of the sort!" I proclaimed emphatically, for I don't like the cold voice of supremacy. "It goes out at 4:09 by the Delaware Bridge, and I'm taking it myself."

The young man got a time-table and saw he was in error; then, with the chronic self-justification that distinguishes the inaccurate, he growled: "Well, she wasn't running last Monday. It's only 468's second trip this season."

"And they call this an Information Bureau!" exclaimed Stanwick.

"Certainly," I said. "Information for the young man. The Pennsylvania road invites co-operation from its patrons."

"Does the Tuskegee Convention—?" began the clergyman mildly.

"Wait for your turn!" barked the young man; I had enraged him, I'm glad to say.

"Smork," said the emigrant again; and on this we left the group.

We moved toward the news-stand, for I wished an afternoon paper. I was, however, not destined to read this.

"Seen my new story?" Stanwick inquired. "Out yesterday." He did not hear my hasty assent. It would have been hard to escape seeing that such a tale existed; the magazine announced it flamboyantly all over the news-stand, with the author's name, and a red and blue locomotive upside-down in a river. "Buy it for you," the author continued. "You can read it in the train and tell me how you like it. It's a peach!" I murmured words of gratitude and anticipation not listened to by him. I now made out in front of the books and periodicals, which he was studying sourly, another literary acquaintance, a critic, whom Stanwick saw at the same time and instantly hailed with one of his claps on the back.

"Hello, Ortley! Going to the shore? I'm bound

for Salamis Park. Best surf on the Jersey coast. Guess you've read my new story. You critic chaps have to keep up with—"

But Ortley, with acid imprudence, cut in: "I've had no time for your new story, and I'm taking the 4:09 to Plantagenet Harbor."

Stanwick clapped him again. "My train! Buy it for you. You'll read it on the way, and I'll get your expert testimony. Ha, ha! Expert testimony!" and he beckoned the news agent, shouting, "Two copies of the July Colossus."

Ortley made his favorite conservative gesture; he stroked the silken cord of his eyeglasses. But he and I and all quiet people are no match for Stanwick. I rather wondered at Ortley's attempting to cope with the author as he returned upon us, a Colossus in each hand, saying: "There you are—cost you nothing. Cost the public ten cents."

"And what, pray, does it cost the magazine?" inquired Ortley—a most foolish method of attack.

Stanwick did not even see it *was* an attack. "Oh, it's expensive for them. I don't know how much they pay for the illustrations, but they have to pay me fifty cents a word."

Ortley winced as the Colossus was thrust into his limp fingers, but he still attempted to cope. "I'm surprised you don't get more."

"Oh, I'm going to on the new series that the

editor of Pan-America has arranged for. Let's go to
the parlor car or there'll be no seats.''

He forged onward through the crowd, through
the gate; and Ortley, following helpless in his powerful wake, held my arm tight and hissed inces-
santly: ''Fifty cents a word! Fifty cents! He shall
have expert testimony.''

II. EXPERT TESTIMONY

I always like to see what kind of locomotive is
going to draw my train; especially on the Pennsylvania Railroad, where, in their struggle for motive
power as efficient as the New York Central's, they
have indefinitely multiplied their types of engine.*
I, accordingly, in the few minutes that remained
after we had secured our seats, strolled along our
short train from the parlor car in the rear to our
locomotive. She was Number 853, class P, with a
Belpaire boiler and medium drivers—sixty-eight
inches at most—not much of a locomotive; the railroad has better than that, though I naturally abstained from any such tactless comments to the engineer. Evidently before my arrival he had given
them the air, the brake testing was over, and he was
down now out of the cab with his oil-can.

''So they don't run an E on this train,'' I began
to him.

*Note. True twenty-five years ago, when this trip on the
''bridge train'' was taken.

Even in this his engineer's pride felt an inferential slight upon 853. "We get all the speed we want."

With that, spoken very quietly in a capable, independent voice, he continued his last preparations before the start.

I watched him drop some oil on the guides, and I put conciliation in my next attempt to talk. "Of course you do! Only they seem to be running E's on all their fast expresses: E's and L's."

To this, which called for no answer, he gave none. He was thirty-three, I suppose, with a face of marked seriousness, and he wore spectacles, something that I never before happened to notice an engineer wearing. But for a certain hammered, weather-beaten courage in his features, he might have passed for some Greek or History professor wearing inappropriate overalls.

Still I didn't give it up. "I suppose with this light train through a country like Jersey you can make any time you please?"

He finished oiling a crank-pin, and looked at me quietly and without encouragement. "We can generally get there," he remarked; and then his eye fell on the Colossus in my hand. He brushed a contemptuous gesture at it with his knuckles, and said: "They've hired a prize liar to write for them." And on my inquiring who, he explained: "There's a railroad story in that thing. The call-boy had it in the roundhouse, and we took it away from him."

"You don't say so!" I exclaimed.

"Yes. We took last month's away from him, too. That one had an engineer putting on full speed to cross a weak bridge. The boy is intending to be a railroad man, and we don't care to have him grow up on fool trash like that."

He actually showed no interest in why I laughed so; he dropped some final drops of oil upon his locomotive. "The author," I now told him, "gets fifty cents a word for it."

And this did at last awake symptoms of some emotion in him. His eyes flashed through the spectacles, though I don't know what with. Anger, it may have been, but never amusement; at any rate, I had seen that his expression could change, which I had begun to doubt. He now had much interest for me, while I, alas! had none for him; he climbed actively into his cab without more notice of me, and made it impossible to ask him how an engineer should cross a weak bridge. I decidedly wished to know!—and how extremely Ortley would wish to know! When you are a boy, I reasoned, and you go skating, you always skate as fast as possible over those thin spots, denoted "tickly-benders." You break through if you don't. Why, then, should not a weak bridge—well, speculation couldn't help me; but what a close miss—and close misses are always the hardest to bear! I fairly grieved to think how near I had grazed possessing knowledge with which not merely to cope with Stanwick, but to slay him outright.

These thoughts had brought me back along the platform to the cars, and were broken by the voice of the newsboy coming to me out of the open windows.

His was a wandering voice, carrying its chant slowly through the train. "Nothing sold after leaving. Buy your reading matter now. Colossus for July. Nothing sold after leaving."

I saw the conductor with his watch at the rear steps of the Pullman, his hand waved a sign, the air-whistle sounded forward in the cab, and our train got into faint motion. I mounted the steps nearest me, and passed on my way to the Pullman between the thick, luxuriant rows of hot passengers, the pink, damp foreheads, the shirt sleeves, the bare necks, the fans. A sudden leaning motion of our train on one of the yard switches tilted me down upon the stout breast of a lady who was reading the Colossus; but after this I steered a straight course to my car and seat. My seat was not at all the kind that I wished to stay in; this forward half of the car was a sleeping-car (a singular arrangement for an afternoon journey of less than three hours, and a

too plain symptom of an economical use of old rolling stock designed for long Western runs); ladies,
nurses and children filled the sections, and I was
glad to escape to the observation half of the car,
where you could sit in a wicker chair, smoke, order
a drink, and be out on the rear platform with a
camp-stool, if you desired. Stanwick had the de-
fenseless Ortley there already, with his Colossus,
and he vigorously beckoned me to come and occupy
the stool he had kept for me. I beckoned back
through the big, clear window that I would stay
where I was; upon which Stanwick came for me and
jovially took me out.

"Ever so much better out here," he declared.
"Fresh air, good view; bring the story along."

So there sat Ortley and myself on two camp-
stools, each with a Colossus, and Stanwick owning
both of us. We were now slowly leaving the West
Philadelphia Station. For fresh air, in that gigantic
railroad yard, we swallowed the smoke of generations of locomotives, and for view we saw these
same locomotives, old and young, freight and passenger, and beyond them the flat, mediocre city.
William Penn and his tower were blotted out in
thick, black Pennsylvania Railroad smoke.

"When you've finished that story," said Stanwick, "I'll tell you about my next one."

Words quite suddenly came from me: "At what

speed should an engineer take his train over a weak bridge?''

"As slow as he can, of course. Why?''

The tunnel stopped me—the tunnel where the New York tracks go under those of the main line— and when we were out of its sulphurous fumes Stanwick was off with his monologue.

"Want to know the technical explanation? Well, it's simple. What kills a bridge is first, vibration, shaking, and then the drag on it—the drag, you see, of the engine's drivers catching the rails as they haul the train—and, of course, the parallelogram of forces is to be reckoned with most. Queer thing —you'd never think it—but you combine the gravity pull with the horizontal pull, and it's a worse strain than just the gravity alone, in spite of the diminished angle. Now, as your gravity pull is a fixed quantity, your point is to have as light a horizontal pull as you can. See? So the engineer shuts off for his bridge, slows down, and gets over it, if he can, on momentum alone.''

I was happy to murmur that I "saw"; and, as Stanwick galloped forward with more monologue, I dimly did see; the parallelogram of forces waked in me college memories of freshman physics; intricate, chilling memories, which I hastened to banish in a more immediate wonder: Which was the barefaced one, Stanwick or the engineer? What possible motive had the engineer for making up for my benefit a story about a bridge which Stanwick had never told? Or could Stanwick be so brazen as to fabricate a whole false and impossible technical procedure when he knew the truth?

The sudden, wide vista from the Delaware Bridge roused me to the fact that we had left the Schuylkill and North Philadelphia behind us. I saw Ortley crossly reading the Colossus, I heard Stanwick still copiously discoursing about himself to me. "You see, I know about these things," he was saying. "I wasn't a railroad man ten years for nothing. Well, I won't keep you from my story any longer."

We had now swung off from the double-track Atlantic City road, and come into that seashore branch which passes through Mount Holly and Whitings on its way to Bay Head. I read Stanwick's title: "Old Irongrip's Last Signal."

"Got the material in California," Stanwick put in. "Happened in the tules during the '94 strike. But I don't want to interrupt you."

What did interrupt me was Jersey's fecund yellow loam, rising, as we swept through West Moorestown, in cloaking clouds, blinding my eyes, turning gritty the pages of my magazine.

"There's no use out here!" I said.

"It's better after this," said Stanwick; "but the

sun's hot." And all three of us came in from the platform.

Stanwick's story began:

" 'Let them dare,' said old Irongrip, as he turned his steel-gray eyes from the time board, and rested them with proud affection upon the blooming slip of a girl who had addressed him."

Yes, it was once more the egregious go, right in the first line; and I counted the pages to see how much of it there was going to be. I presently found that I had read nothing more, but was gazing emptily at the illustrations, which were plentiful, and just like photographs. To be just like photographs is the triumph of magazine art.

"Glad to see you, sir," said the conductor, an acquaintance of several summers in the train. He handed my return coupon back. "You got that, too?" he commented; then his hand, like the engineer's, made a brushing gesture at the Colossus. "Only one thing wrong with that story," and he laughed gaily.

Hope, at these words, stirred in my heart. "What's wrong?"

At his next words my heart leaped. "The printed matter. The illustrations are all right." He again laughed gaily.

His ticket duties took him away from me, but I sat happy; I would get things out of the conductor.

We were only at Hainesport, the train was just
picking up speed again after the bad S curve and
the drawbridge, Jersey corn and farm fields were
not yet merging into Jersey sand and pines; oh,
yes! there was plenty of time for that conductor to
help me cope with Stanwick.

I now sped with haste through old Irongrip's
adventure, and by the time I had read the last
words we were just reaching Whitings. At this
melancholy junction a passenger from the Jersey
Southern got into our car and bellowed at everybody who would look at him, "I've waited an hour
and nineteen minutes!" until somebody fiercely
said: "That's nothing for Whitings," which rendered him silent. But I was grateful to him; the
conductor had to return to our car for his ticket,
and this produced a better arrangement than I had
planned for Stanwick. Instead of seeking the conductor in one of the forward cars where he kept
himself, I had him and his expert information com-
fortably in our midst.

Ortley had finished Irongrip, Stanwick was sipping something with cracked ice that the porter
had brought him, when I began on the conductor.
We had seven or eight minutes before the stop at
Tom's River would take him away from me, and I
started my strategem well. "Do you know, I rather
like this story?" I frankly handed him the Colossus, open.

He held it, looking at it. "Well, the public seem to." His laugh interrupted him. "We railroad men—look here; now I suppose this caught you." He began to read aloud the final sentences, and at the words, and his skillfully blighting tone, all things happened as I wished; Ortley laid down his Colossus and Stanwick took the cracked ice beverage from his lips. " 'Though he well knew what must come (read the conductor) he never stirred from his seat, never took his steady hand from the throttle as the locomotive made its fatal plunge through the trestle. And so they found faithful old Irongrip, still holding that throttle, in the mud and slime. No; it was only his crushed, mortal clay that they found. Heaven had given the white signal to him, and his soul had an open track.' There!" said the conductor. "And the newsboy sells out his stock of that magazine, and a fat lady up front is crying over it right now. She don't know why they happened to find old What's-his-Name—Eagletooth—"

"Irongrip," said Stanwick.

"Dead in his cab at the bottom of the river."

The train slowed, the conductor broke off abruptly; it was Tom's River.

"Oh, come back!" Ortley wailed.

"I'll get a chance," said the conductor, "after we leave Seaside Park."

Ortley elaborately congratulated Stanwick.

"What luxury," he murmured, "to have one's tales appreciated by those they so accurately describe!"

Stanwick was all good humor. "*That's* all right! Do me the favor, when he comes, not to tell my name." He rose. "I simply must see that lady cry. Come on, Ortley."

But the critic sat. "Thank you, I'll take the conductor's word for it."

"Nothing the matter with Ortley," Stanwick remarked to me as I went forward with him, "except that he doesn't get fifty cents a word. Now, where's that old lady?" We traversed two cars, and caught up with the conductor.

"I know her," I told Stanwick, and I took him toward the matron upon whose breast I had fallen.

"Yes, that's her," said the conductor. "Lord, lord, why even the men are fooled by it, too!"

"You don't take these stories as hard as your engineer does," I said. And I related my experience.

"Well, he's taking all life with some emphasis just now," the conductor explained. "He had two hundred dollars in a building association and it busted."

"That lady," said Stanwick, "has a strong, intelligent countenance."

I looked and I could not contradict him. She was lending her Colossus to a neighbor, and a fragment of her words reached me ". . . teach an ideal of duty. So much healthier than most fiction."

Something public in her voice struck me, and I touched the conductor's elbow. "Do you remember where she's going?"

"Temperance Heights," he replied. "Midsummer meeting is on."

I informed Stanwick of this as we turned back. "She will very likely lecture on your story," I said.

Ortley met us here. He hadn't been able to sit alone with his curiosity. "I have counted them," he bitterly said to me. "Seventeen passengers are reading that thing." And we returned to our wicker chairs at the rear.

"Well, I don't want to spoil your enjoyment," said the conductor—we were now running along the narrow sea sand between the Atlantic surf and the great smooth blue inlet—"but the reason they found old Eaglegrip in his cab was because he hadn't time to jump. That's the reason whenever you find an engineer dead in his cab. It ain't like a captain going down with his vessel. He stays to control his crew and get the passengers off. Engineers have nothing like that. When a smash is unavoidable the engineer has only one duty, and that's to save his life if he can, and so be ready to help the injured instead of adding to their number. When he has sounded his whistle, and shut off

steam, and put on the emergency brake, he can do
no more for his train, and his place is on firm ground
if he can get there. Of course, if the cab happens
to be the safest place he stays there. Why,'' pursued the conductor, becoming humorous again, ''if
the Brotherhood was to catch an engineer with a
sense of duty like old Irontooth they'd suspend him
till he got common-sense! Why, to employ such a
fool would be a crime; he'd be dangerous! He belongs in a lunatic asylum! But the newsboy sold
his stock out, and I guess the writer of that story
knows his business. He's not writing for us railroad folks.'' The train was slowing for the flag-
stop at Mantoloking, and the conductor left us.

It had not come out with a handsomeness equal
to my hopes, equal to what the engineer, I felt,
would have made of it if he, with his more emphatic
view of life, could have given us his opinion of the
story and its writer. The lighter-minded conductor
had, with a sophistication that denoted his higher
development, praised Stanwick's knowledge of the
emotional public. Still, Stanwick might feel a trifle
stung by the blast which laid bare his total per-
version of railroad life, and knocked clean away
the underpinning of his hero.

Ortley, I could see plainly, expected to triumph,
and addressed the author with: ''And what have
you to say now?''

But Stanwick had by no means been stung; his good humor gushed. "Say? Why, the conductor has said it all, and said it straight. I could have told him the duties of an engineer: I've been one myself. But I'm an author now, and I write for the sentimental million who don't want realism, but the unreal realistically described. Where's your melodrama in an engineer who jumps? Why, don't you know that the heroic engineer who dies with his engine is one of our biggest popular delusions? He's an ideal with all boys and women, and most men; and if I can make fifty cents a word out of him why should I go and bust him? I couldn't get five cents a word for an engineer who jumped."

"No matter," said Ortley; "the truth before everything."

"But why, Ortley?" I cried, for I was beginning to enjoy the critic. "Why destroy their ideal?"

Stanwick added: "Where's the harm for them to believe an engineer sticks to the throttle—so long as they're not going to be engineers?"

Ortley couldn't see it. "No good ever comes from fraud," he snarled.

Stanwick's good humor fairly bathed the critic. "Ortley, you are simply immense! Well, I must go get a look at those seventeen passengers reading about poor old Irongrip."

III. AT THE Y-SWITCH

You must know that north of Bay Head Station the single track goes immediately upon a trestle across a brown Jersey pond, and then for a few curving yards to a cross-road where a flagman is. A little grove—a Jersey grove of little oaks, little pines and thick, short foliage in general—hides from the engineer what's ahead until he has finished the curve and reached the grove, and may be going pretty fast; for now he has a straight mile or so of double track to Point Pleasant. The grove lasts for perhaps two hundred yards to another road-crossing and a Y-switch. The engines of both the Pennsylvania and Jersey Central trains from New York, which end their run at Point Pleasant, come down to use this Y-switch, and any engine backing from it to the main track is invisible until too late; hence an engineer leaving Bay Head watches the flagman. This afternoon there happened to be the combination of one careless man and one imbecile.

We had left Bay Head, crossed the trestle, come to the grove, and Stanwick was on his feet to go watch his seventeen passengers, when three, four, five—I don't know how many—hoarse, horrible whistles screamed from our locomotive. I saw us all staring at each other, Stanwick shooting forward and catching something; then came a dead, heavy shock. It tipped my wicker chair, objects rattled on the floor, and next we were all stone still, silent, with the little quiet, green Jersey grove outside, a rear vista of track and a flagman staring, joined hurriedly by two more starers, and up front, somewhere, a crazy roar of steam in the silence. A voice outside said, "They're killed," other voices added variously: "You can't see him. He's underneath. Did the fireman jump? No. The other one's all smashed, too. You can't see anything for steam." Somehow we inside were all saying: "You hurt? No. I just fell against the buffet. We're all right. This car's all right." On the track behind the observation platform, the conductor, with a very white face, was speaking: "What time do you make it, gentlemen?" "I make it fifty-six now." "Yes; fifty-six by mine," said a passenger. "We're due here at fifty-five," went on the conductor, still looking at his watch, and writing notes at the same time. "The responsibility for this must be fixed. He has no right to be here with me due. I must have some of your names, gentlemen." He got our names. "How did it occur?" somebody asked. "That Central engineer. Backing on our track and never sent a flag in front of him. So that man down at the road gives us a white flag. So we come right on and into it."

I had begun to live again. It is curious how one can stop living while the mere mechanical part—the

heart, the lungs, the circulation—goes on. I don't
think it is fright. I think it's surprise; but thoughts,
will, attention, all cease, and one is no more than
a vegetable. But now all parts of me were going
again, and I was curious and anxious. I hoped we
should find no awful disaster up ahead. Stanwick
and Ortley and I were walking slowly along together, quite silent, by the empty, open windows of
the train. All the passengers were down, grouping,
dispersing, stopping; and each man and woman
seemed to be relating aloud eagerly their sensations
to everybody, and nobody listened to them. It was
not bad, no passenger was hurt, we were not
wrecked; yet even coming so near was sinister and
numbing for the moment; that roar of steam seemed
like a spout from the world of death that we had
just not entered; the terrible, invisible forces around
us were hissing at us in that steam. And now rustic
Jersey was scantily gathering to the show. Our
crash had happened at the end of the grove, where
the second road crossed and the Y-switch came in.
Here stood a man with a string of fish, talking to
a man with a wagon of vegetables. "I knowed what
was comin' when I heard them whistles." And the
vegetable man said, "I could 'a' told 'em it would
happen with him backin' that way"; while two little girls, who had evidently been wading somewhere, beckoned wildly to three little boys, running

to us across a field. Other natives arrived, and all
expressed the sentiment that they "could have told
you so." Meanwhile, here was the show, not very
terrific to see. On the Y-switch, a few yards off,
where we had knocked it, stood the delinquent
Jersey Central locomotive. She was not hurt; only
one corner of her tank was mashed in, and lifted
a trifle from its frame. We had evidently struck
that corner only, just as it was getting clear of us;
if we had struck it full and square—well, never
mind, that had not happened. Our locomotive was
worse punished on this side—the engineer's side.
Her firebox was ripped open, tank and cab somewhat crunched together in a kind of splintered hill
of broken wood and bent metal, one feed pipe
twisted to a corkscrew. From the gash in the firebox the dying steam was ebbing. Poor old 853 would
not haul us any farther this day; and any human
life that had been caught between cab and tender
when they crushed together would now be crushed
like them.

My eye fell on two very grimy men to whom the
conductor was intimately talking, while the baggage master was offering to sponge the wrist of one
from a bucket somebody had just hastily given him.
He—why, he was the fireman, and the other grimy
man was our serious engineer! The brakeman had
just picked his unbroken spectacles from a bush.

"I remember throwing them before I jumped," said the engineer.

"I'm very glad you got out of it," I said to him.

"If we had jumped half a second later—" said the fireman.

"Yes," said the engineer. "I hadn't much time to lose."

The fireman's wrist was the single hurt between them, nor was it broken, but merely hard struck by something. Washing would almost cure everything that was the matter with them. The engineer looked the worse. In jumping he had been thrown on the cinder ballast, and from numerous digs in his face and forehead blood trickled between a rich plaster of dust and ashes. His appearance was quite shocking, but it was mostly appearance.

I heard exclamations of pity and admiration behind me, and, turning, I beheld the Temperance Heights lady with clasped hands, gazing with passionate benevolence at the engineer. She then hastened away, and some new person offered a bucket to the unknowing object of her solicitude. He plunged his head in the water, after handing his spectacles to the conductor. I saw now that there was a tie of strong fellowship between these two, and that the conductor had been really somewhat unnerved by the narrow escape of his mate. I stood by and witnessed as thorough a ceremony of getting

clean as ever I saw under conditions so limiting.
Buckets were brought, one after the other, fresh
and full, soap had appeared and a second sponge,
and from his plastered grime the engineer was beginning to emerge as does the dawn from night. The
concern for him manifested by the conductor, the
deference paid him plainly by the other train
hands, his acceptance of it as a matter due his position—all this glimpse of disturbed railroad life
held me on the spot, although I could plainly dis-
cern the Temperance Heights lady standing by the
grove, and surrounded by a crowd of passengers
whom she was addressing with vehemence. But one
cannot be in two places at once, and I remained
near the engineer.

"Is it hard to jump?" I presently ventured to
ask him.

He gave me his quiet, expressionless look. "It
comes easy when you have to."

I found myself desirous of expressing sympathy
about the building association; but what business
of mine was that? Stanwick was examining the
locomotive's injuries with a technical eye. Ortley
was looking at his watch.

"When shall we reach Plantagenet Harbor?" he
inquired.

"Dear knows," said the conductor. "I've asked
Point Pleasant for an engine, but the division ends

there, and red tape may keep us any length of time.''

"Why, they can see us!" protested Ortley, waving petulantly at Point Pleasant. "I can count three locomotives up there now."

"So can we all," replied the conductor; "but counting won't bring them."

"Good gracious!" Ortley snapped. "What a way to do things!" And he stepped about in a peppery manner.

I saw the conductor wink at the engineer, but this less frivolous person merely continued to wash, remarking, "That Central man will be out of a job."

"He'll claim it's only our second run," said the baggage master.

"Nothing excuses his sending no flag back," said the conductor. "And we ran all last season."

"The flagman down at the road could have stopped us, anyhow," I suggested.

"He's a Jersey flagman," observed the conductor, in a withering voice.

Stanwick came from inspecting the wounded engine. "Pity she's so light," he said. "An E would have pounded them and stood the shock herself."

"No E could have acted better than she did," retorted the engineer promptly.

I thought I would go and listen to the Temper-

ance Heights lady, but her exhortation must have
been brief. She was approaching us, a little in advance of her recent audience, who seemed to recognize their leader in her. Well, their curiosity was
going to be disappointed if they had come to stare
at the engineer. His sensational grime and blood
were gone, and there was nothing to see now but a
recently washed person with some scratches. He
had, moreover, put on his spectacles, which still
further removed from him the suggestion of disaster.

"I always think of them now," he said to the
conductor. "Once I jumped with them on, and
I thought the oculist would never get through with
me."

The Temperance Heights lady here burst in upon
our small group. "Old Irongrip is not dead," she
began with trained but sincere rhapsody; "he is
here with us. Sir" (she now directly addressed the
engineer), "your deed has spoken to our hearts,
and our hearts go out to you. Defying destruction,
you sat at duty's post with your faithful hand on
the throttle, and shed your blood to save us. Earth
has no fitting reward for such deeds, but" (here
she failed to keep her eloquence quite up) "accept
these one hundred and ninety-seven dollars and
fifty cents from the men and women who thank you
for keeping your faithful hand on the throttle."

Amid general cheers from the passengers I heard

explosive noises beside me. It was Stanwick enjoying himself. His story had splashed like a stone into our pool of humanity, and he was delightedly watching each widening ring of result. Ortley was purple with protest. He was incoherently yelping, "But he jumped, I tell you. He did. They all do," when I clapped my hand upon his mouth. "Don't you dare to destroy their ideal!" I fiercely commanded.

I have already mentioned that a second time came this afternoon when I saw that the engineer's features could express emotion. It was now. His spectacles stared; stupefaction dumbly opened his mouth.

"Do not try to speak," the Temperance Heights lady urged in romantic tones. "We know how weak you must feel. Good-by." And she departed, taking with her the passengers, happy every one. Their ideal had been preserved.

"Oh, he ain't weak, but I am," observed the conductor. He retired to a fence and leaned against it.

The engineer now spoke. "What does all this mean?"

But from the fence the conductor said: "Put the money in your pants, and don't ask questions. Your loss in the building association is covered."

Well, the engineer obeyed the first part of that at once. I can't but think it was later made clear to him how Stanwick's story, already expensive for the Colossus, cost the passengers two hundred extra dollars.

It was two hours before help came to us, but I regret to chronicle that Ortley's outraged feelings had not calmed when he left us at Plantagenet Harbor. His last observation was, "Fifty cents a word!" in a voice of despair for the literature of his country.

As I got off at Shakespeare-by-the-Sea, I asked Stanwick why this was not material for him. He gave me a stare.

"This? Why, where's the sex punch or the thrill or the sob stuff? This would be satire. How can you chew till your teeth come? We must feed our baby on soft foods till it has cut its teeth—and then some—say five hundred years. Come to me then, and maybe I'll talk to you about selling satire to 'em. Glad any day to see you at Salamis Grove. Drop in. Cocktails."

I suppose he does know his business, as the conductor said.

How Doth the
Simple Spelling-Bee

How doth the Simple Spelling-bee
Impruv each shining ower.

OF course, I know not how it may be with you; but with me the mail brings daily a multitude of communications that I have not sought, and do not want; nor do I refer to bills alone; and so, when there came one day a printed card saying:—

Why Heifer?

I tossed it into my waste-paper basket, and remembered it no more. Some days had passed, during which I had worked onward at the index of my forthcoming volume, when my memory was jogged by the arrival of a new absurdity:—

Why not Heffer?

Like its predecessor, this card went at once into my basket. I had nearly finished the B's in my index before the mail brought the following:—

It ought to be your custom now
To simplify, and spell plough plow;

Therefore write quickly on your cuff
From this day forth to spell tough tuff.
A third must follow these first tu,
So you will always spell through thru,
Nor in the midst of things leave off,
But joyfully now make cough coff.
By this time you must clearly noa
Dough can't be doe, do, dow, but doa.

Well, if they purposed to reform our spelling, which has always been a mere rag-bag of lawlessness, I hoped that they would do it right; but I was too deeply immersed in completing the index of my forthcoming volume to spend thought upon this question; nor did I court interruption. My wastepaper basket, therefore, received another willing contribution. And when presently the clue to these cards reached me in the following telegraphic message, just at the outset of my morning's work :—

Chickle University,
Arkansopolis, October 6, 1906.
English spelling rotten to the core. Help us.
Masticator B. Fellows.

I responded, not without satire :—

Utterly prostrated by news. Helpless.
Thomas Greenberry.

And thinking that thus I was rid of him, I proceeded quietly with the index of my forthcoming volume.

But Masticator B. Fellows, president and proprietor of Chickle University, had not done with me so easily. Since his street boyhood, sixty years ago, this ardent personality ('tis thus the daily press describes him) had made his own way, and had his own way; he was his own capital, and there is no record of his ever having sunk a cent of it. Of habits strictly pure, he had never seen a card or a drop of liquor that he had touched, and he had never seen a dollar that he had not touched. He had organized every industry along his path, from paper-selling, boot-blacking, and so upward to his organized lobby at Washington, through which he had caused a heavy tariff to be put upon every commodity necessary to the American people. It was he who had advised his brother organizers to keep Religion on the free list, because, as he assured them, "If we tax it, they'll do without it, while if we don't, they'll trust us for a while yet." And now, at the age of seventy-five, with uncounted millions, and ten United States Senators, and a fourth young wife all in his pocket, he proposed to hand his name to Immortality by simplifying the spelling of English all over the earth. Well, let him do it if he would only do it right.

But this he must do without my assistance; there were other professors, many of them. I did not permit the circulars that now began to pour in from Chickle University to distract me from my index. Striking as these circulars were—and I will instance but one of them:—

Judge, budge, ridge, acknowledge
ARE SLOW
Call in and try our Quick Spelling
Juj. Buj. Rij. Aknolej—

they went into the basket one after another. To this method of suggestion a second was added, and my coat-pockets, as well as my mail, began to be filled with spelling literature. I would go out for a walk, and during this exercise some paper or pamphlet would be slipped into the coat, which I would discover upon my return. I remember pulling out a little book of verse, beginning:—

I am only a primer to teach you to spel,
Which is something that nobody does very
    wel.
A sweet little primer,
A dear little primer,
Sing hel, bel, tel, fel, sel, nel, quel, swel,
    and smel.

I felt, let me confess it, annoyed the next day on returning from my walk to find a new method of

suggestion, in great charcoal letters, on the white
marble of my house-front :—

Such nuisances as
Solemn Comptroller and Wednesday
are preventing
THE KING OF SIAM
from learning English

Nor was my annoyance decreased by the further
announcement that defaced my house-front upon
the day following :—

MILLIONS OF SCHOOL CHILDREN
turn away weeping from
PEOPLE MANOEUVRE DIAPHRAGM

Much should be conceded to the man who is fighting for his Immortality, as was Masticator; but not
too much. And displeasure, it may fairly be said,
began to rise in me, when I found, next morning,
a page of the primer introduced in the midst of
my index :—

Of the bad English spelling you'll surely beware,
When you notice how stair, pear and heir rhyme
with there;
The sad English spelling,
The mad English spelling,
Sing hi! for the mare and the mayor and the prayer.

Next consider, for instance, a word like enhearsed :
Now what business has it to be rhyming with first?
  Sing hi! the old spelling,
  The horrible spelling,
The spelling of nursed and of versed and of worst.

But our simplified speling can cure every il,
And permits nothing foolish like two l's in pil.
  Sing hi! the new speling,
  Our comforting speling,
Sing pil, bil, fil, wil, til, sil, quil, spil, and swil.

Yes, Masticator was going too far—and how had
he managed to tamper with my index? I rang the
bell, and questioned my man Edward sharply. He
knew nothing of it, nor did the housemaid, whom I
also questioned sharply. And I trusted I should be
less harassed on the morrow.

But on the morrow, at breakfast, lifting with my
fork the top buckwheat cake in order to spread butter upon the second, I found a leaflet between the
two cakes inscribed :—

     Phthisis
How can you eat while a word like that is allowed?

I flung the cakes at my man Edward, and in five
minutes I had dismissed every servant in the house.

Quite unable to work, I left the house myself,

and set out to take the air. No, Masticator was not doing it right; he was taking too many sudden liberties, not only with the language, but with myself. Becoming gradually aware that a number of young persons were following me with loud and disconcerting expressions, I stepped into a shop where I am unknown, and where they at once offered to brush off my back. A double mirror showed me these words, chalked plainly :—

He wants a
P
in Consumtion

Being now without servants, I decided that I should be free from persecution in the luxurious wilderness of a great hotel. Upon getting into bed in my room in the twelfth story, a dreadful contact caused me to leap to the floor, where my foot dashed down upon some similar dreadfulness, and the shock threw me flat on my face and stomach only to feel myself instantly plastered with more of the same odious and encasing substance. I believe that I shouted loudly in the dark for some time before hotel employees rushed to my succor; the door was burst open and the light turned on. It was flypaper; and much time was consumed in relieving my person of it. Every piece bore its motto, such as :—

> If you'll but drop the e in pi
> Better on stomach pi will li.

and also :—

> The b in lam
> 's not worth a dam—

and others.

As early as possible the next morning I wired this message of capitulation to Masticator B. Fellows :—

Delighted to serve you. Glad to abolish spelling by derivation. American people demand psychology should be sykology. But also fear pitfalls in phonetics. At dinner lately the lady to my right admired the flowers in the vayz, and the lady to my left spoke of the same ornament as a vahz. Needs ripe judgment and broad outlook. What can I do for you?

And his reply came back :—

Rejoiced that you are with us. All we seek is to serve. Private car train twenty-one Thursday.

The spirit of this message pleased me, except that it was wired collect, and I had of course paid for mine.

The secretary of Masticator was at the steps of the car and presented me at once to a most lovely girl. At the news she was to serve on the Simplified

Spelling Committee with me, my heart bounded, every doubt left me, and I exclaimed:—

"I will spell just as you say."

"Then," she most sweetly returned, "never let us consent to any simplification of kiss." And I counted such answer a very happy omen.

She had come from a woman's college, and her important work on the authorship of Shakespeare's plays had demonstrated, beyond refutation, that the plays had been written by Queen Elizabeth, in collaboration with Sir Walter Raleigh and Lady Jane Grey.

"Shall we be in Harrisburg soon, Mr. Kibosh?" she asked the secretary.

"It will be ten minutes after seven, Miss Appleby."

"And that is a whole three hours!" she cried, with no pleasure in her voice.

"Here is some good chickle," said Kibosh. And when she would take none, "Then I will," he said. "The private stock of Masticator B. Fellows. The public gets nothing like this."

He took a small object from the box that he held and put it in his mouth; and soon, while the train sped on, his large, long jaws were oscillating with a smooth motion, and content, like a lukewarm glaze, overspread his immense bald features.

Thus it came to me what chickle was. "Chewing-gum!" I exclaimed.

Kibosh opened gentle eyes upon me. "We do not employ that word at Arkansopolis." He smiled, removed the plastic morsel from his mouth, and placed it on the window-sill, that he might speak to me without impediment.

"We always say chickle at Arkansopolis. We like that better. Masticator B. Fellows likes that better. When his genius bought up the small plants—"

"Is there a chewing-gum trust, too?" asked Miss Appleby.

"Chickle, Miss Appleby, chickle, if you please. When Masticator's genius organized this noble industry, thereby placing a superior, pure, cheap, and uniform article within the reach of eighty million jaws—"

"But the whole nation does not chew gum!" the lovely girl again, with some spirit, interrupted.

"Chickle, Miss Appleby, if you please. Fifty per cent of our population chickles, and that makes eighty million jaws. When the time came to—ahem—float the proposition, after the bonds, there was an issue of one billion preferred, and two billions of common stock. It did not seem fitting, Miss Appleby, it did not seem dignified, that Wall Street should bandy back and forth such an expression as—ahem—'chewing-gum common.' To the eye, such an expression printed in the financial columns would seem—would—in short, hence chickle, Miss Appleby, noun and verb. Never anything else at Arkansopolis. Will you not chickle now? No? Ah, well. But at least you are with us in the Higher Spelling." His hand sought the window-sill, and then his mouth; and his jaws resumed their placid oscillation.

Miss Appleby had gone out upon the broad rear platform of our car; and there, as she sat alone, I joined her, saying :—

"Shall we talk of the Higher Spelling?"

But she seemed inclined for not much talk upon any subject; and the nearer Harrisburg drew, the more difficult I found it to engage her attention.

"There is nothing to see," I assured her when, as our train entered the station, she left me with something almost like eagerness.

I did not get out during our somewhat long stop, being occupied in my private stateroom with unpacking and disposing my clothes for the journey. As we started again, I emerged to find Miss Appleby in bright conversation with a newcomer.

"Professor Jesse Willows," said Kibosh, "of Paw-Paw University, Mountain Dew City." And as the extraordinarily handsome young man rose, quite six-feet-two, to greet me, Kibosh continued: "The professor's Dictionary of Deadly Weapons, as well as his great work on Bowie-Knives in the Stone Age, makes him a welcome member of our committee."

I felt, I know not why, less glad to see this Professor Willows than Miss Appleby seemed. His long black coat and black tie were fairly proper for a man of erudition; but his hat was soft and broad of brim, and his trousers were of brown corduroy, drawn over high boots.

"And what, sir," I asked him, "may your views be on the Higher Spelling?"

"Bless yore heart, suh," he gayly responded, "what's spellin', anyway? Just alphabet lettuhs fixed like some man chose to fix 'em befo' you an' me were bawn. An' so I say such a man's had his notions more'n long enough, and it's high time we-all took a whirl at the dictionary."

"I admit, sir," I responded, "that our spelling is but a rag-bag of lawlessness. But it has been ratified by a noble army of great writers. They and the daily press have spread it over the world. Therefore we must go slowly. We must do it right. Derivation—"

"Bless yore heart, suh," the impetuous youth interrupted me, "what's derivation? Just conquest follo'd by mispronunciation. Julius Caesuh he lambastes Gaul; and he talks Latin to 'em; he says 'honor,' an' he goes home; an' the Gauls retain Caesuh's idea, as all puffeck gennlemen should, but the nearest they kin git to the Latin is 'honneur.' An' then, whoop they come over to England, an' they lambaste the Anglo-Saxons, an' talk to 'em about 'honneur.' An' the Anglo-Saxons, bein' also puffeck gennlemen, they ketches on to the idea, but be-Jeroosalemmed if they kin say it straight, either; an' so it gits to be 'honour.' An' then comes our glorious Revolution; an' we tell the English, 'Good-by to yo', King Geawge. Good-by to yore iniquitous parliament. Good-by to yore whole dog-goned outfit of tyrants and helots. We-all don' keer how you-all spell anything whatsoever, an' the language of Washington, an' Jeffuhson, an' Patrick Henry, an' all the glorious fathuhs of libuhty, is goin' to spell it honor without a u.' An' there you are, back to yore original Latin."

"I quite agree with you," I said, somewhat tartly, I fear. "I have little value for derivation."

"A noble sentiment, Professor," said Kibosh. "A truly noble sentiment. Will you not join me in a chickle?"

The professor bounded to his full, long height, with all the agility of the felis catus of his own wild, native mountains.

"I'm with you, suh!" he exclaimed. "Be-Jeroosalemmed if I wasn't pow'ful thirsty."

"Chickle is not liquid refreshment," said Kibosh, mildly; and held out the box to his tall guest.

The professor glared at it for a moment. "You

and yore chickle,'' he then began, with alarming
deliberation, ''can go right—''

A quick, girlish cough sounded behind him.

''—to my private cabin in this cyah,'' the professor continued, with no change in countenance or
voice, ''where I will join you, and where we will
find liquid refreshment.''

Kibosh did not dare refuse him, and I came without being asked.

''It's a glorious exercise, suh,'' said the professor
to me, in the private cabin.

''In moderation, yes,'' I answered.

''May I inquiuh to what you-all are referrin'?''
he asked haughtily.

''Why, to this,'' I answered, tapping my glass.

The professor grew more stiff. ''I referred to
simplifyin' the spellin' of our language,'' he said.

''A glorious exercise?'' I repeated vaguely.

''Fo' the imagination, suh. Turn yore eye whah
you will, you'll see words that need refawmin',
words that need our help, words that cry an' clamuh
to be relieved of the stigma of their congested and
nonsensical appearance; nouns, adjectives, verbs,
all stuck in the hopeless mud of antiquity, an'
holdin' out their hands for we-all to drag 'em out
an' bring 'em up to date.'' He now gave me a list.
''Look, suh, at those pore, sufferin', aged cripples,
awaitin' the renewal of their youth.''

"You have a magnificent collection," I remarked
to him, after a glance at the list.

"Pshaw!" he returned. "I could double that in
an hour. I just jotted that down as I came up the
valley from Paw-Paw in the Chattanooga Limited.
Why, just lookin' out of the cyah windo' would
give me notions. I saw a thistle. Down she went on
the list, an' down went whistle next her, suggested
by our locomotive. Thistle. Whistle. Look at those
disgraces. Look at the dead wood in 'em. Are not
they just congested all up with pitfalls for the
young? Once we get to work at Arkansopolis, and
they'll be thissl and wissl, or my name is not Jesse
Willows."

He paused, and I looked at his list again. The
railway journey had given him a number of suggestions; I saw, in hasty writing:—

Freight. That's dopy. Should be frate.
Bridge. Another has-been. Brij.

My perusal was interrupted by his seizing the
list away from me. "The po'tuh has turned the
gas higher," he said. "That gives me another whole
big line of 'em." And he wrote:—

Light should be lite. So also fight, and tight and
others on the same plan.

"Po'tuh!" he called out, "what is yore name?"

"Michael, Colonel," the man answered.

"Another!" exclaimed the professor. And he wrote :—

Michael, Mycle, because cycle.

Bicicle because icicle.

I kept the various doubts to myself, and resolved that such must continue my policy if I were ever to have peace; but, no matter how I might agree to spell bicycle, I was secretly determined never to address my younger brother as Mycle. Imagine thus mutilating a name that had been in our family for generations!

Professor Willows showed his list to Miss Appleby; I saw him, and I saw her evidently add some words to it. But, to my surprise, this seemed to cause them mirth. They did not seek my company, and conversed together without ceasing, in a corner of our car, while Kibosh slumbered; and I wondered if the Higher Spelling was the subject that brought their heads so close to each other. That girl was more and more a disappointment to me; and I retired in no very good humor.

Mycle was not the only word to which, as I dressed myself next morning, I found my opinion to be entirely adverse; frate seemed to me objectionable, nor did I feel any leanings toward brij and lite. And the surprising readiness with which Professor Willows accepted my criticism failed to make

upon me the happy impression which the adoption
of one's views by another is apt to cause.

"You don't like frate, suh?" he said, whipping
out his pencil, and quickly writing on his list.
"Bless yore heart, then we'll just make it frait.
How does that hit yore fancy?"

I thanked him for his amiability, but my fancy
was as little hit by frait as it had been by frate; and
it was still less hit when he came to me with his customary enthusiasm some twenty-five minutes after
breakfast, to show me forty-three more words that
he had simplified since rising from table. Still keeping all thoughts to myself, I read:—

Earth and dearth to irth and dirth, like mirth.
Also worth to wirth. Pheasants whirr. Cats should
pirr.

I passed the list back with I know not what com-
mendations of his rapidity. He retired with it to
the rear platform, where sat Miss Appleby; and
almost immediately I heard egregious peals of
laughter coming from them both. This, for some
reason, kindled in me such annoyance that I put my
head out of the door, and cried loudly to them:
"Do you intend to make flirt flurt, or hurt hirt?
And how about squirt?" And I shut the door sharp
upon my words before they could make answer
to me. But still, even through the closed door and
thick plate-glass windows, their shameless merri-

ment reached me, and seemed, if anything, louder than ever.

The outlook for the Higher Spelling was scarce a bright one, I thought, if the rest of my colleagues, whom I had yet to meet, should approach their solemn responsibilities in anything of the spirit shown by Professor Willows and Miss Appleby. His facile adoption of a new spelling, and equally facile relinquishment of it, gave but poor evidence of any deep thought on this matter; and to see him through the plate-glass as he talked to her on the rear platform, no one would easily be persuaded that spelling was the subject of their colloquy; and lastly, when he fetched a large shawl and hung it across the window outside, so that they were wholly screened from view, I found it no light effort to believe that it was to shield her from the cold blast, as he informed me.

I sought (without great eagerness) the companionship of Kibosh. "Do you not fear," I asked him, "that we may not find ourselves able to reach an agreement as to the system by which this spelling should proceed?"

"What would hinder it?" he inquired.

"Of course, our present spelling is but a rag-bag of lawlessness," I replied, for I was growing fond of my description of it. "But great authors and newspapers have spread it round the globe. The sun never sets on English spelling. We must join the great English universities with us. We must join Canada, India, Australia. We must do it right.''

"England will have to follow us!" he declared.

"If you'll watch England," I said, "I think you'll find she has her own ideas about that."

"Then our publishers and writers will ignore England," he replied.

"If you'll watch our publishers and writers," I again said, "you'll see they'll be slow to let go their English market by making books that would be illegible throughout the British Empire."

"What are authors, anyhow?" he demanded. "It is our business men who are our glory."

"If you'll watch our business men," I repeated, not without acerbity, "you'll find they have London correspondents, and they'll not care to run two sorts of spelling with their stenographers."

Kibosh thought awhile, and then, with his gentle smile, he again removed his chickle and placed it on the window-sill.

"But, nevertheless, Masticator will have gained his point," he said.

"Scarcely so, if a system fails us, and we do nothing," I suggested.

He seemed not to hear me. "And all of the committee, every member, will have gained the point as well."

"You'll pardon me, but what is the point?" I now asked him.

"And the English language," he continued more and more gently, "it will have gained the point, too."

"I must confess," I said, "to utter ignorance of your meaning."

Kibosh smiled for a long while, looking at me very kindly.

"You will readily appreciate," he at length began, "that the greatest need of mankind is Publicity. It is as essential to the German Emperor as it is to the female society leader, or the trick mule. We are no exceptions, we leaders of thought, and teachers of youth, and captains of industry; we too must have Publicity or—ahem—pass under. And as the demand for Publicity increases, the supply of it naturally diminishes. You understand that? Well, now, any association with Masticator B. Fellows means Publicity at once for the lucky individual. But there are times when the vast sweep of economic currents ties up all the available Publicity, and at those times great enterprises languish from its scarcity. It may befall that even such giant operators as Masticator B. Fellows find themselves embarrassed. It is then only the man of genius whose magic hand can smite the rock in some novel way, and cause Publicity again to gush forth fresh and sparkling—it is then only he who is heard from. There has been such a time of late. Publicity was tied up, and Masticator needed some for his—for certain plans he has to benefit the human race. Now, what does Masticator do? He surveys the general situation, he thinks it over, and presently he says 'Spelling Reform.' He smote the rock, and there you have it. You understand me? Well, supposing you gentlemen do fail to—ahem—make any considerable impression upon the English language, you will have made a considerable impression on the public; the rock will have gushed, Masticator's point will be gained. He will have secured the Publicity he needs for his—his benevolent enterprises; each of you gentlemen will have secured Publicity for your names and works; and we mustn't forget the English language. It will have got Publicity, too; it needs it, like all the rest of us. I'm sure you understand me."

Thus Kibosh finished, and it entered my mind to descend at our next stop, and take the first train back to my own place; but this thought I quickly dismissed, remembering Masticator's methods of reaching those whom he wanted. And (although I know this is unworthy) I was becoming very curious to see what we should all do, once we were gathered together. Were all the rest of my colleagues coming for Publicity? I glanced at the window, where the shawl still screened Professor Willows and Miss Appleby, and it seemed to me that they had come rather for Privacy.

"Who are the rest of my colleagues?" I now asked Kibosh.

"Well, now, I'm afraid you've got me," he responded. "There's—let me see—Professor Flawless Nathaniel Maverick, of Fishball University, Massachusetts. He is with us. A profound scholar, sir."

"What is his line?" I asked.

"Well, now, that's another tough one. Let us see. Did he write *The Fuel of the Future?*"

I shook my head, being ignorant.

"Or was it *The Mustard Plaster in Pharaoh's Time?*" Kibosh dreamily pursued.

"What is the fuel of the future?" I asked.

"Pecan nuts. I am certain of that," answered Kibosh. "But whether he's that one, or whether it's Lysander Totts—"

"Who is Lysander Totts?" I inquired.

"Another profound scholar, sir. Of Numa Pompilius University, New York. But we've got them from all around—from Seminole, Florida, Oglethorpe, Georgia, Lafitte, Louisiana, Sandys, Virginia, Graftsburg, Pennsylvania—but you'll meet them to-morrow at Chickle University. All profound scholars, sir. It was Totts, come to think of it."

"Think of what?" I asked.

"Pecan nuts," said Kibosh.

I should have been glad to learn the names of all my colleagues, and what they had written, that I might be better prepared to meet them; but Kibosh could be sure only of Totts and his book; and Professor Willows and Miss Appleby had not heard even of Totts, when I asked them at lunch to enlighten me.

"What mattuh, suh?" cried Willows, cheerily. "They'll tell you quick enough themselves why they're so famous."

At this remark Miss Appleby broke into much gayety.

"Got many words this mawnin', Professuh?" asked Willows of me; and I retorted, with what should have been telling reproof, that I was not of those who can improvise thorough work.

It was extraordinary how much this young man's remarks pleased Miss Appleby. He was but a poor companion for the lovely girl; and when, after lunch, he retired to slumber in his cabin (as he called it) I took my seat beside her on the rear platform. She was most amiable, but bade me first take down the shawl behind us. The cold blasts, she said, had ceased. We talked for some time, and it was easy to see that under proper guidance her mind would open to all befitting things. Not until Professor Willows came out of his cabin and joined us,

did I feel her grow distant again. Without preliminary, he asked: "What does a man who sits down
on a sharp needle most resemble?" And, without
waiting, he answered, "A profane upstart."

Into such levity I could not possibly enter; I
resolved to wait the morrow, and the succeeding
days of our convention at Chickle University, for
opportunities to exert upon this impressionable
young girl my wholesome influence.

We reached our destination during the forenoon
of the next day, and I was amazed when I beheld
spreading out before me the vast institution where
we were to hold our sittings. Chickle University
covered, with its grounds and buildings, four square
miles. Swift electric cars ran everywhere by routes
so well planned that less than four minutes were
consumed between the two most distant points. The
several thousand buildings were of a uniform pattern, but lettered on the outside, so as easily to be
distinguished: House of Latin, House of Chiropody,
House of Marriage and Divorce, and so forth.
Everything was taught here, and had its separate
house; and the courses of instruction were named
on a plan as uniform as the buildings: Get French
Quick, Get Religion Quick, Get Football Quick, and
so forth. The University was open to both sexes. I
saw great crowds of young men and women trying
to push their way into the House of Marriage and

Divorce; and Kibosh informed me that this course was the second in popularity, and in such active demand that a corps of ninety-six instructors was kept lecturing continuously day and night. The football course had overflowed its own building so copiously that it was also filling the houses of Latin, Greek, Music, History, and Literature.

"And what do those students do?" I inquired.

"There have been none," he answered. "We have accommodations for two million students; but if this spelling reform fails to prove the—ahem—you'll remember what we said about rock-smiting, Professor Greenberry—fails to prove the—er—attraction that Masticator anticipates, any idle houses in this University plant can be readily turned into the Chickle plant, which adjoins it."

I asked him, would they not meet great difficulty in finding professors for two million students?

"Professors are our lightest expense," he replied. "We can always pick them up for next to nothing."

So saying, Kibosh led us to the library; and here were some gentlemen assembled whose appearance clearly proclaimed them to be profound scholars, and who were to be our spelling committee. While Kibosh made us known to each other, and we exchanged our formal greetings, the eye of each scholar sought the eye of every other scholar with that thirsty look an author wears, when the hope for compliments upon his writings flutters in his breast. But we were true professors, all of us, and not one had read a word that any of the others had ever written.

Deceit should always be discouraged, nay, firmly punished, in the young; for by reason of their immaturity they have but little judgment when to practise it; but to the old it is frequently of the greatest service. Intending, therefore, to be as agreeable as possible, I approached Professor Lysander Totts with a feigned knowledge of his work. Shaking him cordially by the hand, I said, "Ah, yes; Pecan Nuts!"

"What?" he replied, staring.

"Why, Pecan Nuts!" I repeated. "Let me congratulate—"

"My name is Totts," he interrupted.

"To be sure!" I exclaimed. "Who has not read *The Fuel of the Future?*"

"I haven't," said Totts.

I corrected myself hastily. "What an absurd slip of the tongue!" I gayly ejaculated. "I meant *Mustard Plasters in Pharaoh's Time.*"

"I haven't read that, either," said Totts.

I should now have been at some loss, but a plaintive voice behind me said, "Hup, hup, hup, hup."

I turned, and saw a smiling little old man, with delicate silver locks that hung well-nigh to his collar.

"Hup, hup," said he again, very amiably.

I turned back to Totts in bewilderment.

"He stutters," Totts explained.

The voice behind me now said with a sudden sort of explosion, "I wrote it."

I turned again, and, catching both his hands as a drowning man is said to catch a straw, I wrung them earnestly and long. "A great work!" I called to him, as if he were deaf. "A very great work!" And not well knowing what I did, I further shouted to Miss Appleby, who was passing us: "He wrote it! Pecan Nuts!"

"Hup, hup," said the little man. "Mustard Plasters."

Little as I owe Miss Appleby, I must always hold her memory in gratitude for her coming forward at this extreme moment.

"Of course it is Mustard Plasters!" she said, with delightful sweetness; "and you must write your name in my copy, dear Professor Egghorn."

He extended an eager hand for the volume.

"It is in my trunk," she continued promptly; "and your signature will make a unique gem of what is already a precious treasure. And you, dear Professor Totts, when I am unpacked, you will

surely not refuse me the same honor? Professor
Totts, you know," she added to me, "has proved
that Cleopatra was a man."

"Then who wrote Pecan Nuts?" I whispered to
her hastily.

"He hasn't come yet," she hastily whispered
back.

"I am sure," said Kibosh, leading a tall new arrival among us, "that Professor Camillo Cottsill
needs no introduction here. We all welcome the
man who has said the last word on—the last word
on—on—well, now, really, it escapes me, Professor," he finished, turning his wide, gentle smile
upon the newcomer, who glared at him angrily, and
announced with unnecessary loudness:—

"Nostalgia in the Lobster."

"Thank you, Professor," said Kibosh; "thank
you kindly. I think lunch is now awaiting us in the
House of Bread."

After brief preparation in the rooms assigned to
us, we lunched with the students; and, as I passed
down the hall, I saw Totts and Egghorn signing
their respective volumes for Miss Appleby.

"So quickly unpacked?" I asked her.

"Dear, no!" she returned. "Professor Willows
easily bought them for me at the University Book
Shop."

"I have but one complaint against your exquisite

deceit," I said to her. "Why did you leave me out?"

"Ah!" she said, "who could deceive you?"

I strove, but unsuccessfully, to occupy a seat beside her at table; it was Jesse Willows who got it, the other being taken by Egghorn, while Totts placed himself opposite. Napoleon preferred men with great noses, but that of Totts would have pleased him too well, I think; and Totts blew it continually. It was my hope that supper, or dinner, or whatever they called the next meal, would not be served with the distressing rapidity of this one; one had barely the time to swallow, and the food went whole down one's throat; but the next meal, and all meals, were the same, and, had our convention lasted longer than it did, I should have fallen victim to a grave dyspepsia. This, I learned, was another instance of the vast genius of Masticator B. Fellows: while educating his students, he created in them the need for the product of his own monopoly. He gave them no time to chew at their meals, and chickle was served free in all the houses. For chewing, at some time or other, is necessary to digestion, and among the thousands at Chickle University I saw not one anywhere, boy or girl, whose mouth was not oscillating like a rabbit's; and to judge from this universal motion of the jaws of the American People in trains and all public places,

I see they are learning that great economic principle of Masticator's, which is announced everywhere in the street cars:—

TIME IS MONEY
He who chickles
Saves his nickles—

nickles being the simple spelling of nickels.

This great man allowed us at length to see him next morning, when we assembled to begin our work. We sat round an imposing table some twenty strong—for all the profound scholars were now arrived—and in front of each scholar, on the ample green baize table-cover, was a great dictionary, with a great glass inkstand and writing materials. Tall blackboards stood behind us, waiting to receive the words we should reform; but the best of it was to find myself sitting next Miss Appleby, with Willows quite an agreeable distance away. Kibosh had arranged all our seats, and it is the best thing I know of him.

When Masticator B. Fellows entered to open our convention, it was plain at once whence Kibosh had acquired his manner and his appearance—so far as he could acquire this latter: the secretary might have been an early, bad photograph of the magnate. To see Masticator, he was the creature of brotherly love, the preacher of benign gospels, the teacher of female academies; no smell of Senate or Syndicate hung about him. Bald, with a silken skull-cap, bland, with his ten pointed fingers meeting as if to bless, with a sunrise smile, and a black coat as long and unlovely as conscious virtue, he stood before us in benevolent silence, and we rose as one scholar. But at once he motioned us to sit down.

"I think there's a dollar-sign in his jaw," whispered Miss Appleby to me.

Already Masticator was addressing us, slowly and softly.

"Dear friends," he said, "be welcome. I am worth two hundred and forty-five millions. Thank God that you are not. Thank God that you are poor. Thank God for your scanty meals and clothing, and your ceaseless failure to make both ends meet. Pray God you may die poor. How I envy you all your blessed privilege of struggle! Thank God, and now to business.

"Everything is getting better. Man is getting better. Life, Liberty, Happiness—all getting better. And chickle. Better and better. Then why not English spelling? Dear friends, I expect results from you. Let us sing the Ode."

A gasoline organ began to play at the end of the apartment, and we profound scholars stood up and sang together:—

My spelling, 'tis of thee,
Sweet land of spelling-bee,
Of thee I sing.
Land of the pilgrims' pride,
Land where my fathers dide,
For spelling simplifide
Let freedom ring.

"A beautiful pome," said Lysander Totts, on my other side.

"Where were you educated?" I asked him.

"Surracuse, Noo Yorruk," he responded; and he blew his large nose.

"And now, dear friends," Masticator was saying, "I leave you. Remember the poor foreigners, remember the little children. It is for them that the English language exists; and for them we must, therefore, smooth our spelling's cruel path. I expect results, dear friends." So saying, he was gone.

"Yes, there is a dollar-sign in his jaw," repeated Miss Appleby.

"Suggestions are now in order," said Kibosh, taking the chairman's seat.

Three profound scholars stood up. "The only way—" they began, with one voice.

"Professor Flawless Nathan Maverick has the floor," said Kibosh. "I presume the Professor will think no change in Pecan Nuts necessary." And the chairman smiled sociably at the scholar.

"The only way," said Maverick, "is to abolish all words that foreigners cannot spell."

"You mean cut 'em out of the language, suh?" inquired Jesse Willows.

"I do."

"Phew!" whistled Willows.

"Order, gentlemen," smiled the chairman. "Professor Camillo Cottsill has the floor."

"The only way," said this scholar, "is to abolish all words that children cannot spell."

"Phew!" repeated Willows.

"Order, gentlemen, please," said the chairman, gently tapping an inkstand with a pencil. But he was not heeded.

"Who are you whistling at?" demanded Camillo Cottsill.

"Can't yore children spell?" retorted Willows.

"Can yours?" shouted Cottsill.

At this Jesse Willows blushed a deep red, and so did Miss Appleby.

"He is not married, Professor," said Kibosh, tapping the inkstand soothingly.

"My little daughter Zola B. can spell everything," said Maverick.

"How about the others?" demanded Cottsill.

"My salary only affords me one," stated Maverick, with resignation.

"Then how can you judge?" said Cottsill. "Re-

ceive, and believe, and bereave should be cut out
at once.''

"They should not,'' said Maverick.

"Oh, cut everything out,'' sighed Willows.

"Hup, hup, hup, hup,'' began Professor Egghorn.

"The author of Mustard Plasters has the floor,''
said Kibosh, with civility.

"The only way,'' continued Egghorn, "is to hup,
hup, hup.''

"Start the organ, please,'' said Kibosh to an as-
sistant; and while the gasoline music played, "My
spelling, 'tis of thee,'' Kibosh walked round the
table and gave every one an individual box of
chickle. We chewed in silence, waiting for the
voice of Professor Egghorn to go again.

"Hup, hup,'' said he, at length; "phonetic.''

"I object!'' Cottsill and Maverick called out
loudly together.

"I move it's phonetic,'' said Totts.

"Second the hup, hup,'' said Egghorn.

"Those in favor—'' Kibosh began.

"That's not properly seconded,'' interrupted
Cottsill.

"Motion!'' finished Egghorn, with a shriek. And
we carried phonetic by eighteen to two.

"Since Professor Egghorn has shown us the only
way,'' said Kibosh, "will he not kindly lead off with
his suggestions for a reform list?''

But once again the professor's utterance was transfixed.

"Give the pore gennleman a piece of chalk," said Willows, "and send him to the blackboa'd."

With the blackboard we now made visible progress, which I decided it was best for the present not to interrupt. Let as many suggestions as possible be made; then we could weed them out. Consent was undivided upon a number of words, and some old spelling passed away in peace. The letter u disappeared from honor and favor, although, with much surprise, I overheard Miss Appleby saying to herself that she intended to retain it in all her private correspondence. The k was kicked out of Frederic.

("There's nothing new about that, either," said Miss Appleby, in a whisper.)

"But I shall not permit any such liberty to be taken with my own name," said Professor Maverick, firmly; and this was conceded to him, Professor Totts objecting.

"We shall never reach consistency at this rate," grumbled Lysander Totts.

"Who came here to be consistent?" retorted Maverick.

"We came here for spelling reform," added Camillo Cottsill.

("Good gracious," said Miss Appleby, under her breath.)

Presently it was the letter h that occupied us; and old honour now became onor (some were for oner, but gave in), followed by erb, our, and umor.

"What's that?" demanded Totts, pointing to our.

"Time of day," answered Maverick. "Sixty minutes make one our."

"Then nobody can tell it from our cat, our cow," said Professor Totts.

"We can't help that," said Maverick.

"We're only here for simplification," Cottsill said again.

("Good gracious," repeated Miss Appleby.)

"Make it ower," suggested Cottsill; and this was done.

"Make it minits, too," said Totts; and this was done.

"Make it sekonds," said Maverick; and this was done.

Cottsill turned to Egghorn at the blackboard. "Add eir, umble, otel, and istorical," said he.

"No, he shan't!" cried Totts, fiercely.

"Are we phonetic or not?" demanded Cottsill, turning on him.

("You're a pack of geese," said Miss Appleby.)

"I never said umble in my life!" shouted Totts.

"I reckon he don't feel the sensation," said Willows.

"And if istorical is adopted, I'll resign now," Totts continued.

"Gentlemen, gentlemen," protested Kibosh.

"I move those last h's be laid on the table," said Maverick; and this was done.

"Past participles," Egghorn now wrote on the blackboard. "Termination ed to be changed to t; for instance, blest, exprest, dro—"

"What are you going to do with rest?" interrupted Totts.

"And test?" said some one down the table.

"And nest?" another called out.

"Can't you let him finish?" said Cottsill. And Egghorn continued, "Dropt, stopt, spilt, kilt, and so forth."

("Kilt!" whispered Miss Appleby. "Oh, dear!")

"Rattlet instead of rattled will look funny," observed some one.

"So will mart and wart," remarked Willows, "instead of marred and warred."

"If you have rattlet and mart and wart," yelled Totts, "I'll resign right now, right now, right now!"

"Who thought of having them, having them, having them?" thundered Cottsill.

"Gentlemen! Oh, gentlemen!" wailed Kibosh.

"But consistency—" objected Maverick.

"You cut out consistency yourself," Cottsill reminded him.

We despatched the past participles, and came also without much disturbance through catalog, demagog, and so forth (vogue and rogue made some trouble, and our fundamental principle of inconsistency had once more to be asserted), but when their blood was roused and the fire of simplification grew hot in them, and they adopted the following with cheers and noises of feet:—

Receev, deceev, conceev, beleev, weev, leev, greev, seez, pleez, teez—

I felt that we had really got near the weeding-out point, especially when Jesse Willows rose and added fleez. ''Plural of dogbiter,'' he explained and sat down quietly. At this Miss Appleby gave one brief, happy laugh, but at once resumed a singular tapping of her foot which I had begun to observe. We now thoroughly phoneticked many words: blud, for instance, and wunss (which is so much phoneticker than once!) and the days of the week: Munday, for instance, and Toozday. (I say Tewsday, myself, but I did not mention it to these profound American scholars.)

''My little daughter Zola B.,'' said Professor Maverick, ''can always spell Wednesday.''

''My nine children never can,'' said Totts.

''I withdraw the objection,'' said Maverick; and so it was Wensday.

Skwirl, for squirrel, was next agreed upon, and lepard, and eegl. And as the blood of the scholars grew ever hotter and hotter, Constitooshun, Deklarayshun, and United Staits were adopted.

"But my Zola B.—" began Maverick.

"What are you-all goin' call yore next?" asked Willows.

Maverick sighed. "My salary only affords—"

"Beg yore pardon, suh, I forgot," said Willows, with sympathy.

It was here that I rose. "Gentlemen," I said, "let us do it right. Of course, English spelling is but a rag-bag of lawlessness."

"He has said that before," muttered Jesse Willows.

"But," I continued, "the sun never sets on English spelling."

"I object to these constant, trivial interruptions," stated Cottsill.

"Yes, let us onward," urged the chairman.

"Play ball!" added Totts.

"Chew gum!" finished Cottsill.

"I'm through," Egghorn said, sitting down.

It was beyond my power to guide them. I also sat down. I also was through.

"Through?" exclaimed Totts.

"That reminds me." And running to his blackboard he wrote:—

THRU

"What's that thing?" asked Willows.

"Hup, hup," began Egghorn.

"Through," replied Totts, raising his voice.

"What?" said Willows, raising his voice, too.

"Through, through!" answered the convention in a body.

And Miss Appleby, amid the general din, remarked, "That's the way a pig would spell it if it got the chance."

"Thru, clu, blu, nu, hu," wrote Totts.

"Hu? Hu?" repeated Willows, vacantly; "what's hu?"

"Hup, hup, hup," vainly continued Egghorn, waving his arms.

"Hu's who," explained Cottsill, loudly.

"Who, who!" explained the whole convention to Willows.

"Booh, pooh!" said Willows. And running to the blackboard he added:

"Bu, pu, and stu, also glu."

But Egghorn was now standing on his chair, and screaming, "Hup, hup, hup," with the most energetic violence.

"Oh, write it!" every one cried out to him.

They lifted Egghorn down from his chair, and he ran eagerly to his blackboard, upon which he wrote, "This is illiterate, this is unscholarly."

And again the convention cried out together, "We're not here to be scholarly, we're not here to be literate."

"Have yore way, gennlemen," said Jesse Willows, "I'll stand for anything."

"Well, I can't stand this any longer!" exclaimed Miss Appleby; and rising to her pretty feet, she continued, "Gentlemen, in your charitable solicitude for foreigners, you may be making our spelling easy for Lithuanians (though I doubt it), but you are making it quite impossible for the English."

Upon this a cold silence fell, and then, "And who are the English, madam?" asked Cottsill.

Miss Appleby gave her delightful brief laugh. "I'm sorry you don't know, sir," said she, "for I didn't come here to begin your education." And she sat down. There was an impulse in me to call her Gertrude, but I felt it to be premature.

A general murmuring confusion of consulting and dissenting voices now arose among the scholars.

"But what did you come here for?" I asked Miss Appleby.

"Not to see unbroken puppies put their muddy paws all over the greatest language in the world," she retorted.

"Dear me, dear me," I returned, with soothing deprecation, for she was plainly very much incensed, "then what did you come for?"

"Oh, for reasons," she returned evasively.

Doubts that I could not define began suddenly to

fill my mind, and I said to her, ''Didn't you write
about Shakespeare?''

''A college joke,'' she answered contemptuously.
''I'm writing a poem now. I shall call it, 'How
We Brought the Good Spelling from Ghent to
Aix.' ''

''Then you don't believe in the Higher Spelling?''
I asked.

''No!'' she declared, with defiance.

''Does Professor Willows?'' I pursued.

''Hadn't you better ask him about that?'' she
replied.

I think my face must have turned the reddest
that anger can paint faces; for now, at any rate, I
had no doubts as to how I had been made game of
in the private car. Yes, they had mocked me. The
impudent young man had manufactured absurd
spelling for my serious attention, and he and Miss
Appleby had then made merry together over it,
and over myself. But before I could frame a fitting
rebuke to the frivolous though lovely young woman
beside me, a distracting hubbub of voices was set
up, and through this I heard Kibosh calling :—

''On your blackboards, gentlemen, on your blackboards.''

The convention gradually heard him, too, and
scholar after scholar bounded from his chair, seized
a piece of chalk, and began to write. Only one was

left, who stood at his place, pouring forth the most execrable sounds I have ever heard.

"Professor Dudelsacker has the floor," said Kibosh.

"B u r r meowskreeyiyiwurrburrwowwowmeow," went the professor.

"Turn that Central Pennsylvania Dutch quacker out!" shouted some one.

"I've resigned already meowowwow," squealed Dudelsacker, in a fury; and he took his departure at once.

But this brought us no calm. Twenty pieces of chalk were rattling on the blackboards like a platoon of busy telegraphic instruments. Each scholar was making his own list for the new dictionary of English, and I read the lists of Totts, Maverick, and Cottsill, so far as they had written them. Jesse Willows was writing, too, with sweeping flourishes; but I had ceased to place faith in his integrity.

Surracuse	Beverly Fahms	Cyah
Yurrup	Rud	Cyard
Surrup	But	Cyart
Mawrul	Cut	Gyarden
Sawrul	Grantha	Coat-house
Kwawrul	Anywheres	
Awringe	Everywheres	Cottsill's list
Amurrican	Nowheres	
Tremenjus	Tremendious	

"Awringe," I murmured aloud, in ignorance of its meaning; but my own voice revealed to me that it was our chief Florida fruit, as pronounced by Lysander Totts, of Numa Pompilius, New York, discoverer of Cleopatra's true sex. The whole great West was rattling away on the boards behind me, but what I saw in front of me was enough to hold my attention; and my eyes were straying back and forth between awringe and grantha, when Totts, happening to glance up from his work, beheld the work of Maverick next him.

He stopped abruptly. "Rud?" he inquired of the professor from Fishball University, author of Pecan Nuts.

"Road," explained Maverick, writing out the old spelling. "Road, boat, coat."

"Hm," said Totts, with disapprobation.

"But what is grantha?" I whispered to Miss Appleby.

"Can it be a breakfast food?" she suggested; and again I wished to call her Gertrude.

Totts was still gazing at Maverick's list. "Hm. Yes," he repeated. "Bean talk from Boston. We don't want it."

"Are we phonetic or not?" returned Maverick, sharply.

But Totts had now caught sight of Cottsill's list. "Anywheres?" he read aloud. "Why anywheres? Rub all those out."

"I will not," declared the author of Nostalgia in the Lobster. "I guess if you can be phonetic, I can."

"I'm afraid they're skipping grantha," said Miss Appleby.

"Who says anywheres?" demanded Totts.

"I do," snapped Cottsill.

"Well, I don't," Totts replied. "And, what's more, I won't."

Cottsill raised his voice. "I guess I can be phonetic just as—"

"Anywheres is vulgar," interrupted Totts.

"Vulgar yourself!" screamed Cottsill, jumping up and down.

"Vulgar! Vulgar!" chimed in Maverick, whom the term, bean talk, had nettled.

But Totts had spied the list of Jesse Willows, and was pointing at it disdainfully. "And pray," said he, "what may a coat-house be?"

Now the handsome young man from Paw-Paw was the last person to select for addressing in such a tone as Lysander Totts had taken.

"I beg yore pardon, suh?" he remarked, so politely that I became filled with apprehension.

Miss Appleby was gazing at him with all her eyes. "What do you think of him?" she whispered to me.

I suppose that indignation at his unwarrantable

treatment of me in the car rendered me imprudent. "My dear Miss Appleby," I said to her, "my dear Gertrude, he is as beautiful as Apollo, as ignorant as a congressman, and as dishonest as a plumber."

"How dare you speak of my husband so?" she replied. "We were married this morning. That's all we came for to your silly convention. Good-by." And rising, she swept out of the room.

But her exit was unobserved. The great West was still rattling on its blackboards, Maverick and Cottsill were scowling darkly at Totts. Totts was pointing one finger at coat-house, and Willows was smiling steadily at Totts, in a manner that now convinced me we were approaching the edge of something quite particular. Nor did even the bridegroom know that his bride had left us.

"I beg yore pardon, suh?" he repeated.

"Coat-house. What's that?" said Totts.

"It is whah they'd have you, suh, if they caught you teachin' any o' those railroad accidents o' yore's to the young."

"Yes, indeed; yes, indeed!" cried Maverick and Cottsill, eagerly.

Totts loudly blew his nose. "It shall remain court-house in the dictionary of scholars," he remarked.

Willows ran his eye up and down Totts' list, and then up and down Totts. "Schooling," he softly returned, "has done powerful little for the Amur-rican who sails to Yurrup and puts surrup on his hot cakes."

"Yes, indeed; yes, indeed!" said Cottsill and Maverick again.

"Gentlemen, gentlemen!" pleaded Kibosh, "do not quarrel."

"Kwawrul, you mean," smiled Jesse Willows. "It's immawrul to kwawrul in Surracuse, Noo Yorruk."

Totts now began to show signs of jumping up and down.

"Have we adopted phonetic spelling, or have we not?" he roared.

"Not yore kind," said Willows.

"Yore!" echoed Totts. "Listen to that dialect!" And he blew his nose more loudly.

"Hup, hup," began Egghorn; but his voice stuck as usual.

"You should get a chauffeur," said Cottsill, severely, to him.

"Hup, hup, compromise," finished Egghorn.

"Ah, yes, gentlemen, there we have it!" said Kibosh, earnestly. "Compromise is progress. Let us all accept one another. Thus the cause will profit."

His exhortation produced a brief, a very brief, lull. Each looked at the neighboring blackboards in

silence; and Kibosh, doubtless with the idea of har-
mony, set the organ once more to playing, "My
spelling, 'tis of thee," while the rattling West continued to create a new language behind us.

At length Cottsill sighed. "Very well," he said,
"for the sake of anywheres, I'll vote for surrup."

"That's wise, that's kind, that's good," said Kibosh; and he beat one hand gently on the table.

At this hopeful point, Jesse Willows noticed, for
the first time, that no lady was present, and his long
body made a singular twisting and free motion
beneath his clothes.

"I will vote for rud and anywheres," Totts said.
"But I doubt if I can accept coat-house."

Jesse Willows took him instantly by the nose.
"You'll accept nothin'," said he, with great sweetness; and he shook him forward and back. "I am
weary of you and yore antics," and he shook him
right and left. "You're goin' to rub out everything
you have written," and he shook him round and
round.

"Help," gurgled the struggling Totts. "Help!"

"No, indeed; no, indeed," cried Maverick and
Cottsill, delighted.

"You gentlemen are included," said Willows to
them, and they both hastily covered their noses with
their hands. "I don't mean that way," he continued.
"But you're goin' to rub yore lists out, too. Why

you're the contemptiblest of all the great American frauds. Just because you have written a picayune book on some picayune specialty, you pass for bein' educated in our half-civilized country. Put you among genuine scholars and you would look like old gum shoes. I know my accent is provincial," he paused and looked at Totts for a moment, "but it's a heap prettier'n yore's," and he shook Totts round and round again, "and you and I are jus' goin' to let the English language take care of herself. She has done it for a thousand years, and she'll do it for a thousand more, changin' what she pleases an' keepin' what she pleases, an' doin' it when she pleases."

So saying, the young man, even as one drags a resisting dog by a chain, dragged the howling Totts by his nose to the blackboard, and forced the rubber into his hand; and as Totts hung back his firmly imprisoned organ received a still more acute sensation, whereat he leaped into the air, and erased his Surracuse list at one sweep. And next, since Cottsill and Maverick were hanging back also, one with his arms shielding grantha, while the other shielded anywheres, Totts was conducted to those words. "Out with grantha," commanded Jesse. "We'll keep it grandfather for a while yet, Mr. Bean Talk." They attempted to defend their lists, but vainly; and in the conflict that arose, a rubber flew crooked

and hit one of the Great West sharply in the back
of the neck. He, being under a misapprehension,
thereupon kicked his neighbor savagely, and in a
moment all the profound scholars engaged together
in a blind war, rubbing out one another's lists,
whacking one another's heads, and often rolling by
twos and threes beneath the table, from which dic-
tionaries and inkstands were falling continuously.
It was with the greatest difficulty that I got the
gasoline organ between myself and harm's way.
Jesse Willows had mounted upon the table with the
still faintly bellowing Totts, whom he led slowly
from one end to the other, amid the clouds of chalk
and the general bedlam.

At the first pause which exhaustion brought,
Masticator B. Fellows was perceived to be looking
on quietly.

"Gentlemen," he said, "dear friends" (and these
words stopped everything), "I am well pleased
with what you have accomplished. I expected results, and I have got them. The surgeon awaits you
in the House of Bandages."

No serious wounds were found; but also no scholar
was found to be upon speaking terms with any
other. By the generosity of Masticator each was
sent home separately in a private car, on a special
train, with plenty of chickle.

Masticator had created all the publicity that he

desired. New students swarmed in armies to his University, and he presently issued a billion more shares of Chickle common.

The press of the whole country rang with the enterprise.

SIMPLE SPELLERS WED

was one of the first headlines that greeted me upon my homeward journey. Yes; Jesse Willows and Gertrude Appleby were the exceptions; these two scholars had gone away in the same car together to their honeymoon, while I returned lonely to the index of my forthcoming volume.

Heigho!

THE HONEYMOONSHINERS
OR,
WATCH YOUR THIRST

Opéra Bouffe in Three Acts

The Honeymoonshiners

or,

Watch Your Thirst

Opéra Bouffe in Three Acts

PERSONAGES IN THE PIECE

Jupiter ⎫
Bacchus ⎪
Cupid ⎬ *Gods*
Juno ⎪
Minerva ⎪
Venus ⎭

Lotis ⎫
Daphne ⎬ *Nymphs*
Arethusa ⎭

Ganymede, *a young Trojan*
Zoë Moo, *a Greek girl*
First Citizen, *an Athenian*
First Hoplite ⎫ *Rural Police*
Second Hoplite ⎭

Chorus of nymphs, fauns, and Athenians.

TIME. The end of the Golden Age.

SCENE. Act first, Olympus. Act second, near Athens. Act third, Olympus.

ACT FIRST

Olympus. Clouds, rocks, a throne; near this a table and seats. In one of the clouds a peep-hole by which hangs a telescope. On a bulletin board R, "Uplift Meeting at 10.30"; on a bulletin board L, "This is Sunshine Smiles Week." At rise of curtain DAPHNE *and* ARETHUSA *with* CHORUS *of* NYMPHS *on stage.*

CHORUS

We are minor female deities
  And this lofty habitat,
Unupholstered as you see it is,
  Is none the worse for that.
A god may sit on any stone
And it at once becomes a throne.
  On the earth, as in the sky,
Many others can be met
  Of our pattern, that is why
We and mortals make a set:
  We're politically dry,
  We are personally wet;
  And our simple habitation
  Needs no further decoration:
  For gods may sit on any stone,
  And it at once becomes a throne.

(Enter LOTIS *excitedly.)*

LOTIS

News, girls, news!

ALL

Spit it out!

LOTIS

Then you haven't heard?

DAPHNE

How do we know whether we have heard it or not until you tell us what it is?

ALL

Spit it out!

ARETHUSA

And then we shall have heard it.

LOTIS

(She screams it.)

A perfectly splendid bootlegger!

ALL

Glory be to God!

DAPHNE

Hush, hush! Juno will hear you.
(They all surround LOTIS.*)*

ALL

(They whisper their different questions simultaneously, which produces a general confused hissing.)

What's his name? Who is it? Oh, do tell us! How blissful!

LOTIS

His name is Ganymede.

ARETHUSA

What a lovely name! Ganymede. Has he any real gin?

DAPHNE

Has he any real vermouth? That is so hard to get.

LOTIS

They say he has everything. He supplies all the best families in Athens. He is not in the telephone book. Jupiter has sent Mercury to look him up, and report. Mercury is to telegraph, or send word by aeroplane. We may get in touch to-day.

ALL
(Very loud)

Gin! Vermouth!

ARETHUSA

Quiet! quiet! Juno must suspect nothing.

DAPHNE
(Looking off R)

Her Majesty is late this morning.

LOTIS

Her Majesty is in conference.

ARETHUSA

More House Bills, or a new Amendment to the Constitution?

LOTIS

Reform legislation is set aside for the moment, Minerva is doing her best to correct Her Majesty's language. Her Majesty has been mixing her words up more than usual. In addressing the Federated Spinsters of Uplift at the Social Evil meeting yesterday, Her Majesty said that the hand which rocks the cradle rules the sheriff's pussy. It distracted the Spinsters from the main issue.

DAPHNE

Why do the Spinsters have a married woman for their president?

ARETHUSA

With Jupiter's miscellaneous propensities, any wife he had would class as a near-spinster.

LOTIS
(Looking off R)

Hush! Here comes Her Majesty with Minerva.

CHORUS

Sh! Sh! The Queen draws near,
With her secretary in the rear.
Sh! Sh! She seems severe,
And so does the Secretary in the rear.
Sh! Sh! It would appear
We'd be more comfortable anywhere
than here;

But we are caught,
And so we ought
To be immediately sunk in thought.

(Enter Juno *and* Minerva.*)*

JUNO

My viewpoint is that all the alcoholics
Should swallow legal poison in their frolics.
For traitors I declare an open season,
And every drink's another case of treason.
Inebriates now fill the Solid South full.

CHORUS

O Queen, you certainly have said a mouthful.
'Tis often wise, as we have heard,
To disguise our thoughts by deed and word.
Queen, by your leave, if you are done,
We'll go.

JUNO

Stay here, I've only just begun.
I often wonder how it can be
That nobody's right, excepting me.

MINERVA

If ever I felt like that, I'd flee
To a good big pill and a good M.D.

JUNO

I've said it before, and I say so still:
I'll pass another enforcement bill.

MINERVA

She'll never be satisfied quite until
There's never a joy left over to kill.
And though with herself she does agree
That nobody's right, excepting she,
The rest of us incline to doubt
If anyone else will find that out.

CHORUS

Ten thousand laws our Queen has passed
Since four of the clock on Friday last:
By Friday next, when clocks strike four
She will have passed ten thousand more.

JUNO

I'll just remark that it is my plan
That woman shall be the coming man.

MINERVA

If that is the plan, will you unfurl
Whom you intend as the coming girl?

JUNO

The people are done with the rule of men;
I've said it before, I say it again.

MINERVA

She's said it before, she will say it some more,
She isn't afraid of being a bore—
The point I now would make is, when
We women become the coming men,

Shall we then find the same old bliss
In the coming man and her coming kiss?

CHORUS

Ten thousand laws, etc

JUNO

(Pointing to sign)

What does that say?

CHORUS

This is Sunshine Smiles Week.

JUNO

Then do it. (CHORUS *gives a sickly smile.*) Next
week is Love Your Neighbor Week. You will love him
for seven days. (CHORUS *groans.*) Then you may
resume your customary feelings. (CHORUS *smiles.*)
The week after—Minerva, what's the week after?

MINERVA

No Murders Week.

JUNO

For seven days you must kill nobody, not even
your husband. Chicago papers please copy. Now
go away and leave me in peace.

(*Exit* CHORUS *singing Ten Thousand Laws.*)

JUNO

Jupiter has been out-of-doors all night again. I
waited up till three. Then I sank into a state of
synopsis.

MINERVA

(Checks an impulse to correct her.)
Who is she this time?

JUNO

Let the jade remain anomalous.—You must advertise in the paper.

MINERVA

But Jupiter always comes home.

JUNO

It's not for him. It's for a cook, a butler, and a
housemaid. They complained that we lived too far
from a bootlegger. They departed, hurling blasphemous implications.

MINERVA

And who would blame them?

JUNO

Meanwhile, I will attend to the meals. Bacchus
takes the dining-room, and the Gods will make their
own beds.

MINERVA

That will trouble your husband but seldom.

JUNO

To be Queen of the Home is my noble office. But
Jupiter gets all the co-respondents. There are
times . . . moments . . . but no! No! I am
Queen of the Home.

MINERVA

Why not be Queen of two homes? As an advanced female thinker you demand the same standard for husband and wife.

JUNO

But if Jupiter found out! I don't want to make him happy.

MINERVA

He needn't find out. There are boys in the hills . . . inexperienced . . . their bloom intact . . . give one his experience, and destroy him immediately. Here is the mail. (JUNO *takes it.* MINERVA *lights cigarette.*)

JUNO

(Looks up from mail. Takes cigarette and treads it out.)

Not in my presence. A disgusting habit. A deadly poison. *(Smiles fatuously.)* A petition signed by five thousand Volstead mothers. They offer a new national anthem. So beautiful. So true.

MINERVA

And how does this new national anthem go?

JUNO

"I did not raise my boy to be a bar-keep."

MINERVA

If you think Congress will adopt that, you're mistaken.

JUNO

I come from the Middle West and cannot be mistaken. Have you ever met a Congressman?

MINERVA

How dare you!

JUNO

I knew you must have met some. Then you know how temperamental they are. They will pass any bill I ask.

MINERVA

Because they are temperamental?

JUNO

Exactly. If I don't feel sure of a Congressman, he receives a letter. A letter in a female hand. It names an hour and gives an address. Who would expect them to fall for old stuff like that? But they're all so temperamental! I control a large majority, especially among the mature married members. With their assistance we shall have the millennium soon. Only a few more laws . . . a few more laws . . . more laws . . . *(She is opening mail as she speaks. She has opened a newspaper. She gives a start of outrage. She thrusts the open sheet to* MINERVA.*)*

JUNO

Have you seen the *Daily Stench!*
  Crime is thick on every page.
Here's a murder by a wench
  Scarce eleven months of age.

MINERVA

Yes, these incidents occur.
How prevent them, as it were?

JUNO

Triplets take two doctors' lives;
  Kindergarteners carouse;
Judge and jury heave their knives;
  Aged bishop eats his spouse.

MINERVA

Yes, these incidents occur.
How prevent them, as it were?

JUNO

I've a solution:
Just amend the Constitution.

MINERVA

Not a solution:
Don't amend the Constitution.

Don't you think this making laws
May at times be pushed too **far?**

JUNO

No, I don't at all, because
Law is law—and there you are.

MINERVA

There I am, but where is that?
Sounds like talking through your hat.

JUNO

I've a solution, etc.

MINERVA

Not a solution, etc.

(Sound of drum, triangle and tambourine outside. Enter CUPID, BACCHUS, VENUS, *then* JUPITER, *beating these instruments. Chorus of lesser male gods, fauns, satyrs, follows. They march round the stage and line up.)*

JUPITER

Though busy tongues have wagged behind my
back—

CUPID, BACCHUS, VENUS

Have wagged behind his back—

JUPITER

And used me as a target for attack —

CUPID, BACCHUS, VENUS

A target for attack—

JUPITER

Do I reply?
Do I deny?
My name has been associated
With ladies to my neighbors mated.
Do I reply?
Do I deny?
Not so, not so,
And you all know
The reason why.
I represent
Temperament!
Temperament must have its vent.
Never reply!
Never deny!
Oh!—

CHORUS

We represent
Temperament, etc.

JUPITER

Of how I got Europa you have heard—

CUPID, BACCHUS, VENUS

Oh, yes, we all have heard—

JUPITER

And how I swam to Leda as a bird

CUPID, BACCHUS, VENUS

To Leda as a bird—

JUPITER

Do I reply?
Do I deny?
They say I woo and win my prizes
Through zo-ological disguises.
Do I reply?
Do I deny?
Not so, not so,
And you all know
The reason why.
I represent, etc.

CHORUS
We represent, etc.

JUNO

(Ascends the throne.)
Jupiter, shall I take the meeting?

JUPITER
Take it, my pet, take it.
(He yawns and goes to the telescope.)

JUNO
(Rapping with a gavel)
The meeting will come to order. The secretary
will call the roll.

MINERVA

(She has been rattling her papers as she arranged them.)

Jupiter.

(He does not hear. He is peering down at the earth through the telescope and humming absent-mindedly.)

MINERVA

(She coughs.)

Jupiter.

(No answer.)

JUNO

(In a loud voice)

Jupiter.

JUPITER

(Turns round lazily.)

Yes, my pet?

JUNO

Cease dreaming of your amorous laxatives.

(MINERVA springs up, clutches JUNO's arm, and whispers to her.)

JUNO

That is what I said. Continue the roll.

MINERVA

Venus.

VENUS

Here.

MINERVA

Cupid.

CUPID

Here.

MINERVA

Mercury.

JUPITER

I have sent Mercury to the earth in search of a new butler. I can't get on without a butler.

JUNO

A pre-war butler, I presume. Skip Mercury. Go on.

MINERVA

Bacchus.

BACCHUS

Here.

MINERVA

Apollo. *(No answer.)* Apollo.

JUPITER

(Shuts telescope and hangs it up.)
No sign of Mercury yet. Tiresome. Tiresome.

MINERVA

Apollo.

JUPITER

(As he ascends throne beside JUNO)
Oh, Apollo's at Palm Beach for the week-end.

CUPID
Which end? This is Wednesday I'll tell the world.

JUNO
(Raps with her gavel.)
Skip Apollo. Go on.

MINERVA
Vulcan.

JUPITER
Where's my eagle? Where's my eagle?

CUPID
Aw, haven't ya heard? Leda's got him.

JUPITER
So soon to forget her swan!

JUNO
Minerva. A note please. Nineteenth Amendment.
No person shall marry a bird.

JUPITER
All right. Next time I'll be a fish.

MINERVA
Vulcan.

CUPID
Aw, he's at the Hot Springs.

VENUS

I had no idea my husband was unwell. Has it been long?

JUNO

Has he been sex-rayed?

(MINERVA *springs up, clutches* JUNO'S *arm, and whispers.)*

JUNO

Don't dictionary me every minute. I need no Lexington. *(To Jupiter)* As for your marriage vows . . .

(She snaps her fingers contemptuously.)

JUPITER

Well, pet, how is a man going to help his temperament?

JUNO

You men think you've got a copyright on temperament. Skip Vulcan. Go on.

CUPID

Aw, what's the use? They're all busy. It's Affinity Week.

JUNO

(Points to sign.)

Can't you read yet, you baby?

BACCHUS

Some baby. Ask Psyche.

VENUS

(To JUNO *with dignity)*

Be good enough to leave my child alone.

CUPID

(Points to sign.)

If ya want the sunshine smile, ain't an Affinity
the Limited All Pullman flyer to it?

VENUS

(Dreamily)

To me, every week is Affinity Week. Last night.
Ah, yes. We met in a grove. He was perfectly
charming. I didn't catch his name.

JUNO

Next order of business, the Prohibition Hymn.

(She rises. All rise.)

MINERVA

Millions of victims have planted the vine.

ALL

Planted the vine.

MINERVA

Nobody told them the evils of wine.

ALL

Evils of wine.

MINERVA

Nobody said it would turn them to swine.

ALL

Turn them to swine.

MINERVA

Let us touch nothing like that when we dine.

VENUS, CUPID, BACCHUS, JUNO, JUPITER

Then what shall it be today?
Shall it be curds and whey?

GENERAL CHORUS

Oh say,
Oh pray,
Do let it be curds and whey.
(The gods dance heavily.)

MINERVA

Pleasure, refinement, and prudence unite
In a number of waters refreshing and bright,
Such as Clysmic and Pluto, which always go right,
Whether taken at morning or taken at night.

GENERAL CHORUS

Whether taken at morning or taken at night.

VENUS, CUPID, BACCHUS, JUNO, JUPITER
Then what shall it be today?
Shall it be curds and whey?

GENERAL CHORUS
Oh say,
Oh pray,
Do let it be curds and whey.
(The gods dance heavily.)

MINERVA
Temperance daily converts her recruits.

ALL
'Verts her recruits.

MINERVA
Wine-bibbers gladly renounce their pursuits.

ALL
'Nounce their pursuits.

MINERVA
Oranges, lemons, and all citrus fruits—

ALL
All citrus fruits.

MINERVA
Offer them excellent, safe substitutes.

CHORUS
Vichy, vichy, vichy, vichy, vichy.

MINERVA, CUPID, VENUS, BACCHUS, JUNO, JUPITER
>Then flow ye soda fountains, flow,
>Sarsaparilla, foam and flow,
>Sarsaparilla, cold as snow!
>>So what shall it be today, etc.
>*(All resume their former seats.)*

JUNO

Next order of business: Bills reported favorably by the Federated Spinsters of Uplift.

MINERVA
(Reading)

House Bill 453686. To promote sexual purity. No person shall look at any other person with a naked eye.

JUNO

Those in favor will signify by usual sign.

ALL

No.

JUNO

It is a law.

MINERVA

House Bill 453687. To prevent skin disease. Whereas strawberries if eaten by some persons raise a painful rash, strawberries are hereby outlawed. Second Section. Whereas raw onions are suspected of causing biliousness in some persons, Congress shall vote an appropriation to probe onions.

JUNO

Those in favor of first section—

ALL

No!

JUNO

Strawberries outlawed. Those in favor of second section—

ALL

No!

JUNO

Onions probed.

CUPID
(Jumps up and shouts.)
Twentieth Amendment.

JUNO

Stop him.

ALL

Go on, go on.

CUPID

Twentieth Amendment. Wet nurses are outlawed. All nurses must be dry.

JUNO

(Rising haughtily)

This meeting is declared adjourned.
I'll not be baited, mocked and spurned.

ALL

She says that the meeting is adjourned,
She'll not be baited, mocked and spurned.
Juno! Juno!
With you all earnest ladies vote.
Juno! Juno!
We hail the eternal petticoat:
And startling novelties we learned
Before this meeting was adjourned.

JUNO

My back I turn on this unseemly brawl,
I deeply pity and despise you all.
Minerva, come, the Spinsters wait,
Assembled for today's debate.
On Jupiter and yonder pack
I turn my scorn, and also turn my back.

*(While music continues, JUNO and MINERVA go out;
followed by CHORUS. CUPID lingers.)*

VENUS

Run along, dear, to the Spinsters.

CUPID

I'm no Spinster.

VENUS

I know it, darling, but the Spinsters always love
to have you with them.

CUPID

(As he sulkily obeys)

Aw, but you're the mean momma!

(JUPITER, BACCHUS, *and* VENUS *have been cautiously waiting until they are alone.)*

JUPITER

She's turned her back.

BACCHUS

He's turned his back.

VENUS

They've turned their back.

(BACCHUS *steals right to see if coast is clear.* VENUS
tiptoes left. JUPITER *peeps through telescope.
They then draw together centre.)*

VENUS

*(Producing a hot water bottle from inside her
flowing robes)*

When the cat's away

The mice will play.

BACCHUS

*(Producing a two-ounce medicine bottle from his
wreath of leaves)*

Just a drop of glycerine
For synthetic gin.

VENUS

Put it on the tray.

BACCHUS

Since the cat's away.

JUPITER

(Producing a one-ounce bottle from his crown.)
Since at last the coast is clear,
Oil of juniper is here.

ALL

Let a drop go in
To synthetic gin.

VENUS

Never, while we have supply,
Shall we see Olympus dry.

BACCHUS

Now the cat's away.

ALL

And we have some leavings yet
That can make Olympus wet.
   Let us play, let us play,
    Since the nasty cat's away.

JUPITER

(During this, BACCHUS *and* VENUS *go out.* BACCHUS
*returns with a tray on which stand a shaker, a glass
of orange juice, and three empty cocktail glasses;*
VENUS *carries a pitcher of water and an empty
bottle and spoon.)*

> In purlieus surreptitious,
>   Behind the attic stairs,
> In suit-case unsuspicious,
>   We keep our pretty wares:
> Their influence delicious
>   Dismisses all our cares.

BACCHUS

> In corner confidential
>   We fain would meet a man,
> Some agent influential
>   To carry out our plan.
> We'd furnish the essential,
>   He'd fill our little can.

ALL

> Pour, pour,
>   Prayerfully;
> More, more,
>   Carefully—
> Shaking, shaking,
>   Before taking.

In purlieus surreptitious,
Behind the attic stairs,
In suit-case unsuspicious,
We keep our pretty wares.

(BACCHUS *has filled the three glasses from the shaker; the three stand and silently toast each other.)*

JUPITER

What can be the matter with Mercury?
(He returns to look through telescope, while BACCHUS pours an "extra dividend" into the glasses.)

BACCHUS

Come and get it.

JUPITER

Mercury was to telegraph me at once if he got on the track of the boy.

VENUS

(With interest, putting down her glass)
A boy?

JUPITER

(As he shuts the telescope and returns to the "extra dividend")
He is a young bootlegger from Troy. He supplies Pericles and all the best Athenian families. I understand that his stuff is absolutely reliable.

BACCHUS

Any Scotch?

JUPITER

Everything, I'm told.

VENUS

A boy! I could have found him.

VENUS

(During the song BACCHUS *prepares more cock-*
tails.)

On the morn
That I was born
(Sea-shell, foam and sky)
Lo, a fond
And curly blond
Swimmer, swimming by.
"Beautiful boy
Ahoy, ahoy!
Be thou my joy
Ahoy, ahoy!"
So in my shell
Caught by my spell,
He trembled, trembled, and he fell.
Breezes fanned
O'er the strand
(Kisses at sea, kisses on land)
Boy repined,
Left behind,
Out of sight, out of mind.

Other joys,
Other boys,
Waiting, waiting for me—
(*Kisses on land, kisses at sea*)
In the vales
Nightingales—
(*Stillness, moon, and star*)
In the hills
Splashing rills,
Where white bathers are.
"Beautiful boy
Ahoy, ahoy!
Be thou my joy
Ahoy, ahoy!"
So by my smile,
So by my guile,
Forgetting all, they're mine awhile.
Aphrodite!
Heart's desire,
Foam and fire.
Babel Tower all tongues confused,
Save the word that I have used.
Aphrodite!
Bitter my song,
Bitter and strong.
Aphrodite!
Embers expire,
Dead as desire.

Far away
Is that day
Of foam and spray;
Yet my sea-shell
Still floats well!
Heart's desire,
Foam and fire,
Never shall die till earth herself expire,
And no ear
Is left to hear—
"Beautiful boy
Ahoy, ahoy!
Be thou my joy
Ahoy, ahoy!"

JUPITER
*(He raps his applause on the table with the
pitcher.)*
What an artist!

BACCHUS
I can sing as well as that. Better.

JUPITER
I know it, dear son.
(He starts for telescope.)

VENUS
I don't know it.

BACCHUS
(With violence)
If I am not asked to sing immediately, I shall
sing anyhow.

JUPITER
(Hastening back)
Why, yes, son, yes, son. Sing, my dear son.

BACCHUS
(To the orchestra)
Allegretto, ma non troppo.

My favored votaries I crown,
Their hearts I free from care and trouble.

JUPITER and VENUS
Boom ra-ta-ta ta ta ta, etc.

BACCHUS
Their eyes I blind to fortune's frown,
Her smile I teach them to see double.

JUPITER and VENUS
Boom ra-ta-ta ta ta ta, etc.

BACCHUS
Companioned by my pards I roam,
    I pour my cup for thirsty nations;
In forest glade, by salt sea foam,
    I celebrate my aberrations

With little dryads,
With little naiads,
With little nereids,
With little oreads—

ALL THREE
With little dryads
With little naiads
A-roaming to and fro
Among the islands of the Archipelago.

BACCHUS
Each happy she I do enfold,
    Within the shrine of my embraces,
Be she the pure unminted gold,
    Be she the queen of hardened cases—
If once the nymph has been my flame,
    Romance shall grave it on its pages,
And minstrels hymn the lady's name,
    And make her envied through the ages
        With little dryads, etc.

Though common sense be run to seed,
    And ancient Liberty corroded,
Take it from me, it's guaranteed
    That I shall never be demoded.
Though male females and female males
    May chant and rant and rave together,
I'll navigate their frantic gales,

And come to port despite the weather
With little dryads, etc.

JUPITER
(Beating pitcher on table)
Bravo, dear boy!

VENUS
(Acidly)
Well, if that is art, excuse me.
(BACCHUS *is furious.*)

JUPITER
(Intervening with agitation)
Dear son, forget it. Dear girl . . . These intimate family scenes . . . I am too old . . . I should
not be exposed to them . . .

CUPID
*(Suddenly bursts in. All start and stand in front
of the cocktails; but in vain.)*
So that is why I was sent away. You're the mean
bunch, I'll tell the world.
*(A toy aeroplane flies through the peep-hole and
falls on the floor.)*

JUPITER
Mercury's message!
(He opens a yellow telegram and reads.)

THE OTHERS

Well?

JUPITER
(Reading aloud)

"Name, Ganymede. Nationality, Trojan. Age, nineteen. Best Athenian references." H'm. Cautiously worded. Prudent of Mercury. I must see this boy. Cupid, pack my suit-case.

CUPID

Me? Ya gotta guess again.

JUPITER

Dear boy, the servants are all gone.

CUPID

I get ya. Wantya dinner-coat?

FINALE

JUPITER

My purpose is to travel light
And do no dining out at night—
In fact to go
Incognito,
Avoiding social invitations,
And visits from my poor relations.

THE OTHERS

'Tis best to go
Incognito;

In consequence of his flirtations
He has so many poor relations.

JUPITER

Put in a change of underwear,
Of woolen socks an extra pair.

VENUS

Permit me also to advise
A dozen handkerchiefs and ties.

CUPID

May I suggest it will not hurt
To add some collars and a shirt?

JUPITER

No, no; no, no,
For I shall go
Incognito.

THE OTHERS

Ah, that is so;
He means to go
Incognito.

BACCHUS

Your silk pyjamas, what about them?

JUPITER

I'm likely to get on without them.
And then I may
Return today.
I leave at home
My brush and comb.

THE OTHERS

Good gracious! leave your brush and comb?

(CUPID *is going out on his errand.*)

JUPITER

Stay, Cupid, Cupid, stay, come back!
There are some other things to pack.
(CUPID *returns.*)
Throw in a bunch of thunderbolts
To give the human race some jolts;
And you may add a thunder sheet
To be convincing and complete—
And see the metal isn't rusted;
The last I had was nearly busted.
And from the left-hand closet, as you pass,
Just fetch my Wandering Willie alias.

CUPID

Shall I procure your ticket, sir?
And shall you need a Baedeker?

JUPITER

Pack any guide book that will show
The Grecian Archipelago,
And aid me to locate the boy
Reported to have come from Troy.
Call in at Cook's and get a berth
On anything that sails for Earth.
(*Exit* CUPID.)

THE OTHERS

The seasoned traveller always looks
For rates and routes at Thomas Cook's.

JUPITER

It's good advice you'll need
    When you sail to a foreign shore,
For many a sight will not be quite
    What you have seen before.
So what and which to choose,
    And whither and when to go,
And what it's about you had best find out
    From those who really know.
A careful man should form some plan
    Ere ever his trip is begun,
By seeing Thomas Cook and Son,
    Established in 1841.

THE OTHERS
In 1841.

JUPITER

When leaving your hotel,
    You will pass by an army corps
In expectant ranks to accept your thanks
    Assembled at the door.
To valet and to maid
    You'll extend a small douceur;
But to tip by a fluke the wife of a duke
    Might well occasion stir.

A careful man will always plan,
    Before this gauntlet is run,
To call on Thomas Cook and Son,
    Who've avoided flukes since '41.

THE OTHERS
Since 1841.

(*Enter* CUPID, *holding a pair of Jaeger drawers
and a pair of red flannel drawers.* JUPITER *selects
the red flannel. Exit* CUPID.)

JUPITER
    Along the boulevard
As you walk your prudent way,
Through the shadows of night by electric light
    You'll hear some person say:
"Does monsieur need a guide,
The life of the town for to see?"
And ladies will greet you on the street
    With "bonsoir, mon chéri."
A careful man will always plan
    What pitfalls he should shun,
By asking Thomas Cook and Son,
    Who have shunned them all since '41.

THE OTHERS
Since 1841.

(*Enter* CUPID *with large blue woolen socks, a tin thunder sheet, a sponge and soap-box.* JUPITER *selects the socks and thunder, and rejects the rest. Exit* CUPID.)

JUPITER

You'll visit Notre Dame
If a high-brow you would be,
And the blondes and brunettes of the Tintorets
In the Louvre Galleree.
More recent blondes abound
Amid wine and dance and song;
And livelier far the American bar
At the Ritz in the rue Cambong.
If you're a man who fain would plan
The right thing to be done,
Inquire of Thomas Cook and Son
Who have done it since 1841.

THE OTHERS
Since 1841.

(*Enter* CUPID *with a battered and disreputable travelling bag, and the Wandering Willie disguise, consisting of a long yellow duster, a ragged long-haired wig, a black sombrero, and a pair of smoked goggles. All begin to assist* JUPITER *to put these articles on. As they finish, enter* JUNO, *followed by* MINERVA *and by the whole chorus.*)

JUNO

And what may this be, I should like to know?
(She advances upon the cocktails.)
Synthetic gin!

CHORUS

Synthetic gin!

CUPID

Synthetic gin!
Synthetic gin!
To general business we'll go in;
We'll fabricate
And circulate
A line of articles up-to-date.
Synthetic ham,
Synthetic lamb,
Synthetic jam,
Synthetic yam,
Synthetic hops,
Synthetic chops—
You'll find them soon in all the shops.

JUNO

Am I then mocked, am I defied?
And is Olympus to be open wide?

JUPITER, BACCHUS, VENUS

We hope you're mocked, we hope you'll be defied,
We hope Olympus will be open wide.

CUPID

Synthetic salt,
Synthetic malt,
We shall be watchful to a fault;
Synthetic cheese,
Synthetic teas,
Our motto is, "We strive to please."
Synthetic meats,
Synthetic wheats,
Synthetic sweets,
Synthetic beets,
Synthetic gum,
Synthetic rum,
We'll make our commissariat hum.

JUNO

Am I then mocked, etc.

THE OTHERS

We hope you're mocked, etc.

JUNO

Cease this din.
Minerva, confiscate that gin.

(MINERVA *goes to the cocktails and drinks what re-mains in the shaker.*)

JUNO

Minerva! You're dismissed.
I strike you off my list.

MINERVA

I'm off her list.

BACCHUS, VENUS, CUPID

She's off her list.

(JUNO retires with dignity and sits on the throne.)

BACCHUS

(To MINERVA)

Hist!

Whist!

I'm an optimist;

It is much better so, I do insist.

She'll

Squeal

When we make her feel

That the queen of the home must be genteel.

CHORUS

Hist!

Whist!

He's an optimist, etc.

JUNO

(Notices telegram and points to it from throne.)

Say,

Pray,

Will you display

Your telegram that you hide away?

BACCHUS

Here,
Dear,
We are all sincere,
Read it through, you will find its meaning clear.

JUPITER

(*Elaborately presenting message to* JUNO)
Do
You
Cipher out a clue
To a marital ruse that escapes the view?
Fret,
Pet,
For I freely bet
That your heart on a grievance sure is set.

JUNO

(*She has been reading the message.*)
Though he's but a boy,
Him I might employ. . . .
Joy, Joy, Joy!
See
He
May turn out to be
A person I'd agree
To take on as a butler if he's satisfactoree.

JUPITER, BACCHUS, CUPID, VENUS
To take on as a butler if he's satisfactoree.

(JUNO *becomes absorbed in telegram.*)

MINERVA
Something's getting by
That escapes my eye . . .
Why
Try
To enact the spy?
They'll tell me by-and-by.

JUPITER, BACCHUS, CUPID, VENUS
No need to play the spy,
You'll know it by-and-by.

BACCHUS, VENUS, CUPID, MINERVA
(*As* CUPID *hands* JUPITER *the suit-case*)
Slide,
Glide,
From the Great Divide,
Till you come to the plain and the ocean-side.
So
Go
To the earth below,
And return with the tidings we would know.

(*They begin to push* JUPITER *out.*)

JUPITER

Ho,
No,
I shall not be slow, etc.

JUNO

So, so.
Let him not be slow, etc.

CHORUS

So, So, etc.

(Curtain.)

ACT SECOND

A grove in Greece. Moonlight shines upon a slender altar of white stone. FIRST *and* SECOND HOPLITE *stand by the altar R and L in stiff military attitude. Each has a toy bicycle.*

FIRST HOPLITE
We are conscientious, unpretentious guardsmen
    Of the people and the laws.

SECOND HOPLITE
For our exemplary tutelary zeal
    A humble salary we draws.

FIRST HOPLITE
Though this customary honorari-um
    Is not what might be termed obese—

SECOND HOPLITE
We meet with happy snappy scrappy opportunities
    Our paltry stipend to increase.

BOTH
Our sti—
Our sti—
Our stipend to increase.

(They ride off L, while music continues. Enter R the first families of Athens, disguised as Ku Klux.

*The men cannot be told from the women. The men
come forward.)*

THE MEN

(They disclose empty jugs.)
We're pillars of the State,
We're citizens of weight,
We're presidents of boards in the metropolis;
And every Sabbath morn
Ourselves we do adorn
To pass the plate in church at the Acropolis.
In our domestic lives
We're lavish to our wives,
To have a happy fireside we endeavor all;
We heap our loving mates
With diamonds and fêtes—
It is our custom to indulge in several.
So—
Late, late
In the forest glade
We wait, wait,
Though we are afraid
Some tête-à-tête
Has delayed
The sacerdotal maid—

*(A signal light flashes from some distance in the
wood. The men raise jugs above their heads, then
kneel, placing jugs round altar.)*

Bacchus, hail! Dionysus, hail,
      Give heed!
      Make speed!
      We plead!
      Our need
   Is sore indeed.

(The men rise. The women come forward, disclos-
ing empty jugs.)

THE WOMEN

Ulysses sailed the foam,
Penelope stayed home;
She heard about Calypso and of Circe too.
   And, like her, we are mum,
   When back our husbands come
From business trips to Paris and New Jersey too.
   Few husbands ever walk
   A snowy line of chalk;
Society is made of mediocrities;
   We ladies find it wise
   To swallow decent lies,
And never play Xantippe to our Socrates.
      So—
   Late, late, etc.

(Second signal light. Same business with jugs,
men join women in kneeling. All sing Bacchus hail!
etc. At end of this chorus, re-enter the HOPLITES *L,*
on bicycles, singing. The ATHENIANS *continue to*

kneel without taking any notice of them. HOPLITES
dismount.)

BOTH HOPLITES

We are conscientious, unpretentious guardsmen
    Of the people and the laws.
*(As they sing, they pass round among the kneeling
citizens, extending a receptive hand to each one,
who places a gratuity in it without other sign of being aware of the transaction.)*
For our necessary tutelary zeal
    A humble salary we draws.
Though this customary honorari-um
    Is not what might be termed obese—
We meet with happy snappy scrappy opportunities
    Our paltry stipend to increase.
(By the end of their duo, the HOPLITES *have col-
lected their tribute and once more go off L. As they
disappear, the chorus of citizens rise and sing as
loudly as possible.)*
    Bacchus, hail! Dionysus, hail!

FIRST CITIZEN
(Looking off in direction of signal)
We must wait for the third sign.

CHORUS

We must.

FIRST CITIZEN

It should come soon.

CHORUS

Yes.

FIRST CITIZEN

How solitary is this forest! We have not seen a soul.

CHORUS

No.

FIRST CITIZEN

Yet still the high cost of living goes on, and on, and on.
(Enter JUPITER *in his disguise. They avoid notice of him. He coughs slightly.)*

FIRST CITIZEN
(Keeping his back to JUPITER*)*

Nobody is present. We have already seen them. They are satisfied. Go away, please. The high cost of living—

JUPITER
(Interrupts him.)

But my dear sir, my kind sir—

FIRST CITIZEN
(Turns round angrily.)

What are you?

JUPITER

Believe me, good sirs, I have known better days.

　　To see me now, how should you guess
That I was supple once, and slender?
　　Immortal gods, and men not less,
Held me a credit to my gender.
　　　　I sported,
　　　　I courted,
My gallantries provoked some scandal.
　　　Why does life's game
　　　Though still the same,
To me no longer seem quite worth the candle?
　　　　I see!
There's nothing changed, excepting me.

CHORUS

　　How very sad this old man's tale!
　　To move our hearts it scarce can fail.

JUPITER

　　Still do the kings and aces fall,
Still roll the dice, still shift the winnings,
　　Still youth attends to beauty's call
Until the dawn, and has his innings.
　　　In olden days,
　　　In golden days,
Where all the boys were, there was I, too.
　　　But now I find
　　　Me more inclined
To seek a lonely bed and sleep, or try to.

I see!
There's nothing changed excepting me.

CHORUS
How very sad this old man's tale!
To move our hearts it scarce can fail.

JUPITER
(Removes his hat.)
Behold a poor old harmless man,
Above whose head have poured deep waters.
The carefullest of fathers can
Trust me with any of his daughters.
I'll not conceal
That my last meal
Was Friday week, and half a plateful.
And if some friend
Would kindly lend
The price of one black coffee, I'd be grateful.
(He holds out his hat to the CHORUS. *All turn their backs with a gentle gesture of refusal.)*

JUPITER
I see!
There's no small change today for me.

FIRST CITIZEN
(To the CHORUS)
Do you understand him to have mentioned coffee?

CHORUS

We do. He did.

JUPITER

(Lifting his arms)

O Bacchus, O Dionysus, god of the flowing bowl, if nevermore are my parched lips to taste of thy bounty, if never again I am to feel in my veins that joyous tide divine, which only the flood of love surpasses, let me die tonight.

FIRST CITIZEN

Our Government has forbidden drink.

JUPITER

Does a tyrant govern Greece?

FIRST CITIZEN

Yes; a Demockery. That old hag Juno—

JUPITER

Ha, ha! Old hag! Ha, ha!

FIRST CITIZEN

(Turns to JUPITER.)

I beg your pardon?

JUPITER

No remark, sir. It is a nervous affection. Ha! Ha! Bear with me, it will pass in a moment. Ha! Now it is gone.

(The distant light flashes through the wood.)

Oh, what is that?

FIRST CITIZEN

(He addresses the CHORUS.*)*

The third signal. Have you ready the final tribute?

CHORUS

We have.

(They go to the altar and each places upon it a purse.)

FIRST CITIZEN

The hour is come. Bacchus deigns to be kind.

JUPITER

Do you offer money to a god?

FIRST CITIZEN

Well, they seem to appreciate it.

JUPITER

Are you quite sure that it is a god?

FIRST CITIZEN

It is better to think so, and to ask no questions. Zoë Moo is quite the sort of peach that has generally been very close to Dionysus.

(He looks off into the wood.)

She comes. Do as we do, venerable sir.

(After a few bars of folk music, enter ZOË MOO *tip-toeing prettily. Her hair is light gold, her eyes gay, her slim body appealing, her lips pout a little. She is in hunting dress. All have drawn together at a*

*distance from the altar and watch her with devout
respect. She trips round the altar, gracefully picking up purse after purse, shaking it, listening to the
chink of coin, looking in to make sure, and then
dropping the purses one by one into a large reticule
which dangles from her arm. As the last falls in,
she sings.)*

Ye men of Athens of the first
    Society,
The god commends your faithful thirst
    And piety;
His further gifts next week shall win
    Your gratitude,
If you, next week, continue in
    This attitude.

FIRST CITIZEN AND CHORUS
From day to day,
And night to night,
In unison we say
United we shall pray
To Dionysus, god of joy, and giver of delight.

ZOË MOO
Let me convey
A warning quite
Important; while you pray,
Do not omit to pay
The customary honorarium for your delight.

FIRST CITIZEN AND CHORUS
The customary honorarium . . .
We'll not forget to pray.

ZOË MOO
But don't omit to pay.

JUPITER
It's plain she's acting for the boy
Reported as from Troy.

FIRST CITIZEN
Come, come, old man, we must away;
It is unwholesome here to stay.

JUPITER
I'll come away.

ZOË MOO
Yes, go away.

JUPITER
I'll go away.

(FIRST CITIZEN *leads* CHORUS *off R;* JUPITER *follows them with reluctance, after advances to* ZOË MOO, *who drives him away. Music continues. When* ZOË MOO *is satisfied that they have all gone, she cups her hands to her lips and sings towards the forest.*)

ZOË MOO
Cuckoo! Your bird is on her nest.
(She listens.)

VOICE OF GANYMEDE
Cuckoo! Cuckoo!

ZOË MOO
Cuckoo! fly here and do the rest.
Cuckoo, cuckoo!
Bright eggs of gold.
Cuckoo, cuckoo!
Fly here and behold!

(GANYMEDE *steals in cautiously. He is a slim youth of dazzling beauty and grace. A leopard skin is all he wears, his hair is short, of golden bronze, and crowned with vine leaves. They embrace warily.*)

BOTH
Cuckoo! Cuckoo!

GANYMEDE
I'm a certified bootlegger—

ZOË MOO
I'm his soul mate—

GANYMEDE
And when such a bootlegger—

ZOË MOO
With his soul mate—

GANYMEDE
Is a busy young bootlegger—

ZOË MOO
With his soul mate—

GANYMEDE
He'll become a rich bootlegger—

ZOË MOO
With his soul mate—

BOTH
For oh! We're onward-bound for a run
From a place in the moon to a place in the sun.

GANYMEDE
Though we are both wet—

ZOË MOO
We're acquainted with drys —

GANYMEDE
And both being wet

ZOË MOO
We're occasioned surprise—

GANYMEDE
By the way that some persons—

ZOË MOO
Who call themselves drys—

GANYMEDE
In the presence of cocktails—

ZOË MOO
Forget they are drys.

BOTH
For oh! etc.

GANYMEDE
When a wet goes to dinner—

ZOË MOO
With scrupulous drys—

GANYMEDE
They drink to that sinner—

ZOË MOO
With only their eyes.

GANYMEDE
But when those same drys—

ZOË MOO
Go to dine with that wet—

GANYMEDE
They lap up whatever—

ZOË MOO
Before them is set.

BOTH
For oh! etc.

GANYMEDE
Now if all of the wets—

ZOË MOO

Were converted to drys—

GANYMEDE

What then would occur—

ZOË MOO

Is not hard to surmise—

GANYMEDE

For the drys would turn wet—

ZOË MOO

When the wets became drys—

GANYMEDE

And thus solve the problem—

ZOË MOO

Of future supplies.

BOTH

For oh! etc.

ZOË MOO

(She pulls him to her. Passionate embrace.)
There! Until the next one. *(She hands him the reticule.)* Now it's time for the next one.

GANYMEDE

(Interested in the money)
Business first, sweetheart.

ZOË MOO

But I'm part of your business.
(She kisses him.)

GANYMEDE

Don't distract me, love. I'm only mortal.

ZOË MOO

You're a god to me!

GANYMEDE

Haven't I proved I was mortal already tonight?
We must count our money now. Later, I will con-
tinue to prove that I am mortal.
*(He pats her hair. There is a flash, followed by
thunder and voices of dismay. Zoë Moo faints.
Ganymede hides the money. Enter Jupiter.)*

JUPITER

Boy, look at me.

GANYMEDE

(After a long, searching look)
Well . . . Can you beat it!

JUPITER

What is your name, boy?

GANYMEDE

Roger Williams.

JUPITER

That is a very nice name. What is your business?

GANYMEDE

Travelling salesman. What's yours?

JUPITER

Travelling husband. Boy, aren't you scared the cops will pinch you?

GANYMEDE

Aw, who's afraid of them, you old alibi!

JUPITER

When did you catch on to me?

GANYMEDE

Soon as I heard your fireworks bluffing those guys.

JUPITER
(Noticing ZOË MOO *for the first time)*
Does your wife often have fits?

ZOË MOO
(She sits up instantly.)
I'm not his wife, and I never have fits.

JUPITER

Devoted child.
            (He pats her head.)

ZOË MOO

We are soul mates.

GANYMEDE

For the moment.
            (He pats her head.)

ZOË MOO

We believe in free love.

JUPITER

Brave little girl.
            (He pats her head.)

ZOË MOO

If I should get tired of him . . .

GANYMEDE

Or I of her—

ZOË MOO
            (Very sharply)
I'd just like to see you try it!

GANYMEDE

There spoke a true little woman!
            (He pats her head.)

ZOË MOO
            (To JUPITER)
Please, mister, you don't believe in marriage?

JUPITER

Well, you know, I—um—I—um—I'm married
myself.

ZOË MOO

I suppose a god must be behind the times.

JUPITER

That is the price we pay for being eternal. But we husbands who are anchored by the golden chains of wedlock, sometimes swing a bit at the anchor.

GANYMEDE

That's it! Swing at the anchor.

JUPITER AND GANYMEDE

Swing at the anchor.
        (They both pat ZOË MOO's *head.)*
Nice little girl!

JUPITER

Bring your Scotch. After that, we may talk business. I could send my eagle for you.

ZOË MOO

Eagle nothing! Leda wouldn't let him go. Mister, is that bird of yours married?

JUPITER

He has a number of legitimate great-grandchildren.

ZOË MOO

Well, he's swinging at the anchor all right, all right.

JUPITER

Temperament! Temperament!

GANYMEDE

Your messenger liked my Scotch.

JUPITER

Mercury. He sent me a wire about you.

GANYMEDE

He is sleeping it off. He will have no headache.

ZOË MOO

He was very gay. So I introduced him to my sister.

JUPITER

Temperament! Everybody! Everywhere! Go fetch your Scotch.

GANYMEDE

(*Observing* JUPITER *wink at* ZOË MOO)

Say, if there's to be any temperament here . . .

JUPITER

(Points peremptorily.)

That Scotch!

GANYMEDE

What's the pay to be?

JUPITER

Olympus is full of beautiful goddesses . . .

GANYMEDE

Goddesses! Me for them . . . Paris had his luck on Mount Ida . . . In Olympus I . . . these god-

desses . . . I am every bit as temperamental as
Paris . . . *(Exit.)*

ZOË MOO
*(She has been getting the hidden reticule and has
not heard. She speaks suspiciously.)*
What was my soul mate saying to you?

FINALE

JUPITER
(He tickles Zoë Moo *under the chin.)*
Pretty, pretty, will you fly
Up with me into the sky?

ZOË MOO
No or yes? No or yes?
Jupiter, that yourself must guess.

JUPITER
Does this answer indicate
Future plans to leave your mate?

ZOË MOO
No or yes? No or yes?
Jupiter, that yourself must guess.

JUPITER
Did I wear some other form,
Might I hope your heart to storm?

ZOË MOO

No or yes? No or yes?
Jupiter, that yourself must guess.

JUPITER

Why thus do I find you
Obdurate and inhuman?

ZOË MOO

Pray let me remind you
That I'm an honest woman.

JUPITER

Less of personal virtue
  More of social prestige,
Surely never could hurt you.

ZOË MOO

Ah, but noblesse oblige!
(JUPITER *suddenly puts on the smoked goggles.*)
  Remove those eyes! their burning light
  Prevents my telling wrong from right;
  The more I think, the less I'm wise—
  Remove those eyes, remove those eyes!
  Remove those eyes! their fatal gaze
  Affects me with a wild amaze;
  My heart in supplication cries,
  Remove those eyes, remove those eyes!
(ZOË MOO *has swayed into the arms of* JUPITER,
where she suddenly clutches off his goggles. She im-

*mediately frees herself from his embrace. At the
same moment* GANYMEDE *re-enters from the wood.
He drags behind a rolling buffet such as is wheeled
along the platforms of the large French railway
stations where trains stop a few minutes; only the
bottles are concealed in boots. He stands at attention, salutes, and then makes a graceful and sweeping gesture toward his load.* JUPITER *looks at the
buffet, then at* GANYMEDE; ZOË MOO *hands him the
goggles; he puts them on and takes another look,
shakes his head, and removes the goggles.)*

JUPITER

If that's a joke, it is obscure,
And you'll regret it.

ZOË MOO

(She has taken a bottle which GANYMEDE *has given
her.)*

O sir, we're feeling rather sure
You will abet it.

JUPITER

Is it Scotch? Then let me taste it.

ZOË MOO

Taste and see! You'll not forget it.

JUPITER

Do be careful not to waste it!
Pour it slowly, don't upset it!

(During the above and the following, ZOË MOO *has taken* JUPITER *by the hand and led him to the buffet, while* GANYMEDE *draws the cork from the bottle and produces a glass and siphon. He pours a little into the glass, fills from siphon, and hands it to* JUPITER, *who lifts it to his lips.)*

ZOË MOO

Notice how the mere aroma,
   Even ere a drop is swallowed,
Inculcates a dreamy coma,
   By ecstatic visions followed.

JUPITER

(He has sipped the liquor and then gulped it down; he now stands with a beaming expression and raises his glass on high. On one side of him is ZOË MOO, *on the other* GANYMEDE, *who remains by his boots.)*

Maid of Athens, ere we part,
I present you with my heart.
In exchange I shall employ
In my dining room this boy.
(ZOË MOO *gives a jump of alarm*)
Punch for me shall he distill,
And my cup for ever fill.
Soul mates of exalted birth
Shall console him for the earth.

(At these words GANYMEDE *gives his leg a resounding and joyful slap;* ZOË MOO *rushes across to him*

and winds her arm round his neck. FIRST CITIZEN
has entered, timidly and respectfully followed by
the CHORUS.)

FIRST CITIZEN
(*With a warning gesture to* ZOË MOO)
Seek not to evade the god,
Lest perchance you feel his rod.

CHORUS
Beware the god,
Beware his rod:
Though he be odd,
Obey his nod.

(*During the above,* ZOË MOO *has remained holding*
firmly to GANYMEDE, *who pays no attention to her,*
but has his eyes fixed upon JUPITER *with eager ex-*
pectancy. JUPITER *now places his empty glass on*
the altar, walks to GANYMEDE, *and lays one hand*
upon his shoulder, pointing upward with the other.)

JUPITER
Mortal, I have enrolled thee
Immortal, and no less.
Soft arms shall soothe and hold thee,
Soft lips on thine shall press;
Secrets divine be told thee—
Canst thou not half guess?

FIRST CITIZEN AND CHORUS
Ah, most freely we confess,
Every one of us can guess.

ZOË MOO
(She rushes to the CHORUS, *to whom she appeals.)*
Ye men of Athens, take my part,
My urgent accents heed!
He's welcome to his stale old heart,
He's past the zenith of his art,
Give me my profitable cart,
Give me my Ganymede!

FIRST CITIZEN AND CHORUS
Her reckless language makes us start.
What pious man could take her part?

FIRST CITIZEN
Zoë Moo!
Other fish are in the sea,
Zoë Moo!
Other fish as good as he.
Zoë Moo!
Why not take a look at me,
Zoë Moo?
What is free love if it is not free?

JUPITER
That is true!
If free love is really best,
Zoë Moo,

As you claim with so much zest,
　　Zoë Moo,
Delicately I suggest,
　　Zoë Moo,
Surely it should stand the acid test!
(Zoë Moo *rushes back and seizes* Ganymede, First
Citizen *rushes and seizes her.*)

ZOË MOO

No no! No no! No no! no no;
　I will not have it so!
No no! no no! no no! no no!
　I will not let him go!
And by the way, and by the way,
What is Juno going to say?
Ho ho! ha ha! Just answer that!
How will you fool your mean old cat!

FIRST CITIZEN AND CHORUS

O blasphemous! O frightful! O what next!
How candid! How deplorably unsexed!
　　(They fall upon their knees.)

JUPITER

Rise up, and have no fear: I am not vexed.
　　(He pats zoë moo's *head.)*
Nice little girl! and such soft hair!

ZOË MOO

.Of course it is. But I don't care
At such a time for your hot air.

Your eagle's here, and he and I
Will shadow you into your sky.
This deal has not been on the square—
I'll say it here, and everywhere.

JUPITER

If in Olympus you appear,
You shall receive our welcome, dear.

(Points to buffet.)

This precious and assorted store
Belongs to those upon this shore.
These dames and gentlemen shall not forget
We found them dry and left them wet.
So crack the ice and fill the glasses.

CHORUS
Fill the glasses!

JUPITER
Circulate them through the masses.

CHORUS
Through the masses!

JUPITER
Let the members of all classes
Drink to the Scotch.
Drink to the rye.

CHORUS

Here's to the Scotch.
Here's to the rye.
Health to the wet and death to the dry!
(All now have glasses filled from the buffet, except
ZOË MOO *who refuses and stands apart.* GANYMEDE
comes forward.)

GANYMEDE

Ye Athenian City Fathers!
    Though your shining glasses clink,
Ye will meet very few who'll tell you
    Exactly what they think.
Here are one or two suggestions,
    In your ears better let them sink:
You will not change human nature
    By shedding drops of ink.

CHORUS

We cannot change, etc.

GANYMEDE

Ye may outlaw Evolution,
    And prohibit the Missing Link,
Make the girls wear longer dresses
    When skating on the rink;
Ye may forbid the boys to kiss them,
    Or to greet them with a wink—
But you don't change human nature
By shedding drops of ink.

CHORUS

But we don't, etc.

GANYMEDE

Cigarettes, cards, all enjoyments,
Ye may force them to hide and slink—
If you hope you can tramp out pleasure,
Your brains are on the blink:
Ye may fill up the Constitution
With Amendments to its brink,
You may lead a man to water,
But you can't stop his drink—

CHORUS

But we don't, etc.

JUPITER

And now, we'll have a parting toast
To all the dwellers on this coast.

JUPITER WITH CHORUS

To all true souls of all the ages,
Peace and plenty be their dole;
In their Life's tale be none but sunny pages,
Each part glow bright within the perfect whole!

JUPITER

Golden Age!
For thee we long and yearn;
Golden Age!

Say, wilt thou e'er return?
Golden Age!
In what far world, in what far sky dost burn?
Are gods and men thy glories nevermore to learn?

ALL

Golden Age! etc.

ZOË MOO

Farewell, O Ganymede, farewell!

ALL

To all true souls, etc.
(GANYMEDE *mounts buffet.* JUPITER *wheels him off.*
Enter HOPLITES.)

BOTH HOPLITES

We are conscientious unpretentious guardsmen
    Of the people and the laws.
For our necessary tutelary zeal
    A humble salary we draws.
(While singing they approach the bottles left by
JUPITER, *pour themselves refreshments, and the*
CHORUS *joins them.)*

ALL

Though $\begin{cases} \text{our} \\ \text{their} \end{cases}$ customary honorari-um, etc.

(Curtain falls on general fraternization between
HOPLITES *and* ATHENIAN CITIZENS.)

We are again on Olympus, in the home of the gods. It is Thursday morning, twenty-four hours since our last sight of the heavenly mansion. There is no change (as yet) in the moral or intellectual atmosphere, and there are but few changes in anything. The same august clouds veil the dwelling of the immortals from profane eyes, the same peephole and telescope offer facilities to such as care for a look at the earth, the throne is there, and the sign board of the week. After a few measures of gentle music, the curtain rises, disclosing to us all the gods we have met, except JUPITER. JUNO *is looking through the telescope,* MINERVA *is moving various cups, saucers, plates and dishes which are on the table, as if preparing to take away the breakfast things.* BACCHUS, VENUS *and* CUPID *are sitting on chairs pushed away from the table.* BACCHUS *has the morning paper. They sing quietly.*

ALL

'Tis strange that mortals are inclined
　　To envy us
A life so many of us find
　　Monotonous.
Except for human aberration,
We all should perish with stagnation.

333

Therefore we hail from our immortal dearth
Any excitement that is bred on earth;
All pestilence, disaster, famine, blight,
We welcome as diversions for our sight;
                In them we see
Alleviation in our huge ennui.
Yet still these mortals are inclined
                To envy us
This life so many of us find
                Monotonous.
                They never see
'Tis they that save us from our huge ennui.

*(During the gentle measures of music which pro-
long themselves for a moment after the voices have
ceased, JUNO shuts the telescope and comes forward.)*

BACCHUS

*(Laying down his paper, speaks to JUNO with a
gesture toward the peephole, while CUPID and
VENUS pick up the paper and look it over.)*

Anything to be seen?

JUNO

Nothing. Anything in the paper?

BACCHUS

Not a single cook. No domestic help at all.

CUPID

I'd sooner have a cook than a butler.

JUNO

What is behind that remark?

CUPID

Aw, I'm sick of your cuisine!

JUNO

Then suck your bottle. Babies mustn't be greedy pedicures.

VENUS

Let my child alone.

JUNO

Your baby's talk is superoregoratory.

MINERVA

At it again!

(An aeroplane flies through the peephole. JUNO catches it and takes telegram.)

News from Jupiter. *(Reads the address.)* Why, it is not for me.

MINERVA

Then don't open it.   '

JUNO

It is for the eagle.

ALL

Then don't open it.

JUNO

Certainly I shall. Merely a bird! *(She reads aloud.)* ''Come back, sweetheart, and all shall be forgiven. Your Leda.'' I notice you're all listening. The eagle shall have it.

MINERVA

Leda will never be able to hold that bird. He is very flighty.

VENUS

Temperament! But where can he be? What can he be doing?

(Enter JUPITER. *He still wears his Wandering Willie disguise.)*

JUPITER

Sorry to keep you all waiting. But I have brought a butler.

ALL

Let him come in.

JUNO

Cupid, go get him.

CUPID

I wish he was a cook. *(Exit.)*

BACCHUS

In polished households 'tis the plan
To keep at least one indoor man,
And often two, and sometimes three:
But we shall see what we shall see.

VENUS AND CUPID

Parents and guardians never taught
Us to be useful as we ought;
And none their negligence can rue
More than we would, more than we do.

(*During the above,* CUPID *has re-entered, drawing* GANYMEDE *on the buffet, on which he reclines. He wears a broad hat and is wrapped in an ample fur coat, which also evidently conceals the goods with which the buffet is now re-loaded. Some of the* CHORUS, *which follows slowly in a procession, help to push the buffet. The music continues softly during the following dialogue.*)

JUNO

But why in a car?

JUPITER

He is very tired.

MINERVA

And why in the coon-coat?

JUPITER

He got wet. High floods through the country.
Several poets drowned on Parnassus. I still fear
lest he have a congestive chill.

(GANYMEDE *coughs heavily.*)

Only listen to that.

JUNO

Poor boy! He must have some hot instantaneous
purum. What is your name?

GANYMEDE
(In a hoarse voice)

Ganymede, your Majesty.

JUNO

Try your skill on purum. Make some for us all.
Take some yourself. And remove those garments.
We must see more of you. Cupid, show him the
pantry. Show him the box of purum. Two spoon-
fuls to the cup. Boiling water. Stir . . . and hasten
back.

GANYMEDE

I will hasten, your Majesty.

(CUPID *drags* GANYMEDE *out.*)

BACCHUS, MINERVA, VENUS

We rather hope she'll find she can
Engage this promising young man,

Whose countenance seems frank and free:
But we shall see what we shall see.

(Re-enter Cupid. Jupiter *and* Juno *ascend the throne.)*

Parents and guardians never taught
Us to be useful, as we ought;
And none their negligence can rue
More than we would, more than we do.

*(Re-enter .*Ganymede *in the full glory of his youth and beauty, his hair wreathed with vine leaves, the leopard skin about his loins. He bears a tray with beaker and goblets, carries it among the gods after serving* Jupiter *and* Juno *first. All sip. Signs of gratification. Glances of admiration from* Venus. *Absorbed attention from* Juno. *During this business* Chorus *sings quietly.)*

CHORUS
Ah, sure he is an ornamental lad
To make us glad;
His predecessor whom we lately had
Was rather sad.

(The gods extend their goblets for more purum. Ganymede *inverts beaker to show it is empty.* Ganymede *is obliged to go out and refill the beaker. This serving of the purum proceeds while the following sextette is sung.)*

JUPITER, JUNO, VENUS, CUPID, BACCHUS, MINERVA
Soft, soft upon my sense
  Day dreams are lightly stealing;
Slow, slow, their influence
  Creeps silent through my feeling.

CUPID AND VENUS
Bright drops! shine and fall;
  Clear drops! now aid me;
Pure drops, warm drops, all!
  Lull me, pervade me!

ALL
Bright drops, etc.

CHORUS
Now sure he is the ornamental lad
To make us glad.

(The music keeps pace with the livelier mood of the gods. JUNO stands up and sings. JUPITER slyly fills up her goblet.)

JUNO
Why, why have Scotch or rye,
When purum to all homes is nigh?
  Let sinners to purum come.

CHORUS
(Presenting hip pocket receptacles)
Give us some, give us some.

JUNO

Who needs Baccardi rum
When here we have Elysium?
So, why try rye,
Since purum is near by?
(JUNO *reseats herself and drinks.*)

GENERAL CHORUS

Why, why have Scotch or rye, etc.
(GANYMEDE *goes out again to fill his beaker, and
returns at the first words of the general chorus, at
which point* JUPITER *descends the throne, flinging
off his Wandering Willie disguise and appearing in
royal glory.* BACCHUS *hastens to him and shakes
him by the hand.)*

BACCHUS

All excitement, all impatience
To extend congratulations.
What a flavor!
What a savor!
Diet had become a question
Full of menace to digestion.

VENUS

(She too shakes JUPITER's *hand.)*
Nourishment is now a pleasure,
Swallowing a perfect bliss.
'Tis impossible to measure
Developments to follow this.

MINERVA

(She shakes hands with JUPITER.*)*
Developments will follow
If another cup I swallow.

CUPID

(He shakes hands with JUPITER.*)*
I mean to imbibe just one or two more.
(GANYMEDE *returns with the pot refilled. All hold
out their cups to him.)*

JUNO

(She hastens down from the throne with her cup.)
There's nothing can be harmful
In a beverage so charmful.

VENUS AND CUPID

We think we've met something like this before.

MINERVA

Rosy sights my vision greet,
Wandering whimsies fill my feet.

ALL

(They join hands and circle round JUPITER *and*
GANYMEDE.*)*
All excitement, all impatience,
We extend congratulations.

GANYMEDE

*(Who is quite aware of the love glances which are
being cast upon him by various ladies.)*

Interesting situation
For a young man of my station!
  Zoë Moo could hardly blame,
Should I once or twice forget her—
At another time I'll pet her—
  In my place she'd do the same,
  And I hope she'll play the game.

MINERVA
(Flirting with GANYMEDE*)*
I hope that she engages
Him no matter what his age is.

VENUS
(Flirting with GANYMEDE*)*
I do not like them too mature.

MINERVA
Modern servants are such fumblers
With the soup plates and the tumblers.

VENUS
China's a stuff will not endure,
Glass is as bad, of that I'm sure.

CHORUS OF NYMPHS
We approve this adolescent,
His appearance is so pleasant,
  Sympathetic and attractive!

CHORUS OF FAUNS

What we all are quite agreed is
That this young man Ganymede is
As a butler highly active.

GENERAL CHORUS

So—
Quickly let us go;
Soon, soon we shall know
If he's to stay or return below.
All excitement, all impatience, etc.

VENUS

(Lifting cup to GANYMEDE*)*
Love!

GANYMEDE

(Drinking to VENUS*)*
Love!

MINERVA

(Lifting cup to GANYMEDE*)*
Love!

GANYMEDE

(Drinking to MINERVA*)*
Love!

CHORUS OF NYMPHS
Love!

GANYMEDE

(Drinking to everybody)
Love!

(JUNO has been busily making herself up with a vanity box, and now, from the throne, by a gesture during the closing measures of the ensemble, orders every one out. They obey, VENUS bringing up the rear. GANYMEDE would follow at her invitation, but a motion from JUNO stops him. He and JUNO are now alone. The effect of the purum upon JUNO is to melt away her usual austerity and render her smiling and friendly.)

GANYMEDE
(Accounting for his attempted departure)
I expected Your Majesty would wish me to set to work in the pantry.

JUNO
You forget I have not seen your references.

GANYMEDE
I will bring them.
(Is hastening out.)

JUNO
Stay, Ganymede. Your references can wait.

GANYMEDE
(Still near the exit)
They're in my coat—right out there.

JUNO
Stay, Ganymede. To me there is something of

more importance than references. Do you know what I mean?

GANYMEDE
(He is puzzled.)
Why—why—

JUNO
Can you not guess?

GANYMEDE
Your Majesty—

JUNO
Come a little nearer. *(He takes a few steps, still puzzled. Suddenly an illuminating thought strikes him and stops him short. He dismisses it with a gesture.)* Nearer, Ganymede.

GANYMEDE
(As he obeys, bewildered, to himself)
It's not possible. She? Never!

JUNO
(As he reaches the throne)
I spoke of something more important than references. Have you ever . . . kissed *sub rosa?*

GANYMEDE
(With fearless and sincere denial)
Your Majesty, I never so much as heard of her.

JUNO

Not so loud. Nearer. You need not address me
as Your Majesty when we are alone.

GANYMEDE

(Anxiously looking over his shoulder)
Zoë Moo . . . that eagle . . . if she has bribed
him to bring her . . . she had all our money . . .

JUNO

I should like you to forget Zoë-what's-her-name.

GANYMEDE

I only hope she will let me forget her!

JUNO

Hear me, Ganymede.

A husband who's philandered—

GANYMEDE

Now what does she mean by that?

JUNO

Deserves the single standard.

GANYMEDE

Now what does she mean by that?

JUNO

When wives have been neglected
'Tis but to be expected

That some fine day
They'll find some way—
And that's what I mean by that.

GANYMEDE

So that's what she means by that!
So that's what she would be at!
And I'm the way
She means to find today,
And it's me that she would be at!

JUNO

Temperament! Temperament!
Who can prevent
Their temperament?

GANYMEDE

Temperament! Temperament!
To what extent
Should I consent?

JUNO

Though you count none but young years yet,

GANYMEDE

O Lady!

JUNO

Though you have suffered few fears yet,

GANYMEDE

O Lady!

JUNO
Even now
Though that brow
Time has not shorn with his shears yet—

GANYMEDE
O Lady!

BOTH
Even so
Do you know
How sweet and bitter, and weal and woe,
Mingle their waters, mingle and flow.
Even so
There below
Love and loathing, light and gloom,
Like bride and groom
Together go.

JUNO
Kneel then, and learn that to do here

GANYMEDE
What I do here—

JUNO
That which was false there is true here;

GANYMEDE
Is true here—

JUNO
Kneel and feel
Weal is weal,
Thorns do not tear them that woo here.

GANYMEDE
I'll woo here.
(JUNO *here makes* GANYMEDE *kneel.)*

JUNO
Under the rose
Soft repose,
Curtains of bliss, your eyes shall close—
Rise, now arise,
See, grow wise;
(JUNO *during this makes* GANYMEDE *get up.)*
Bend on your Queen and slave those eyes.
(She now descends from the throne and makes him
take her place upon it.)

BOTH
Under the rose
There's none that knows
What lover comes, what lover goes!
Under the rose
Raptures enclose!
Come, my adored one, under the rose.
(During the following JUNO *sinks down before*
GANYMEDE *and embraces his knees. He leans his*
head down against hers, clasping her.)

Not upon the uncertain sorrowful earth,
But here alone, are kisses kissing worth.

(*Enter violently* Zoë Moo.)

ZOË MOO

Help! Help! Oh dear!
Oh everybody! Just look here!
(The gods enter precipitately, in succession.)

ALL

Well, well! here's a fuss!
　Here's a fall!
Who'd have thought that after all
　She's merely one of us?

BACCHUS

(Dancing gaily)
All excitement, all impatience,
To extend congratulations.
　Juno . . .
　You know . . .
Gossip . . . sensations . . .

JUPITER

(He dances.)
Telegrams to all the nations
Will elicit speculations.

CUPID AND VENUS
(They also dance.)
Ganymede's a perfect treasure,
  Such a sight I wouldn't miss,
'Tis impossible to measure
  Developments to follow this.

MINERVA
With laws and lectures she encumbered us.

ALL
She did.

MINERVA
By many virtues she outnumbered us.

ALL
She did.

MINERVA
Now, upon my word,
If it isn't too absurd!
Who'd have ever thought she would be
No better than she should be?
Is it not absurd?

ALL
We never thought she would be
No better than she should be.
It is most absurd.

BACCHUS
She said we were all sinners natively.

ALL

She did.

BACCHUS

She tried to change us legislatively.

ALL

She did.

BACCHUS

Now, upon my word,
Who'd believe it if they heard!
Who'd have ever thought, etc.

JUPITER

Wine bibbers she denounced as truculent.

ALL

She did.

JUPITER

But still she found flirtation succulent.

ALL

She did.

JUPITER

Now, upon my word,
She has turned out quite a bird!
Who'd have ever thought, etc.

GANYMEDE
(To JUPITER)
I have ruined your home. Take a thunderbolt
and strike me dead.

ZOË MOO
Don't do anything of the sort.

JUPITER
(He pats her head.)
Nice little girl. There is no trouble.

JUNO
*(Reviving from where she has remained collapsed
by the throne, and speaking tragically.)*
No trouble!

JUPITER
None whatever, pet.—Cupid, my boy, bring in
the buffet.—I make this young lady immortal. We
shall find both her and her lover useful. (CUPID *has
gone out.)* We'll call her Hebe.

JUPITER AND GANYMEDE
(They pat ZOË MOO's head.)
Nice little girl!

JUNO
I am ruined.

JUPITER
Nay, my pet. Not at all. We will make a little
deal with you.

MINERVA

As you do with the mature married members of Congress. Temperament!

(Re-enter CUPID with buffet glittering with bottles.)

JUPITER

See? *(Points to buffet.)* You will be quiet about that—and we'll be quiet about *(points to* GANY-MEDE)—that! And to keep the people in absolute ignorance of the truth, we will order a congressional investigation.

FINALE

Then fill each glass and all shall drink a health.

ALL

Now let us drink a health.

JUPITER

To common sense within this commonwealth.

ALL

Within this commonwealth.

JUPITER

Let no one try
To keep us dry.
Our name has been associated
With those reputed dissipated.

Do we reply?
Do we deny?
Not so, not so,
And you all know
The reason why.
We represent
Temperament;
Temperament must have its vent.
Never reply
Never deny.

ALL

We represent
Temperament, etc.

(During the above, GANYMEDE and HEBE take bottles and glasses and carry them round among the gods.)

(Curtain.)